# CARNOVSKY'S RETREAT

# CARNOVSKY'S RETREAT

a novel by

## LARRY DUBERSTEIN

℘

THE PERMANENT PRESS
Noyac Road, Sag Harbor, NY 11963

*to my father, with love*

Grateful acknowledgement is made to the following for permission to reprint from previously published work:

to Alfred A. Knopf, for a quotation from Dashiell Hammett, THE MALTESE FALCON, copyright © 1929, Alfred A. Knopf, Inc.

to New Directions Publishing Corp., for a quotation from William Carlos Williams, THE AUTOBIOGRAPHY OF WILLIAM CARLOS WILLIAMS, Copyright © 1951, William Carlos Williams.

Library of Congress Number: 87-62806
International Standard Book Number: 0-932966-83-7

Manufactured in the United States of America

THE PERMANENT PRESS
RD2 Noyac Road
Sag Harbor, New York 11963

—This is human life: this is the infinitely precious stuff issued in a narrow roll to us now, and then withdrawn for ever; and we spend it thus.

—Virginia Woolf, July 1926

—The mass of men lead lives of public transportation.

—Wally Wiley, July 1956

My uncle Oscar Carnovsky, my mother's brother, died last July even though we had planned a trip to Saratoga Springs in August, he and I, to see some racing. Nothing could have been more unlikely, more out of character for Oscar than to miss a day at the races, except perhaps for the dying itself. I cancelled my half of the trip too; it was the thought of the racetrack without him, any racetrack, that made me realize how much I cared for Oscar, and how much I would miss him. Certainly I could not imagine going upstate to Saratoga without him, or with anyone else for that matter.

But the two most vivid memories I have of my uncle have nothing to do with horse racing. Each struck me at once with the news of his passing and each went far back, long before the time we became friends and would do the city together several times a year. The first occurred when I was only four years old, in fact, and Oscar must have been in his middle thirties, though to me then he was in the way of an elderly relation.

While he always deserved to be my favorite uncle—as indeed he was—the truth is that Oscar purchased the status initially; he gave me a dollar. It was my first acquisition of the kind and believe me when I say that this was truly The Almighty Dollar, for it had never crossed my mind I could have one of my own, a soft green *paper* dollar. And somehow having one made me not merely rich but also more of a person. It certified me. Money can do that.

My second recollection went back a mere thirty years to

the time when Oscar was in his late forties, living with my Aunt Tanya in Brooklyn, a short ride from Oscar's warehouse. He ran his own business importing and distributing beer, and would go off to the warehouse every morning in much the same way. They had a routine, as most couples will, in which they drank a cup of coffee together, then rationed the morning paper right there on the stoop into his and hers (his was Sports and hers was Features and the devil take the news of the day) after which he would kiss her cheek and start down the block. At the corner Oscar would look back and wave once. Then, and only then, even on the coldest morning in January, would my aunt go back inside the house.

Not terribly riveting, I know, and yet much was to be made of the fact that this quite ordinary scene, this little play, was enacted with all the usual stops and turns on the morning my uncle vanished into thin air. Because one fine day, as they say in stories, Oscar waved from the corner and was seen no more. Not that evening, nor the next morning; neither the next month nor the next year. Poof!

He had said nothing to give either Tanya or my mother the least hint of his intentions—if he had any, for of course there were initial fears of foul play—nor did any communication reach them during the more than two years he was away. And then he did return, again without fanfare or explanation, on a rainy day in October of 1957, on the eve of Tanya's birthday as it happened, though not because he had remembered it. The occasion had been chosen at random; the dozen yellow roses he admitted were only a "gesture". And that was it.

Time elapsed was in fact two years plus four months— roughly nine calendar seasons. A few ballplayers had retired (most notably Jackie Robinson) and one or two old movie queens might have died, but Ike was still President and Uncle Oscar was "home". Thus the gestation period of a Returnee. I was seventeen, my own life just beginning.

As far as I could tell then it might not begin for some time yet (and sometimes sitting quietly by myself at night I catch myself wondering if it ever has) but I can remember seeing Oscar soon after his return and finding him as sweet and funny as ever. He was always a very affectionate man. And naturally he gave me a dollar that time too, for it had become a tradition with us, and in 1957 a dollar was still money.

Like my parents, I was consumed with curiosity, eager for the story. What had happened to Uncle Oscar? Where had he gone, and why? My sister Barbara said Aunt Tanya "smelled" and that was why; I could not completely ignore her analysis for we had long agreed there was an aroma, albeit one I no longer felt certain I disliked. But could that really have been it? If so, what brought him back? Surely Tanya had not submitted herself to an extensive fumigation in the interim?

Frivolities aside, I did not rouse my limited courage to ask Oscar at the time, and I knew that nothing in the whole creation could be more patently futile than to ask my parents. I did ask eventually, at age nineteen and then throughout my twenties, and I was still asking a decade later though only in jest. By then we both knew, Oscar and I, what his answer would always be: a grin and a one-dollar bill. As the dollar grew smaller (with inflation and because by now I made my own) the grin grew wider, the joke richer. The bill became a source of giddy hilarity to him, such that he might bring himself to tears of laughter in the attempt to make this presentation with a straight face, to his favorite nephew, now thirty-five years old, now forty-one.

And then he was gone again—this time for good—dead at the age of seventy-six and at his funeral my aunt handed me a package. It was flat and rectangular, a cardboard manuscript-box in fact, though what she handed over was wrapped in layers of the rough brown paper and wide tan tape I recognized from the old warehouse, so that nothing inside rattled audibly. A legacy left not in his Will, where I was also remembered, but in trust with Tanya. Did she know what it was?

She said not, and I did and do believe that was the case, though her curiosity must have been boundless. Or perhaps not. Perhaps in real grief and shock, the box could not mean a damned thing to her whatever the contents. She probably assumed it was a dusty collection of old racing sheets anyway, or some idiotic betting "system" for beating the races. To me it was treasure.

Literally so, for when I got it home and opened it later that night I found right on top a crisp freshly-minted two-dollar bill, within the very texture of which I could discern my uncle's laughter. Inflation factored in at last! But beneath the bill, a last playful laugh to share, lay more serious secrets: the Daybooks of Oscar Carnovsky. The missing years, day by day, month by month. Oscar in absentia had kept a journal, and he had kept it ever since—not in the sense that he had added to it (the final entry was dated some two months prior to his return, in 1957) but merely saved it, for me apparently. He wanted someone to see it someday and I turned out to be that someone, to my great delight.

To me the text is absolutely fascinating and endlessly provocative. This is not to say as much would be true for anyone else. But all my life, since the time of Oscar's curious program, my consideration of the larger questions (such as it has been) has always referred back to the "missing years". As far as I know nobody, including Tanya, ever learned a thing about them. It is also true that no one other than myself seems to have much cared, but I have, and I do, and as I say with always the softminded assumption that if there *were* answers or even clues to the larger questions concerning the Purpose or Meaning of life, those answers were tied irrevocably to the mystery of Oscar Carnovsky.

Or the three mysteries I should say—for there were three—at times of a piece in my thinking and at other times quite separate considerations. 1. Why he went, in the peculiar fashion described. 2. What he did while away. 3. Why he came back. Now as a successful, relatively urbane middle-aged businessman, the man to whom Tanya most dutifully did hand the magical package on the morning of the funeral, even as that man I was convinced that I suddenly held the key to these mysteries of Oscar Carnovsky and therefore to the mystery of life itself.

Credulous? Puerile? Certainly you could say so. And though I hesitate to digress, it may be worth a few lines here to tell something of who I am, or appear to be, other than the kid with the dotty disappearing uncle. To put the matter in its simplest form, I am Walter Ford, Jr., born 1940, dirty blond hair, clean gray mind. I am very much what in my youth was derisively called a White Anglo-Saxon Protestant, though my mother was at one time Florence Carnovsky, Oscar's little sister. I do not imagine she thinks of herself that way very often, now (and long since) at two removes from it. This might have been different (and different for myself as well) because in 1935 my mother married a man named Louis Schecter in the Temple Emanuel in Brooklyn, and this was just as God intended I am sure.

The trouble was that in 1937, two scant years later, that young gentleman died "of a heart" and so became in time a curio of sorts to my mother, mere ancient dust to my father who never knew him, and a rather intriguing ghost to me. In 1939 Florence Schecter (née Carnovsky) married again, this time my flesh-and-bloodline father Walter Ford, and just one year later she had become "Flo Ford" and he had become Walter Ford, Senior. Unlike myself, they had each had some choice in these matters.

Never have I felt anything toward my progenitor save warmth, respect, and gratitude. He was always a good father to me and yet at some juncture in my youth I did

also begin to feel that something had gone wrong. I suspect mine was like the experience of a youth who gradually
becomes aware of his own homosexuality, and sees that all
the small differences he has perceived in confusion are
explained by the single unchanging over-arching circumstance. Put it this way: I am a creature of chance, as we all
must be, but of chance gone itself awry—chance to the
second power—because I should have been born two years
earlier, to two different parents, Florence and Louis, in
which case I would be older than I am now not merely by
two years but older in some ways by centuries. I should be
a Jew. I should be Harvey Schecter.

To be Walter Ford, Jr. has never quite fit me, like a suit of
the wrong size, and makes me a changeling before the
fact—before the cradle or the stoop, before even the
womb. A preconceived changeling then, exchanged in the
playful mind of God, the Big Guy, grimacing at Hitler's
advances in Europe, chagrined by Chamberlain's Munich
Appeasement, spinning his magnetized dice in quest of
comic relief. Walter Ford, Jr.

To this day I believe that Schecter is trapped somewhere
inside me, a man as I say slightly older and more emotive
(a worrier really, as I see him) but dark-haired and kindly,
like Oscar I suppose, or like Cissy's older brother Leon.
(Cissy, or Cecilia, is my wife.) I am Schecter suppressed,
enclosed, and it is this lifelong suppression that makes me
what I am: boring. Oh yes, I know it.

Funny thing, growing up Walter I knew Harvey Schec-
ters, lots of them, by various names, and I know for
certain that many wished they had been Walter Fords. I
didn't *not* wish it, I simply wasn't it, like those hypothetical homosexuals who at the first shock of recognition
must have cried inwardly, Oh no not me, for they knew it
was cast in granite, it was what was. At a large conference
in Detroit last month, in a crowded banquet room, I heard
someone call out "Harv!" and spun around to see who it
was wanted my attention.

All right, I have exaggerated all this, been carried away in the telling. It is more a whimsical wisp of a thing, an amusement if you like, and not the governing neurosis of my personality. Of that flat unflappable self myself. I am a great success, you see, flat unflappable success of the most familiar sort—did well in school and never misbehaved. None of this imagined identity confusion deterred my straightline march to status and security. I have never been the kind of success Harvey Schecter might have been, that's all; nary a drop of creative aggression fermenting inside me.

I break stocks, or broker them for a living, and even that is Oscar's joke, not mine. I am a stockbroker, quite the competent one, and I make money at it, so much so that we have houses both in Greenwich and in the Berkshires. Stockbreaking from Stockbridge by telephone, I still make money. Thousands in a few minutes. A fine fellow I am I am. It even comes naturally to me, without effort. Successful slob father of _____ and _____; devoted son to _____ and _____; loving husband of _____. The obituary line is solid, unimpeachable. They'll never suspect it was Harvey they buried, dark-haired Harv in Walter's drab blond body.

All I am telling you, really, is that I am terribly different from the uncle I so loved and admired. That Oscar and I are opposites, or so I see it. Did he see it that way too? And did he leave me with these secrets as a corrective, a lesson before too late, or merely as a kindness, knowing the depth of my interest? For here I sit in my comfortable office suite and nothing can move me; even if I despised my life I'd stay the course. Yet Oscar loved that shabby little office of his and walked away. We fall on the leaning side, that is all one can say, as there are men who will kill without apparent cause and others incapable of the slightest violence though fiendishly provoked.

Just this morning we were in here discussing this whole befuddling nuclear business, and Bill Aarons was saying he felt agonized dealing shares for Niagara-Mohawk's new nuclear plant—that he felt tainted, an accomplice before the fact of some future nuclear disaster. And when I was alone I found myself at the window, looking down thirty-one stories and trying to imagine The Bomb exploding (although we had discussed only the energy side). A vast expanse of Manhattan is visible from up here and yet I could imagine just a piddling blast, a gasoline bomb, that took apart a few storefronts, kicking up chunks of side-walk and filling the air briefly with glass. Nothing sub-stantial. And I felt safe because I could *see* the whole explosion, so small and decorously self-contained that I was never engulfed by it, never included in the damage.

Unimaginable to me that an object dropped here could even rend Central Park, much less devastate the landscape of Massapequa or kill all the shop-keepers where they stand in Nyack and Peekskill, or as far north as Albany. I simply don't feel large things, or better (though ungram-matic) I don't feel things large. The threat of nuclear disaster is to me trifling alongside the threat of the milk going sour.

And that is why I have been so fascinated by Oscar and by what he did, for *until* he did what he did my uncle might have been taken for a timid soul himself. His shoes were nailed as firmly to the kitchen floor as anyone's. Just picture that ritual of departure, every morning for years and years—the kiss and the wave from the corner. How very radical it was, not just that he left (if that's what he did, and it wasn't, as he didn't, finally) but rather *how* he left. In a puff of smoke.

How strange to conceive or be capable of executing such an exit. Think of Tanya that first evening, and the next, and the next. Think of my mother and the other frantic siblings. Think of the long chain of liquor stores on the Island crying out for their Carlsberg and Heineken. See ya fuckin later.

I was there and can well recall how the inconceivability

of Oscar's action was far more discussed than was the act itself, almost as though they resented his methods more than they mourned the loss of his companionship. Granted it was a sea-change, just as wondrous as when some quiet young church-deacon goes ape, swinging naked from lamp-posts and raping shop-girls there in the moonlight.

Yet it did happen. Moreover, as I learned in reading my uncle's journal, it is something of a syndrome. In the early stages of his new existence Oscar was apparently fascinated himself by what he had done, and sought out random examples in life and literature of others who had sunk their boats without trace. Who had waved cheerfully from the corner, as it were, and kept on going. He clearly believed the "Walkaway" was a definite exotic species and set himself to gathering and recording all available lore, like Melville cataloguing the trivia of whales—or more like Noddy Boffin's gallery of misers, since Oscar belonged to the genus even as he researched and compiled it. And belonging, he seems neither horrified nor charmed, merely interested. A student and critic of the possibilities of the form.

Of course one could argue that this "rare" phenomenon is nothing but a variation on the commoner forms of separation and divorce, that those categorized as Walkaways stand linked by some incalculable coefficient of correlation to those others who simply walk out in conventional fashion (after much disputation and grief) and possibly also to the myriad who never go at all yet wish to. "The mass of men lead lives of public transportation," as Oscar's friend and associate Wally Wiley puts the matter in these pages. But I am inclined to agree with my uncle that there is a difference in kind, something unique here, just as all men walk but very few walk the high wire.

Now I offer these notes to the world with no true sense of their value to anyone other than myself. Although the chronological nature of their accumulation makes it possible to posit a beginning, middle and end of sorts, they do not purport to tell a story. And while they do more or less provide answers to the three mysteries of Oscar Carnovsky, the answers themselves do not involve thrills or chills; he never fell in with pirates or princes, or proved ready to die for perfect love. So perhaps it is all quite drab.

In fairness to Oscar, the journal was never shaped or edited, nor was it originally intended for anyone's eyes but his own. It came to me strewn with blots and doodles and cross-outs—a pile of paper. If it fails the tests of literature, the fault is not Oscar's but mine, for presenting it as such. I will say, though, that words nowadays are "processed," like fake cheese, and these words, Oscar's, are not. They are him, no "cheese product" but rather the real cheese. There is a voice in these pages that becomes more and more Oscar to me as I listen to it.

My uncle did not believe he spoke "like a Jew," and he disliked the speech of relatives who did so broadly. He chose consciously to do otherwise, melting his voice into the potpourri, and I am sure he would not like to know that I detect in his "scribble" (as I did in his speech), the lilt and language of his forebears. This is not a literary voice, it is Oscar's literal voice. I don't read these notes really, I *hear* them sounding in the room.

Though he clearly found it a chore at times, it is equally clear that Oscar enjoyed recording his impressions, that it satisfied some whimsy of his to wax literary, as I confess it has done for me too in these pages I usurp. Indeed I have gone so far as to divide the text into three parts, arbitrarily I know, and to assign these parts titles. Likewise the title this volume bears is my contribution to it and warrants one final explanation, because although the words come from Oscar, they do not (as the other headings all do), come from his daybooks.

I know the word "retreat" suggests many things, chiefly

monks and the flight of armies. What I must add, that you cannot know, is that my uncle was quite a chess player in the parks and cafés as a young man and he had a habit of giving jocular names— parodies really of the names for gambits in chess—to the erratic and often deliberately self-defeating strategems he employed in our years of competitive checkers.

On one occasion he kept moving his men backward, toward an implied box-canyon where I with my several advancing kings would surely corner them, but then with the rout most imminent he suddenly effected a stunning triple jump, seizing three kings at a single stroke and sending me down to a crashing defeat. (I told you I was credulous, though he did almost always let me win.)

I had completely forgotten the game, and the name he had given his winning gambit, until we found ourselves playing the same game under the exact same conditions about one year later. We sat at the cluttered weatherbeaten table in Oscar's freezing office, and a Saturday morning sleet was sinking past the big drafty windows into the harbor waters below, and the exact same sequence unfolded (with the exact same result).

And Oscar moved his head sadly, almost gravely, in reference to the "gambit" he had expected me to recognize.

"Carnovsky's Retreat!" he said. "You never learn, dear Walter, you must watch for Carnovsky's Retreat."

# I

## A Hole in the Water

### Summer 1955–

Well I kept going, just as I imagined it possible, and now I'm gone. Not far—I never meant to go very far. I'm no world explorer, not a tourist of some kind, just an every-day joey who crossed the Brooklyn Bridge. This is still my territory here, smells like saltwater and diesel, feels all right to me, and the people speak my language. Of course I know the neighborhood, since Kramer re-located here years back.

This hotel is nothing but a dump, for drunken sailors and two-bit crooks I'm sure. The Bedbug Hilton. They can't even offer the use of a tub or shower, but I will be gone from here too, as soon as I have worked out a few minor details. Such as where I go instead. I look for a place the oldfashioned way, knock on every door. Because the newspaper is a big waste of time. Anything good in there gets snatched up while you are still fishing a nickel for the phone-call.

This notebook will be my diary, to keep track of things, keep tabs on myself, as time races away and nothing is left behind. A man who goes overboard and drowns is just a hole in the water, and it will close over him fast. Likewise something might occur yet by the very next week you lost track of what it was. And it was your life.

Dear diary. You see that keeping a record like this gives you something to do, it obligates you, and can also serve to absorb your worst fears. For instance I worry about the

Missing Persons. I stagger around with sugarwater in my gas-tank thinking, Oh my God what if Tanya has called in the Missing Persons! Of course I am not missing, I am right here, but she doesn't know that until she gets to the bank and finds all the money.

So I peek through the filthy curtains of the Bedbug Hilton like an escaped convict, and I peek around every streetcorner before advancing, to see if the FBI has got me staked out. No wonder I woke up this a.m. and suffered a nice bout of going back—thinking, drop the whole idea and hustle back there before the soup really thickens. If I turn tail today then nothing has changed. Just the drummer fell asleep and missed a beat. It is possible I didn't lose a single order yet. Go down to the office, make my calls, and erase it from the record with some little story. It never happened.

The diary is my salvation. If I start to put it all down, start to talk about it, then I will not do it. I'll get calmed down and put my nerves on the back burner till after breakfast. And so I am talking to my diary (this is me talking right now) and I am not going to the office to make my calls. I am going elsewhere—out to Jamaica to make the first post.

Same night. On the beam out there. I had a feeling for the 7-horse in today's feature. She got bumped early last time and drifted way back, so there she was at 10-1 in the morning line and I knew better than that. So did a few others, and bet her down to 3-1 at post, but it was still pretty good. Then for the hell of it I hit a quinella on my way out the door and took home a few hundred altogether.

Also, in the meanwhile, I stopped worrying. Out there my nerves are steadied. Someone this hot the F.B.I. won't find even if they are looking. And I recalled my friend Tannenbaum, the criminal lawyer, who told us the bad guys always went to some little town upstate to hide, East Flat Rock or Horseshoe Junction, where they stood out like a tuxedo in a nudist colony. Manhattan is the place to play lose-me, he said, and no one is smart enough to know it. Well I am. So I was set to pick up one of those phony Groucho-noses, with the glasses and eyebrows attached, at a joke-shop near here, but decided to stand on my dignity instead. And I got back and sat down in the Battery Park reading my evening paper, just like a person who isn't missing in the first place.

Tomorrow I get to take a peek at the room on Battersea. Here's hoping I like it and it likes me, because for one thing I could use a bath. Play with fire you get burnt, live in a ditch you get a little messy.

I might take my penny and march myself up to the public baths on 1st Avenue and then again I might not. It's warm enough I could splash in the sea at Coney Island and get clean (if you call that clean) and I'm sure no soul would recognize me at the beach. I haven't bared my chest in public for ten years. Still I could be spotted on the train, a sitting duck, that's where the risk would lie.

Another thought I had (though just a joke, like Groucho's nose) is on Tanya's dancing afternoon sneak in my own house and enjoy a nice hot shower. Like a ghost, float in. A wraith, the invisible mensch, that's me.

But Mrs. Getz would get me. She would spot me for sure and start yelling out her kitchen window, Oscar Oscar, good to see you home safe and sound! Anyway it's not for real. I would never go near the place, it's too rough on Tanya. When I am sitting here and thinking about there, then I am just a kid playing a game, that's all. And what's the name of the game? You run away from home, of course.

Saturday. I am in "first position" for the room at 10 Battersea Street. Whatever the hell that means. I think it means I hustle back there in the morning and offer the little weasel six months rent cash in advance if I want the place. Because your credit is not so hot, your credentials, when you must answer "Current Address" with The Bedbug Hilton.

Sunday. Yes I got the room. I was right. Without a job or an automobile registered, without so much as a goddamned suitcase, a man is not a good risk. Face it, a liability, he doesn't impress. Either they let him out of prison last week or else they haven't quite gotten around to putting him in there.

How do you turn a liability like this into a benefit? How do you make a good impression in this city? Show your money.

I let him have three months in advance and a phony name and I can move in next weekend. Last time I moved house I ordered up the biggest truck they had—this time it will take two shopping bags, maybe three.

Touched down at the library as it opened up today, then out to the track in time for lunch. Hearn very much excited about Price Tag in the first and bet his shirt. (Lucky thing he's got more shirts at home.) I had no big opinions myself but made out a little anyway.

Riding back on the train I remembered how right after the War I was going only now and then to the track, and playing a few races with Kramer. I was too busy then, getting ahead in life. Maybe I put a thousand a year on the line, maybe I got twelve hundred back. I know I never in my life had put so much as fifty dollars on a single horse, or never but once and that was a horse I dreamed about the night before. In the dream I watched this nag, Silly Ginger, crossing the wire with about ten lengths on the favorite. So I took a fifty-dollar flyer and so did the horse. That saved me from getting religion.

Anyhow it was that way for years, I was just *playing* the races, and then somewhere along the line I began taking the Morning Telegraph at the warehouse, delivered fresh every morning, and heading out to the Island a few afternoons a week. And I got a little reckless too—I didn't mind. One day win big, next day give it back, hundreds every day one way or the other.

A man on the edge, that was me, in love with danger. Look now—my business sits rotting across the East River and here I sit feeling no pain. The thrill, however, did not come from danger at all. In truth the reverse. The thrill came from the fact that I could sense *no* danger. I risked nothing because the money didn't matter to me. I didn't love the money so much anymore (who knows why) and that made it into a game, a child's play again. If you don't love the money, then let five hundred go, let one thousand. Doesn't hurt you.

And that was the real thrill, finding out there was no danger to fear. The discovery that *nothing matters*. Because that is freedom.


Now when you choose to maintain a diary you are holding yourself accountable. I detect in my latest that "nothing matters." But it gives me pause to read it, where it gave only the greatest pleasure to write it down.

Can it be such a cause for joy that "nothing matters"? If nothing matters will a person find happiness? Where? So something is wrong here.


A test I conducted today. Because I can *say* that nothing

matters but does nothing matter in fact? I can say I'm Roy Campanella but that don't make me roly-poly. So I went out there and for the first time in my life I bet what Hearn calls a dime—what I call a thousand bucks. Will I not care a damn if I go stony broke and don't have the price of a hot dog and a watery coffee?

Unfortunately for science I had no chance to sweat on this one. Too smart a bet. Peashooter was good at 4-1 in the morning but he was already an underlay at 2-1 when I took him a thousand bucks worth and thanks in part to me he went off at 7-5. An underlay is my most nervous bet, even for a fiver, because I never expect a horse to carry the flood of late money from the panic-buyers, the band-wagonmasters. It's like extra weight on his back.

Today however the smart money was smart and he went wire to wire in a cool breeze. I broke it up in little pieces, my big bet, because you don't want to attract anyone's attention and you never know where Uncle is. They make you sign in with Uncle and pay your taxes on the spot only if the odds are very long, but a ghost must put some thought into all his large transactions.

And this was large—the down payment on Buckingham Palace. Yet it fouled up my test. I started parlaying it back in pieces too, on the jockey, on the barn, on the five-hole—wild bets I was happy to lose, if only because a handicapper hates luck, or dumb luck, until it leaves him. I was not handicapping, though, just gambling, and I gave back most of the dough before I was done for the day.

Still it did not test my theory because this was play money, someone else's money I was spraying. Wasn't money I felt a strong attachment to. Easy come easy go dough, that's all it was today. Yet such a nice day. A sea breeze and clear sunshine on every square inch of the world including my heart.


Tomorrow's the day. I take up occupancy at 10 Battersea

Street, hence this is my last night at the Hilton. History in the making, Oscar Carnovsky slept here! (Though he has slept better elsewhere.)

I was not looking forward to copying out the doctor's story—anything over twenty minutes I get writer's cramp. But Mrs. K. at the library saved my bacon. She used her thermofax to provide me with my own personal copy—I can just file it here and have plenty of time left over to pack up my toothbrush.

There is no scandal on Skid Row. In a very real sense all scandal occurs in high places, for it is the very height of the place that lends the whiff of scandal. And one of the sniffiest in some time is now unfolding in the exclusive upper-crusty Connecticut shore village of Deephaven.

At the center of the storm stood the once and future Dr. Mark Widmer, who five years ago was a wealthy, highly regarded obstetrician with practices in Deephaven and New Haven and a summer home in Peacham, Vermont. Handsome and charming, the patrician Dr. Widmer was "a man you liked and trusted instantly." He had the bedside manner. He also had three children and a wife of twenty years.

Once and future Widmer, though, because for the last five years, during which time he was missing and deemed legally dead, he was Harold "Hal" Prince of Savannah, Georgia. This is how it happened:

On a bright windy March morning in 1950, Dr. Widmer strolled some two miles along the private strip of beach from his home to the ocean marina, cooperatively maintained, where he and a few other families moored small craft. The boats were not in the water. The attendant's shed and gashouse below were shuttered. Inside the shed at this time of year would be "maybe a few pennants and a rusty anchor, nothing much," according to Widmer's longtime friend and associate Dr. Frank Parsons, also of Deephaven.

Upon the sturdy oaken dock were found (some twelve hours later that night) the doctor's clothing and shoes—every stitch and seam—and a pair of binoculars he used for viewing sea-birds, a hobby. The binoculars were a personal treasure of

Widmer's for having once belonged to President Theodore Roosevelt.

The inescapable conclusion was that Mark Widmer had gone in the water and never come out.

Whether he went voluntarily, on a whim, or because of unknown foul players, it did not seem he could be anyplace else. He might have washed up farther down the coast, or been rescued by an outward bound fishing vessel, but the general assumption was he had drowned.

Moreover, though they could find no motive for it, the police believed that suicide was indicated. Captain Sherman of the Connecticut State Police continued to believe even after the insurance companies agreed to pay full damages on the double indemnity clause, that the careful placement of clothing on the dock constituted "a note of sorts, a clear enough message." Not himself a swimmer in any season, Captain Sherman could not be persuaded a man might dive into the sea for pleasure on a cold March morning when the water temperature was 39° Fahrenheit.

Against the trooper's instincts there arose the full weight of unanimous testimony from Deephaven's elite that the very idea was ludicrous. Widmer was simply too vital, life-loving, beloved by friends and family, valued by the town, a pillar of the church, and so on right down the line. And so the verdict, taken in the absence of any proof to the contrary, was accidental death by drowning.

The records were filed away and Louise Widmer set about the difficult task of caring for three teenaged children in a large house, admittedly wealthier by $100,000 yet still reeling emotionally from the shocking loss of a man she had loved "all my life, it seemed."

Meanwhile, the pillar of the church was living it up down in Florida with his beautiful young girlfriend.

For as it came to light last month (when he returned some five years after the moving pageantry of his own ritzy funeral), Dr. Widmer had not drowned that day. He had not even got his tootsies wet. Instead he had unpacked a bundle of clothing on the dock, tossed his well-known binoculars on top for effect, and cut through the fringe of pinewoods lead-

ing back to the road where a woman who shall be called
"Catherine" here (that is not her actual name) was waiting for
him in her 1946 Packard. In the trunk of the car were suit-
cases, a portable radio, and a canvas bag containing 500 ten-
dollar bills.

They put up for two weeks in a motel on the Gulf in St.
Petersburg, where Widmer read on the beach and Catherine
went to watch the baseball players train. Then after a trip
through the Blue Ridge Mountains, they settled in Savannah
where he worked, under his own whimsically chosen
monicker Hal Prince, in a marine biology laboratory, reading
slides. The life they carved out in Savannah—rented homes,
jobs, two small children—was the one they shared more or
less up to the time Prince returned, or Widmer did, to Deephaven last month. He told his wife over the telephone that he
had a lot to say to her so they should perhaps plan on having
dinner in the city that evening. She had not remarried.

Catherine had been the doctor's patient. She was young
(24), pregnant, and unwed. She didn't even have a steady
boyfriend. The baby's father had been "passing through." But
she was a very pretty girl and she was also a bit of a Bohemian, having worked chiefly as an artist's model in New
Haven. Though her family was well-to-do, her father in fact a
banker, they had not heard from her in years.

Widmer fell in love with the girl and she accepted his
protection, medically at first and then in every way. They
carried on their affair in his Deephaven office until the baby
had begun to show and the doctor had begun to plot his
disappearance. Just so, in a Georgia coffee shop this Spring, he
began to draw up a scheme for returning.

He missed the practice of medicine. Having had two small
children to raise, he wished very much to see his three grown
ones, and he wished to be with his wife again, walking the
familiar strand, birding, clamming . . .

It should also be mentioned that Catherine had taken the
children and left him for a young man of nineteen, a roust-
about. Now that she was close to thirty and Widmer in his late
fifties, the thing had become unseemly to her and she reminded him that he had no *legal* connection to the children—

that he was in fact the biological father of just one. ("Oh. 'Just one, then,' she expected me to say, I suppose.")

It never crossed Hal's mind that he perhaps ought not return, that there might be other, better directions to take. He was certain Louise would forgive and welcome him back home; he only hoped she had maintained the boats and retrieved in good fettle his T.R. binoculars.

Their life together had, after all, been rather perfect in his recollection. But Louise had different memories and, possessed of the facts, did not feel up to welcoming him home. In fact her initial impulse was "to kill him, to finish the job—that would keep things neat at least."

The insurance proceedings were closed to the public but the criminal fraud prosecution is just underway in New Haven Superior Court and Hal Prince (the name taken from Shakespeare's Prince Hal, a rather more quixotic figure) has been playing to packed houses all week.

And up in the remote, ornate balconies of this old Victorian pile, several spectators have been seen focussing binoculars on the leading man, admittedly a rare bird in any field.

I have yet to find another word on this case anywhere in the library, so this constitutes the whole story so far as I know it. Maybe try the Connecticut papers. But I can explain this man and I will do so at my earliest. At the moment, I am going to organize my belongings, and doze.

Moving out of the Bedbug Hilton, hoping the bedbugs stay put and don't move with me. I was over there, the new room, once already today and the key worked. The place was empty, *exactly* empty like a barren plain. Okay so at least there is nothing bad in there—not a mouse, not a louse. (Until I take up occupancy.) But of course it will need a lot of things, I never stopped to realize. Bed, chair, table, at the minimum.

So I thought of the basement in Brooklyn, where I have jammed in beds, chairs, tables, and more. All the extra furniture, decent enough some of it, and there it sits being wasted. Likewise I went to wondering if Tanya took the trouble to cancel the racing papers. A lot of dough if she didn't, and subscriptions are the least of it. But I came to my senses, such as they are. What I am doing, what I did, is not good fiscal policy. Efficient it ain't, nor practical in the slightest. No point worrying over the mailbox and the bills and what's in the basement back there. Kiss it goodbye. Stop thinking and go buy a bed, only give it a good shake to make sure no bugs.

Tuesday night. I'm in and very pleased with my new address. (Went mid-town for dinner in celebration.) All the comforts for fifteen a week, including my own tub and a plug-in hotplate for cooking. The dishes must be done in the bathroom sink but it's not a big problem for a one-dish family like me. Also I like some sunlight inside the house and this one is blotted out by the apartment building behind. But what the hell, I can step outside for sunlight and the place is nice and cool on a doublebroiler day like today. So why quibble?

I said that to Kramer once, why quibble, and he said Because you're a Jew, Oscar. If you don't quibble then no one will and we will lose track of the details. Maybe so but there is also the reverse—that you lose track of the Big Picture if you sit picking nits.

I like being located close to the water. It's a skip and a jump from here to Coentes Slip or over to Battery Park and I am in plain sight of the Brooklyn Bridge. I still have the smell of sea-water and the fresh fish-catch, along with the music of the tug-boats in the basin. From the roof of this building, not easily attained, I could see clear across to the Heights and maybe if I had Teddy Roosevelt's binoculars with me I could look right in the window of my office and see Giselle in there trying to make some sense of the bookkeeping I left behind.

You think of a Walkaway and you think Timbuktoo or the Himalayas, but it is not necessary. This is a big world and a big city. You can be a stranger three blocks from your house, because nobody leaves the neighborhood. My friends don't cross the Bridge. Tanya did it twice in ten years, to my knowledge, and both times on my arm. This is another planet here, a world away, and I am not looking back over my shoulder anymore. I just go about my business.

And Tanya I'm sure goes about hers. The weather is so good and the Dodgers are headed for the World Series, and between the Hadassah and her dancing I can't help thinking Tanya must be well. Maybe even glad to have me out of there.


With Widmer they all talk about the money he had, the big connections, the pretty girl. It's all beachfronts and mountaintops and fun in the sun with a highpowered dinghy. Not one bit are they fazed by what this guy did— that he could lift off without a sound. He slipped the traces, flew the coop, and never said a mumbling word. Do they think this is normal? Do they believe it's easy?

Clothes on the dock. It wouldn't fool a little boy with a plastic detectives kit. And now they think that the point of the story is that he left on account of a girl. What else is new? That's also why he came back, when it was finished with the girl.

They leave all the time, every day, because of Blondie. A little strange leg and it's lights out America. But they agonize about it. They sweat and confess and after they do battle-royal they always settle up the money. What they do *not* do is drop a nice outfit, slacks and a sweater, on the dock and tip-toe through the tulips to Saint Pete. That's crazy stuff. And that is the point.

But I can explain this man. First off of course he did settle up. He left plenty behind, made the arrangements. He did not choose to consult the wife about it, and that's a doctor for you every time. He figures there's no need to put anything to a vote when he is always in the know. This particular doctor, however, is also ashamed of himself. Proud of himself I'm sure, very cock-of-the walk with a smooth little backside in his bed, yet ashamed before the world. And before he will suffer the world's opinion he would rather erase himself from the record.

This can happen when you get too high up. Everyone must sooner or later drop down in class— a baseball great, movie queen—must take the backward step and it hurts. There's a poem about it that you read in high school, to the athlete dying young. Either you die young or you die going downhill from your prime, that's the story. Pay the nickel and take the choice.

But Doctor won't choose. He wants to eat his cake and have it too. He must be "dead" in order to keep his place up there on the pedestal he made for himself. So he appoints himself the silver-haired hero of the funeral and leaves everyone happy he could die so well-born.

The man spent his time making a reputation. Now he wants to make a life but can't waste the work he put in on the reputation. A charming man they all agree, I'm sure in Savannah too.


I shouldn't have to worry if I get a little bout of home-sick because freedom means I can board the boat for Spain early tomorrow, or take the parachute jump at Coney Island without a parachute if I prefer it that way. But it also means I could go to my old house, sit down on my chair in the living room, and take a look at the sports page. *If that's*

*where freedom takes me.* You don't want to stop yourself in
life—let something else stop you. (For example, Tanya
might say Get lost, as Mrs. Wid did, but that would be for
*her* to decide.)

As far as the parachute jump at Steeplechase Park, I
never took a notion even with the parachute. Not for me.
Put my life in the hands of a bag of wind? When my dear
nephew Walter asked me to take him up, I was very relieved his old man nixed it. Saved me admitting I would
never. (Uncles must stand for adventure.)


Completed interior decorating today with a nice brass
lamp—standup kind—from the flea market on Bowling
Green. A package of two light bulbs at the hardware cost
me the same money as the lamp did. Figure that one.

Figure this one too, a new vice to report. Two nights
back I got an eyeful of my girl neighbor across the alleyway, and then last night the same again. And it is as they
say: the Devil made me do it the first time but the second
time I did it on my own. Let the record show I looked.


Saturday night, so what? I feel like I should be on to
something and I'm not even close. If I was home we would
eat, the two of us or possibly in a restaurant with Morris
and the Mrs., and then we would walk and talk (if Morris
then politics, if the two of us then family) and afterwards
settle down to the business of bed.

So what does a single man do? Prowl the city like an
alleycat? Bowl a few strings and wash down the week's
dust at a tavern? Maybe. Or sit home and say So what,
and wait till his neighbor gets ready for beddie.


They say the last one to know he is crazy is always the
crazy man himself. He feels sharp as a tack, sees it all

clearly, like a newborn genius. That's me to a tee. I can feel my brain waking up. I am seeing the world in a new way— and I don't mean Seeing the World like from the Eiffel Tower or London Bridge, I mean seeing it right here under my own nose where it's always been. And if they told me I was crazy I would definitely refuse to believe them. If they came to reel me in, the men in the white suits, I would kick and scream and tell them Hands off the newborn genius.

All right, tonight's subject is Oscar Fish, a new man in town. Who is this Fish?

It's me of course—I am Fish. It's the phony name I gave, my nom de guerre or de plume, whatever. It's a little bit for hiding behind, naturally, but also for fun. Brooklyn is across the water but it is not across the water like Paris is and supposing a detective did come over to Manhattan, suppose he did nothing more brilliant than browse around with his index finger on the rooming-house logbooks, or crummy hotels like The Bedbug Hilton? He might take the trouble.

Or suppose he has friends and sets their ears to the tune "Carnovsky," tells them Give me a bang on the telephone if you happen to catch these syllables. It could happen. Fish is the precaution.

A new life rates a new name in any case. Hal Prince got one. So did Pierce, the man in the detective story, which I must put in soon. They keep the names simple for two reasons—easy to remember (for you) and hard to notice (for them). Who minds a Prince or a Pierce?

Of course you have the license, be anyone you want. Just keep a straight face when you say it. So do I want to be an eye-talian tonight? Whoops, I am Dino Rinaldi. A Greco? Make me Spyros Skyros. Or polish your teeth, paint on a pencil-thin moustache, and watch out for Clark Hutton, Leading Man. The self-named man.

I considered putting hair on my face, add a beard and

look like the ancestors. You can hide behind a nice bushy beard, like the ones on the cough-drop boys. Buy Fish Brothers Cough-Drops, they stick to your beard! But in the end no new hair and just the name of Fish. It fits somehow.

Good to be comfy with a new name, to feel it belongs with you, and if you are changing over at an advanced age this is no easy proposition. Fish came to me from the neighborhood, it's no great inspiration, just short and easy to say. You couldn't argue with it the way you might argue with Katzenjammer Junior or Burlingame the Fourth. It's silly but quick off the tongue: Fish, like a fact unvarnished.

Oscar Fish, I say, and I even believe it myself. Because it's over before you can argue, perfectly real.


Tonight I will enter into the record the tale of Flitcraft (Pierce), a good one, from the detective book. And credit to my friend Mrs. Kearney at the library desk who had it in mind when I first asked about the topic and then went and located it. How wonderful to recall something from a book read years ago. I never could.


A man named Flitcraft had left his real-estate office, in Tacoma, to go to luncheon one day and had never returned. He did not keep an engagement to play golf after four that afternoon, though he had taken the initiative in making the engagement less than half an hour before he went out to luncheon. His wife and children never saw him again. His wife and he were supposed to be on the best of terms. He had two children, boys, one five and the other three. He owned his house in a Tacoma suburb, a new Packard, and the rest of the appurtenances of successful American living.

Flitcraft had inherited seventy thousand dollars from his father and, with his success in real estate, was worth something in the neighborhood of two hundred thousand dollars at the time he vanished. His affairs were in order, though there were enough loose ends to indicate that he had not been setting them in order preparatory to vanishing. A deal that would have brought him an attractive profit, for instance, was to have been concluded the day after the one on which he disappeared. There was nothing to suggest that he had more than fifty or sixty dollars in his immediate possession at the time of his going.

He went like that, like a fist when you open your hand.

That was in 1922. In 1927 I was with one of the big detective agencies in Seattle. Mrs. Flitcraft came in and told us somebody had seen a man in Spokane who looked a lot like her husband. I went over there. It was Flitcraft all right. He had been living in Spokane for a couple of years as Charles Pierce. He had an automobile business that was netting him twenty or twenty-five thousand a year, a wife, a baby son, owned his own home in a Spokane suburb, and usually got away to play golf after four in the afternoon during the season.

Here's what happened to him. Going to lunch he passed an office-building that was being put up—just the skeleton. A beam or something fell eight or ten stories down and smacked the sidewalk alongside him. It brushed pretty close to him, but didn't touch him, though a piece of the sidewalk glanced off his cheek. He was scared stiff of course, he said, but he was more shocked than really frightened. He felt like somebody had taken the lid off life and let him look at the works.

He, the good-citizen-husband-father, could be wiped out between office and restaurant by the accident of a falling beam. He knew then that men die at haphazard like that, and lived only while blind chance spared them.

It was not, primarily, the injustice of it that disturbed him: he accepted that after the first shock. What disturbed him was the discovery that in sensibly ordering his affairs he had gone out of step, and not into step, with life. He said he knew before he had gone twenty feet from the fallen beam that he would never know peace again until he had adjusted himself to this new glimpse of life. By the time he had eaten his luncheon he had found the means of adjustment. Life could be ended for him at random by a falling beam: he would change his life at random by simply going away.

He went to Seattle that afternoon and from there by boat to San Francisco. For a couple of years he wandered around and then drifted back to the Northwest, and settled in Spokane and got married. His second wife didn't look like the first, but they were more alike than different. You know, the kind of woman that play fair games of golf and bridge and like new salad-recipes. He wasn't sorry for what he had done. It seemed reasonable enough to him. I don't think he even knew he had settled back naturally into the same groove he had jumped out of in Tacoma. But that's the part of it I always liked. He adjusted himself to beams falling, and then no more of them fell, and he adjusted to them not falling.

And that's Flitcraft, not exactly a sentimental fellow. He leaves behind the beloved country club, and a wife should never be surprised, but I am interested that these men can leave behind their children. A child expects so much, it's a piece of his heart every time you disappoint him. I believe that for me a child would alter the matter.

Of course I haven't got one and not only that—I was never nicked by a steel beam or rolled in the hay by a cute little blonde either.

Quiet morning with newspapers, noisy afternoon at Belmont Park. Found just one race worth playing all day, an absolute certainty which got there very late, by a nose hair. I was sure we got photoed out until they put the number up. They forgave me all my misconceptions and handed me the money.

Flitcraft's story reminded me very much of a couple of things that happened to me recently. Trivial matters, nothing along the lines of a steel beam, but I'll put them in the record.

Last winter I was coming down the access road to the loading dock, the steep part where the pavement is always rutted with ice so you go very slow, taking baby steps and yet all of a sudden my feet fly right up in my face. A flash of magic, like a film with a few frames cut out in the middle. Walking and *carefully,* but before I know it I am upside down in the air ass-over-teakettle and seeing my shoe-tops. The crash landing woke up my ass-bone forever and cracked the left elbow for good measure.

I was kayoed pretty good. The shock of flying and the shock of landing makes your stomach light and I just sat there awhile, first confused and then hurting. And when I regained a few of my senses, I confess my first move was to check and see were there any witnesses to this humiliation. Relieved to see none, but I stayed down for the count and got a little thinking done right there on the ground. I can't say exactly what I thought, or what I concluded—maybe what fools we are so easily shown to be as in our presumed dignity we parade, something along these lines.

But reading Flitcraft transported me right back there. I could feel the cold coming through the seat of my pants just as though I was still sitting and thinking. Flitcraft got a real scare, his life was threatened, but I got a scare too. Not so dramatic of course. In fact the reverse—I felt like an idiot, a clumsy fool, and so it took me longer than just "luncheon" to put the matter straight in my head. Nonetheless I concluded that my life was threatened too and it was this experience, along with one other, that gave me a good kick.

So you never know which are the small matters and which are large. Because the other one is even smaller, non-existing, could not be a more trivial moment in any man's life—and yet it did a job on me. Also last winter on a Tuesday so things were dead at the office, nothing coming in, nothing going out, and the phone is just a black lump on the desk. I puff on a Gonzales to stay awake and look over what's up at Hialeah. Kill time. A day like that when

Walter was little I might grab him for a few hours, take him around. Or eat a sandwich with Benny Herz, who's not so busy himself these days.

That day I prowled around, good and restless. Say hello to the girls downstairs, say hello to Freddie upstairs—nothing. Finally I decide I will do a cleanup, sweep the floor. I'll capture the big dustbunnies that move around on you with the cold drafts. I spend a few minutes at this and now I've got them gathered in a nice gray pillow on the floor and set out to search for the dustpan. No can find, so I try for a magazine, shirt cardboard, anything flat. (Newspaper doesn't do it.) I end up ripping the back cover off the phone-book and I scoop up the pile—*but this is my morning's activity!*

Nor is it done with, because next I am wandering the halls looking for the damn wastebasket. I have the fuzz balanced on the flat and I am shielding it from drafts with body english because God forbid it should whisk away on me and escape back to the floor and then suddenly it hits me smacko that I am some kind of lunatic. Look where I put my time and energy! I could drop dead this very second, on the spot from a heart attack like my father's brother Abe (on the spot in his own den, with a glass of fresh-steeped tea in his hand—he was alive, he was dead) and what if it was so? What if my life ended right then and there, wandering the corridor and holding my breath for fear a plate of filthy fuzz and mouse-droppings should blow away! What would they give me for a monument?

And I flipped it, like a pancake, and walked away. Kept on walking two solid hours in zero degree weather, coldest day of the year, around Wallabout Market as deserted as a ghost town and back down to the waterfront again. You could have broken my ears off like a dry biscuit.

Everyone must have such moments, many of them. I know that what I did was look too close, I put a microscope on it. Yet what stayed with me was this. The

cleanup, the dustbunnies, I was doing out of sheer emp-
tiness in the first place. If I wasn't doing that, I was doing
nothing at all. And if you do nothing you *are* nothing, so
you try to keep something happening.

Plenty of people will overeat because of this rule. They
find time on their hands so they move around the house
searching and all they find is food. So they eat it, it's
something to do. It's why Lottie is so fat. If she had a
couple of kids to chase around that place she would not be
poking her face into the frigidaire every ten seconds, and I
told her as much. (To which she replied, "What do *you*
know?" But what else would she say?)

Anyway I saw my life that day and it starts you thinking.
Like the steel beam, it's a wakeup call and thinking makes
you think in just the same way not-thinking makes you not
think. You can get lulled, day by day. That's why I tell
Florrie please, not so much of the television for Walter. If
he watches loony tunes all day he will go nowhere in this
world, he'll just go blind.


I'm liking my new neighborhood. This block is all
residential but in New York nothing is far away. On Water
Street there is a pharmacy, nice grocer, everything. I use
the laundry there too—cheap, fast, and a good job. The
Chinaman knows me already and knows how I like it
done. Fine by him. Anything I ask, he has the same
response—"No problem." It may be his only English. He
writes the price on the wrapping and when I pay he smiles,
and if I say thank you very much he will give me one more
chorus of "No problem" and leave it at that. Fine by me.
Loose lips sink ships, but here it's no problem.

Across from Wing-Wang is Bulkitis' News Stand. A hut,
a raft with a roof, floating there on the streetcorner. Every
morning Bulkitis himself sets out a rack of papers, magazines, comics etc. on the curb. Inside he keeps tobacco,

candy, soda and the rest of the magazines. I pick up my Racing Form there and chat with Bulkitis, who is a Giants fan but likable. Sometimes he will ask me to bring him back a soup from the diner, or a coffee and buttered muffin, bran or cranberry. Tanya would shoot me first and ask questions later if she found out I was hobnobbing with a Giants fan, but I try to give him understanding. I say, Tell me Bulkitis, is it that your mama didn't love you enough? Because you must understand a Giants fan is a disturbed individual who may require some sympathy. Not his fault if mother's milk was sour. So treat him like a human, it can't cost us any ballgames.

I take my breakfast at the South Street Diner. The fishermen are out early, then comes a wave of longshoremen, and then the smoke clears by nine, when I arrive. A bummy bunch in there at that hour, Bowery stragglers, but you can find an empty stool and read your papers in comfort while they fry the food. Two pleasant men who smile hello and dish it up and though you don't hear them saying much their hands never stop. The food is good and they keep the place nice—a shine on the marble counters, a polish on the cherrywood cases—so their business booms all morning.

I like sausage and eggs, toast and coffee, and sometimes splurge on the fresh-squeezed orange juice. But I have sampled the house special—fried fish, fried potatoes, toast and coffee for 65¢. Plenty of fish on the plate and none fresher, because these guys stroll down in person and take it off the boat still flapping.

Reading back my fight with the dustbunnies it sounds as though I don't care for my work. Not so. I take pride in Carnovsky's Fine Liquors and also I enjoy the business. That was just what occurred on one particular Tuesday, my slow day.

It's no palace there. If a windowpane goes, no one comes to put it back, and plenty are gone, though mostly in the empty rooms. The furniture will impress no one. It was all left behind when I came there and it hasn't gotten any younger. The walls I paper with calendars that come in the mail—guns and dogs, waterfalls, girls in bathing-suits, girls in birthday-suits. Whatever they send me I'll put it up, to cut down the drafts. And up on the roof, where I like to go once in a while for a look-out over the water, up there you find yourself standing on a white beach of bird-droppings. It would take a crew of ten men a month to scrape the shit away and still it keeps coming, like an all-year snow.

But so what. Makes no difference, no one ever visits. My business is all on the phone and in the field selling. I make a call, I get a call, and my boys head out in the truck. I will miss the life. Miss sitting at my desk with my Form and a Gonzales and maybe even a cup of Ryker's poisonous coffee that he brews up with old motor oil. Miss the hubbub of the boats and longshoremen bitching—music to my ears.

I built that business and I would rather move beer off a boat than sit on the 117th floor downtown with a stethoscope on my neck nodding sagely. You can have your doctors and lawyers, mama, I'd rather sell beer.


I get a lot of walking done these days, and utilize the library. Then I take the train to Belmont Park and that's my day's work, come and go as I please.

Two straight days out there without a favorite on top, which happens, though it always makes a sour house when it does. I don't mind. I never favor a favorite too much. I like a 5-1 horse who shows me he might be ready. Favorites I might pair up in a quinella now and then, to take a shot at the pot.

Meanwhile they are all talking up the match race in Chicago. I liked Nashua very much, especially after his run in the Wood, but back then Summer Tan was the horse to beat. No one knew Swaps from Heigh-Ho Silver. Now if you saw the Derby you must throw out all the big races Nashua won. A horse of a horse in the Belmont, where he was strictly the one, yet versus Swaps he was clearly second best. And in a match race, second place is last place.

My friend and ally Mrs. Kearney has taken me up as a cause. Whatever she thinks I am (and God only knows) she treats me like a scholar. She will catch my eye as I pick up The Post and say, Oh Mr. Fish, I believe I have something for you today. A nice lady, Tanya's age I would say, though not so nice-looking. She is not too accurate with her lipstick, drifts wide at both corners and ends up resembling Emmett Kelly. (It might take an anonymous note to set her straight on this minor point.)

So it's Mr. Fish I think I have something for you today and then Mr. Fish takes the Something very gratefully to his study. This is a wide armchair behind a wall of geography books, each book the size of a piece of rock-lath. On the other side I have a tall window overlooking the plaza which is sunny, if anything is sunny, at my time of the morning. And here I check the Something over.

Today it is Mr. Jones, who has turned up after three months in Purgatory. Where has Mr. Jones been? Why he couldn't say. (Mind, he never touches drink.) Recalls not a thing because he was smitten with amnesia the whole time, forgot his way home and forgot the sound of his name and even lost his wallet so he could not peek inside for a clue.

Mr. Jones is not a Walkaway, only a stray. They'll round him up shortly. It's probably an old war wound, says Doctor What-not, which happens never to have given him a minute's trouble in the twelve years since he left the Air Force. Come to think of it the old war wound was in the shoulder, but of course the shoulderbone connected to the neck-bone, neck-bone connected to the headbone, and I hear the Word of the Lord.

I don't argue that the brain is not a delicate instrument, or that it shouldn't be expected to sometimes go out of tune like my carburetor. I just say that Jonesy knew his name the same way Widmer's feet stayed dry. And I am a man, when it comes to knowing, who has been cashing winners all month.

Another one she found me, on the subject of runaway children. Not the little ones, but teenaged. I gave her my thanks, naturally, and took the magazine into my study where I stared at the pages with my most serious and scholarly frown. I even scratched down a few notes for her benefit. She should feel she accomplished a librarian's mission in life.

But every kid runs away and even with the teenaged, where it is admittedly more serious, it's not what I mean. Because they *run* away. This differs from those who walk—there's a speed factor here. If you are a runaway you are saying by your action: find me, help me, make my life bearable.

Whereas when you are a Walkaway it is saying: goodbye, please don't ask, believe me when I tell you I cannot explain, you can't help, I don't need any help I'm fine so don't ask, goodbye and please no hard feelings there is money in the bank.


Do women do it? They must, why not? Tanya might have beat me to the punch, packed up her blue satchel for the beach and kept drifting clear across the water to Europe.

I thought I had spotted one today and maybe it was so.

She was nicely dressed, an attractive lady who somehow looked uncomfortable inside her skin—and who carried a small valise instead of a purse. And she was not going anywhere. Killing time by her lonesome. Possibly a rendezvous and she got stood up by the party of the first part. But I should have checked up, and gotten to the bottom of things. I left her in the Chock-Full-O-Nuts with her valise sitting on the stool beside her like an old friend. I should have sat down on that stool myself and greeted her as a comrade-in-arms. Oscar Fish conducts the interview!

Tell me please madam, did you leave your best clothes on the dock? Did you leave your children lunch money for the next fifteen years? Give us just a few details for our records if you would be so kind.


The girl across the alleyway undresses in her window. She does it every night (which makes only sense—who doesn't?) but I mean to say she is like clockwork, same *time* every night, and which just happens to be the time I am crawling into bed myself, as I have at half-past-ten for the past few decades. The way our windows are arranged I would have to change my habits to avoid peeping at her. At least that's part of the problem. The rest of it is I don't wish to avoid.

Does this make me a criminal? If so then here I am confessing, but I'm not so sure. I feel a need to explain, and to begin at the beginning because I never was sinful and never lustful and I am only truthful when testifying that my wife is the only woman I have ever accompanied to bed. With a few tiny exceptions I could add she is also the only one I have glimpsed intimately from top to bottom close up in the flesh. What you don't know can't hurt you, said my late mother, and quite correctly.

There is an old story in which a man gets the key to a

house full of beauties, a beauty behind every door and each one ready for action. And the man goes crazy—from confusion, not lust. He can try a different door every hour on the hour but it won't make him happy, just busy.

One woman holds the power to make you happy and not so busy that you don't have time for the ponies, or shoot snooker, whatever is your hobby. That's my background on sex. Stay away from the burlesque houses, steer past a prostitute, and ignore the insinuating glances of Kronstein's busty cousin. Look to your wife.

When I married Tanya she was a show. The legs of a dancer, face from an artist's painting, and the head of hair everyone admired, black with copper in the sunlight. A *famous* head of hair, in the borough of Brooklyn. I married her for love and I still love her after many years. If this were not so, there would be no need to walk away—I could run.

She still has her beauty, her legs and the rest of it. There isn't a wrinkle or a bubble or a bump on the backside and I'm glad the truth can be so kind if I must write it down here. I would hate to criticize even in private for God knows I am no Adonis myself. But if anyone is made for sex it's Tanya, and yet she doesn't care for it. She's neutral.

She allows me, once a week, because that is her interpretation of the marriage contract: twice a week would not be fair to her, zero is no good for me, so once. My Saturday night tittle and that does it for the week. It's enough. By now I wouldn't know how to do it on a Wednesday. If she was to suggest it all of a sudden on a Wednesday after dinner—Hey Oscar let's go at it—I would probably faint. Like Pavlov's Doggie, I have become a creature of habits.

All these years, however, I have kept a curiosity. Not a lust that I would plan to act upon, merely a curiosity that was not so idle—to learn a little more about this business. I would never go for such a reason the way Widmer did it and yet having gone I might say let's now take it under advisement, and not be so stubborn or shy as not to learn. I never sowed wild oats but tame oats like these, why not? Thus comes my bare girl to the window across the alley. How far away is she? Not far. I could toss her a beanbag from here. So what choice do I have? But I'm not justifying, I'm confessing. Why do I watch? In order to see. You won't get an education in these matters if you pretend to yourself or to the world that the subject holds no interest.

It is not only that she shows up at the same moment each night, she will also perform the exact same ritual. It's like a Broadway show, rehearsed with hash marks, count on it.

At 10:30 sharp the lights come on and I see her—though only from the shoulders down, since her window is set half a level lower than mine—I see her head for the bureau and begin off-loading jewelry. A little pile of beads and rings and ear-hoops, and then like a shot she pulls the dress over her head and stands there in a little white slip. A real shocker the first time I saw this move—and saw bare legs and shoulders with the shiny smooth that only a woman's skin has.

Before you have time to think it's up and off with the slip, so that now she stands in tiny black underwear, top and bottom. Never a change in this, the white slip and the black scanties, the colors of her secret uniform. Next she flexes her back into two long strips of muscle and gives a little shrug and a tug that wiggles off the top half. It's a lot of white meat. She starts brushing her hair, so you catch a glimpse of breast swaying this way and that before she turns around and shines them both right on you, and heads for her bed below the window.

Fiddles the bedspread, plumps up the pillows, and once in a while she will touch lightly her own breasts. (Maybe that having them on the loose excites them and she likes to get in on it?) As soon as the bedding suits her standards, however, she hits the lights and what remains to be done is done in darkness. I can see her pulling off the panties and tossing it like a hanky, but I am seeing a silhouette, and a silhouette is like clothing. It is the texture of skin, I have learned, that makes naked nude.

My bare girl goes out on Saturday (like me in the old days, for her once-a-week?) and the show closes down for one night. Reopens on Sunday and runs through the week with never a change in the schedule. No changes in the ritual, not even slight, no visitors, no matinées. And no head on her shoulders. You might think she could drop an earring and bend her head down into the frame to retrieve it, but never.

Today at Belmont Park I learned a few things about my friend Billy from Queens. (Amazing to gather such evidence after knowing this man ten years or more.) Billy is in the roofing business, and you can see his truck with the red and black lettering out in the big lot every afternoon. A roofer can't work in the broad sunlight. He works early and late, and knocks off the hours in between, when the heat hits the asphalt. So you see Billy here and you don't think twice—he is taking his afternoon sunshine break, that's all, and the kid knows how to handicap a race. He does it as well as anyone smalltime out here, although modesty forbids me to record the obvious: that Carnovsky, sometimes known as Fish, has had the unbroken history of nothing but winning years dating back to 1939.*

I see my friend Billy with a hot dog in his hand and hope

*Knowing what I know, let me interject that to my uncle a "winning year" was one in which he lost less than $500. There is something to this, inasmuch as he would wager thousands and to drop a mere $500 meant he was protecting his income while footing the bill for his own entertainment. And while he was occasionally a few hundred in the red, he could be (and often was) thousands in the black.

—Walter Ford, Jr.

in his heart and the sun buttering up his face, and always I took for granted that this boy was living the good life in America. A happy-go-lucky with yet a nice reliable business (who is it that doesn't need a roof fixed up now and then?) and also has a family, two nice boys he mentions, living in a bungalow near the Aqueduct track. And not only that, he has a leg up on today's Daily Double, so everything is perfect when he suddenly confides in me that he wishes he were dead. He is miserable, miserably unhappy and it does not show at all. And for some reason today, following a decade of silence, he wants to tell me his life-story.

He got ahead early in life as a kid working with the rumrunners in Sheepshead Bay. This was 1928 when the booze business was illegal so naturally it paid well. (I was not in the booze business when it was illegal and paid well. At that time I was selling shirts on DeKalb Avenue in the City of Brooklyn.) When Prohibition closed up shop he drifted away from the bad boys, still just a kid, and then he bought himself a carry-all from an old roofer who was retiring. It had the words ASPHALT ROOFING painted on the rib-cage. And before he got around to painting out these two words the kid was getting offers to work on roofs, from people in the street.

And said yes to one, as though he knew the first thing about it. He went to his cousin, a handyman, for a few pointers and showed up with some shingles the next day. Did the work, got paid for it, the roof didn't leak, and one thing led to another. He never did get around to painting out the two words. You can see them, plus a few others, on the nice new carry-all he bought himself year before last.

For twenty years he made his living on the roof, for twenty years did nothing else, and then one day woke up to the realization that he hated this work more than anything. He never liked it, it wasn't his idea in the first place, and by now he hated it so much he had a block. Climbing around with the bundles of shingles, buckets of tar, rolls of sheet metal—these things he had done thousands of times without a second thought were now unbearable to him, so he hid out.

How could he tell his wife (a worrier) that he had not worked a single day in what were usually his busiest months? How could he tell her he would never do it again, when it was all he knew how to do, his only way to turn a buck? So Billy was living and dying all summer at the racetrack. A good day and his secret was safe awhile, a bad day and he had the shakes.

And now he wants my advice. Which naturally I didn't have any. This is the price of hearing someone else's life-story. Of course out here I am neither Carnovsky nor Fish, I am just Oscar, because you don't have a surname among the sports. Or if you have a last name, then you don't get a first, like Hearn. Either way it's one to a customer. Out here you have friends but they don't come to your home for dinner. The same way I knew Billy was happy in his bungalow in Queens, he knows I am happy in my bungalow in Brooklyn—no one visits back and forth. However we are all solid citizens out here, so Billy would like to have my advice.

It occurs to me he knows I am in the booze business, that he used to be, and that maybe he is asking me for a job. This breaks the code, it's like coming to your home for dinner, but the real problem is I'm not hiring today. I'm unemployed myself. I tell him,

"Billy I hate to tell you the truth, you know I do, but I am out of business too. I finished with it."

"You're kidding. You sold out?"

"Well, ended. So we are in the same boat."

"And it's sinking fast. Oscar, we should have swapped— I sell the beer and you nail up the shingles. What about that?"

"Too late for that, thank God. I don't like to stand on a roof that isn't flat."

"So what will you do? Have you got something lined up?"

"Nothing."

And that's that. I almost wished I could say to him, here, take the keys, you drive with Ramsey. But Ramsey left anyway, he retired on me, and if he hadn't I might still be stuck there. The young guys didn't need me or my job—they don't care what they do nine to five, only what they do after hours matters to them at this point in life.

But imagine this man going to work every day for twenty years and not even knowing if he likes his job (and he doesn't) and all because of two words written on a truck he bought. Locked in and they swallowed the key. Well, I never wished for myself as strongly as I wished for Billy this afternoon, and though he didn't hit the Double he came out okay on the day.

Another thing. A 39-year-old man with kids of his own should not be called Billy. William, or Bill maybe, but Billy is a kid's name you outgrow. The name was locked in too, however, because he is "Billy the Roofer, Serving Queens for Two Decades." He can't dodge the bullet.

Like the Empire State Building or the Statue of Liberty, the name is what you trade on. Label her the Green Girl instead and suddenly nobody rides the boat out to see her, nobody wants to buy a souvenir.


As a lesson in humility as well as in the perils of handicapping, the match race is a gemstone. So easy to forget that a two-horse race is always a different proposition. There is room to run and the psychology is easy—you want it or you don't.

And another lesson too, you can toss out the Derby. It comes up too early for the real horses, and a speed freak can steal it on a sunny day. Which is not to say that Swaps wasn't game. He stuck a long time at a breakneck pace. But Nashua was on the muscle for this one, too much horse. He ran the red colt down and left him gasping for air seven lengths back. Nashua would have run through a wall of fire to get the California horse this time—I had the feeling he read all the papers and didn't care for what he saw.

More surprises in store. For the first time since the fall of the Holy Roman Empire, Brooklyn wins the World Series. And what's more, they beat the damn Yankees to do it. Having ached for such a moment since I was a little boy, I still never believed it could happen. I knew they could be the best team, by far, and *still* never win the Series. It was a skill they lacked.

Now when I am barely looking, and hardly caring, they go out and just do it. I am tickled of course, though not so much for myself. For Tanya and for Walter (who must be bouncing off the walls) and for Reese and Robinson and Newk and the Duke, and long live Sandy Amoros I'm sure. Baseball is not on my mind, that's all, I had stopped following the last month of the season.

I was tempted to call up and congratulate, but again for her sake only. Unlike the temptations of early days at the Bedbug Hilton. I did think one night last week, What would it take to get me back? An operation might do it, Walter in the hospital with a concussion. Injuries might get me back, tragedies. The happy times can only tempt a little, they waken an instinct, because you're connected.

At the same time I can hear what Tanya is saying: Oscar must be dead. Could not be certain up to now, but if the Dodgers take the World Series and still he doesn't show his face then he must be completely dead. What she means is she is disappointed. She thought when they won I might call or come by or drop a line in the mail, but I am very sorry my love I cannot do it.

Stunned to find out today that Bulkitis was all for Brooklyn. "Who else?" he says. "The Yankees?"

"Sure the Yankees. Anyone. How could a Giants fan go for Brooklyn? It's unnatural, Bulkitis."

"I always go for them once they're in the Series. You don't mean you rooted for Cleveland last year?"

"But desperately. The Giants killed us all year and I wanted to see them get theirs."

"That's funny."

"Funny to you, with Cleveland dropping four straight."

It takes all kinds to make a world. I'm one kind and Bulkitis is another. And I am afraid he is the better.

I am a voyeur. I have avoided the subject but meanwhile looked it up in the dictionary and that's what I am. Maybe Mrs. Kearney will be kind enough to find me the research materials in this area too. But fate has made me one as surely as fate made Billy a roofer. I didn't put the girl in that window, I just sit here guilt-ridden, a criminal in my own room.

And yet I am only normal. The world's original normal boy, you can go to the Form, read it in the past performances. Carnovsky: not a winner, or a loser, runs his race in the middle of the pack. You could not find anywhere a man more average. He is not rich or poor, not black or white, no scholar and yet no dope (he has had a little schooling). Also not elderly nor youthful—go right down the line and I am right down the middle, Oscar Everyman.

Here I can detect the voice of my late mother complaining. "You're not this, you're not that—all I hear is what you are not. Say what you *are*, Oscar, say you are a Jew."

I'm sure. But I never was. Never had a flicker of light in the area of religion, as dark to me as the first Thursday in December at Belmont Park. "Our people have a history, Oscar, a long important past." Again I'm sure it is gospel, except I have never taken an interest in the comings and goings of Pharaohs, it's Greek to me. I'm from the school of common sense.

There was a gelding called The Pharaoh ran at Hialeah years back, and won twice or three times at a distance. That, to me, is history. That's the past. The tote board is my Torah, mama forgive a good boy when fate takes a hand.

But this is important about normal and not normal. I am uncomfy on the subject of sex, yet still I am certain it is normal and correct. Look at an animal. Is an animal shy? Doesn't even introduce himself, he just mounts you. I can imagine myself in consultation with Doctor.

"Doc I got a problem."

"Yeah so what is this problem?"

"It's this. I like to look at the young lady next door, when she takes off her clothing."

"Yeah and so what is the problem? She won't take it off?"

Of course I try to see it that way—that it is good and natural like the doggies in the street—and I can believe in this point of view as easily as in my guilt. In which case why not join her over there, knock once on her door and mount her? Sex is not like a letter from Uncle at tax time, it doesn't come looking for you, you go out and get it the way you get a bottle of milk, with a purpose. I should do it, knock on her door. To her it would be a piece of normal life too—a man asking—and I am not so horrible to look at. Not even balding on the top.

But I won't be knocking. I don't want to. I have never seen her face and who knows, maybe she is the one going bald. I have suspected so once or twice when no boyfriend appears to worship the splendid figure. She could throw open the door and stand there looking like the Bride of Frankenstein. Surprise!

Much easier with one of the prostitutes in the neighborhood. I see them, I know what it is they do. I can also talk, and I've got a five-dollar bill in my poke like anyone else. Why not pick up a piece of education on the street if I'm so normal?

The truth: I am embarrassed. I don't want anyone to *know* I am normal, human. It's a big secret, safe with me. So I am a gelding too, like the Pharaoh.

Last night I played the Professor. The intellect. Because there is food for thought in my bare girl's methods. She shows herself and she does not. She must know the world is full of windows, she feels the breeze come in, so why not darken the room a little sooner? Why wait till she's half undressed? Of course she can't see in the dark, she is not a cat after all, so the light lets her see what she is doing.

Still I see a psychology behind little patterns. To my bare girl the breasts are expendable, they are there for teasing and can be shared at times. Like Tanya who went to bed with me for the first time upon our wedding night, June 16, 1935, yet two years before was allowing me to touch her breasts. It is the rest that is sacred and so becomes an object of fear. We must darken the room before these other, lower extremities are unveiled. The brassiere my bare girl tosses off like she's dealing cards, not so the little panties.

She could get careless and just once forget, and if so I will be on the spot to record the data. Give! Let's have a peek, young lady, be fair, since we are stuck here together anyway. Let's brighten up these mysterious hind-quarters!

Such dignity. May be just the temptation in the wilderness, as I have by this time missed more than a few of my Saturday nights with Tanya.

Meanwhile it has turned cold. Not all at once—it was lovely but I wasn't writing much down for a while. (I will improve.) Now though, my radiator came on for its maiden voyage like an old tug-boat getting underway, clanking and blowing off steam. Settled down after a while and gets warm to the touch but this ancient device will not be throwing a lot of heat into the corners in January.

I wondered about the Plymouth. If Tanya left it sitting that will be one hell of a waste. The block will crack for sure with no anti-freeze and she will get neither the use of the car nor the money. Nothing I can do about this, however.

My girl Friday is still on the case at the library. In fact I think she is having some fun with it. Today she handed me the autobiography of a poet (who is a doctor in his spare time!) with the following in it regarding a friend of his—

Later she married him and went to Central America with him where he bought and rebuilt a seagoing craft of some sort. One evening, having triumphantly finished the job, he got into it to try it out in the bay before supper. He never returned. Pregnant on the shore, she watched the small ship move steadily away into the distance. For years she thought to see him again—that was, how long ago? What? Thirty-five years!

I guess he took a notion on the ocean. Or maybe he didn't know how to get the boat turned around. That can be tricky. And by the time he figured it out he was someplace else and took it from there. From the sound of it, these were people who lived this way—poets and painters, bohemians. The kind who have three wives at the same time, and pet lizards, and dance all night on the French Riviera.

It takes all kinds to make a world. It also takes all kinds to fill up this building. Desperate characters inhabit these walls with me—my neighbors!

On the first floor left side, coming in, are the Holy Rollers (two Johnsons) with a big flowery motto tacked on the door

As you go past you can always hear them inside, picking up steam for their heavenly journey. I'm coming Jesus, they yell, as they fry up a little bacon. Lord I'm coming, they cry, as they carry out the trash. They can never shut up about it.

Once in a while they drift off down the block to the Holy Roller Church for a little relief. They are two nice-looking old colored people, neat dressers, and very solemn as they get underway. Then they look at each other and they are suddenly overcome. "Praise the Lord! I'm coming Jesus! People get ready!"

So they make a little noise. I wouldn't mind if they put their money where their mouth is on the Christianity bit, but it's all noise. He's got a mean streak, this Johnson, and picks on the children who live across the hall.

These children are Myers and judging from what you hear up the airshaft their mama picks on them too. She likes to scream and swear at them. The father works late—

or maybe works a regular shift and then meets his buddies at the bar—arrives home late in any case and then she screams at him too.

In fact she won't let him in. He stands in the hallway yelling "Let me in!" and she is on the other side of their door yelling "Get lost or I'll call the cops on you. Get out of here, the kids are trying to sleep."

Fat chance anyone in lower Manhattan is sleeping. The kids I'm sure are hiding under the bed. I would do the same. Meanwhile these two heavyweights keep going, fifteen rounds every night, arguing over whose house it is.

"It's my home!"

"It's my home too!"

The missus, however, has inside position. She is never stranded out in the hallway, so she is always the winner. Myers can kick his front door but not apparently open it.

None of these people are shy when it comes to advertising their moods. They don't care who watches or hears, nor do they mind filling the ears of their offspring with the foulest obscenities. The lady of the house has a voice to stop traffic in Times Square. A bull ape in captivity—incredible bedlam she turns on them—and yet the little ones don't seem to notice. By now they should be basket-cases. Instead they go laughing down the block to play because you can get used to anything I guess.

There's more of this. Up in Number Three, above the Holy Rollers, lives a fat man and his mama. She does all the talking for them, cries poverty all day long. And it's no wonder if they find themselves a little short since no one goes to work down there. He dresses up early, snap-brim hat and spiffed-up shoes, and strolls out to take the morning air. A boulevardier. Sharp as a fat tack he meanders the streets until it's lunchtime and he's home. This man has never missed a meal. A complete stranger to work, who yet has the cash to sit in the barber's chair on Water Street and have somebody else shave his cheeks.

Don't ask me how he can walk so many miles and stay as fat as Happy Felton, although it may have something to do with eight meals a day plus snacks. And his mother is always at my door crying poverty and asking for a helping hand with her tougher chores, such as changing a light bulb. Last week she could not manage to open a can of coffee, so next thing I know she'll have me down there flushing the toilet for her and the whole time I'm there she is crying poverty while at the same time telling me in plain English she has got one thousand dollars in a stocking. Crazy? Of course this thousand cannot be touched, it's her "burying money." Oh, says Oscar the Good Neighbor, I see—your *burying* money.

Craziest by far is when they interact. These players work out some comedy routines together. For example. The fat man likes to prowl around, and he keeps right on prowling in the flat after the witching hour. His feet come down like so many medicine-balls on the old floor-boards—like an air raid on the Johnsons below—so Johnson wakes up angry and sends back a message with a baseball bat on the ceiling. So now it's clump clump clump and then boom boom boom in the middle of the night, the whole building can hear, and does the fat man politely pipe down? Oh no, he takes offense, and turns up the volume of his big feet to CLUMP CLUMP CLUMP and Johnson must go looking for a sledge hammer so he can reply BOOM BOOM BOOM and they go on like this for an hour.

All I have written is just the tip of the iceberg here at 10 Battersea, but it's enough for now. I will just add, on the bright side, that the Myers boy has come in to visit a couple of times. Not counting Bulkitis and Kramer, he is my first friend in Manhattan.


Still more material for the archives, a poem and a picture. Credit Mrs. K. with the poem—her contacts in mid-town turned it up. It's light stuff, however. She is scraping bottom I'm afraid.

> There was a fine fellow from Greece
> Whose wife never granted him peace
> Till one night while she slumbered
> He left unencumbered
> Without by your leave or valise.

Cute stuff but light. The old joke, a nagging wife and the husband who takes it just so long and then makes a run for it. Driven out. The picture is also a joke. I know, because it's my own. I found this photo in a book The Sidewalks of Chicago and I'm the one who gave it a caption.

VIEW OF A WALKAWAY, WALKING AWAY

I don't mind adopting a sense of humor about this thing either. Up to now I'm like a man with a disease. Not sick, just obsessed, like my old friend Hollenbeck the tailor with his arthritis. He used to discuss anything, the gamut of life from garment union to baseball to the two homely daughters who won't leave his house. Since he started suffering from the arthritis, however, he has only one subject, one interest. All he wants now is the arthritis news.

Naturally he is a tailor and he fears for the use of his hands, but he devours all the phony cures in the tabloids, samples all the latest pills, and bends his ear to every fellow sufferer. Oh yes? It's sometimes in one elbow and not the other? Hollenbeck can talk joints inflamed for as long as you can sit still and listen. And his own attention never flags if you should happen to be a member of the club. That's how I am too because when you suffer from a particular condition, only those who suffer it with you can see the wrinkles in the fabric.

You hope to learn from a fellow sufferer's experience— you study his case history to illuminate your own, that's all, whether it is your wrists and elbows, like Hollenbeck, or your heart and soul, like some others.


Stinking weather, sleet and slop. Nothing unexpected in this, it's just the coming of winter. The time has raced past and now it is standing fast, time on my hands. With the racetrack shut down till April I have to try a few new pursuits.

I tried reading. Not the papers or a magazine, but books, like The House of 7 Gables—Hawthorne. I dipped into a popular one concerning a pimply teenager who uses bad language in place of good sense. That one was no go, so Mrs. Kearney says Try the Classics and I say, Sure, just point me. And I took home The House.

These Gables are as intriguing to me, however, as the bottoms of my feet. Try again, she says, and hands off The Last of the Mohicans. Again, nothing doing. These people don't speak my language. So now Mrs. K. says maybe fiction is not your area of interest. Maybe not, I agree. Another thing I tried, a matinée movie. The usual sleet-slop afternoon (Thursday) so I ducked inside and found the sun shining in technicolor, palm trees swaying, clean wide streets of California. Plus one very pretty girl, Grace Kelly. This worked out all right, better than reading the Classics, although I had a problem with self-consciousness. I was afraid someone might spot me going into the theatre. Not someone who knows me either, not here—I mean someone who don't know me.

I paid my money, didn't sneak in past the usher, but to me it is not moral entering a movie-house in the daytime. It's okay for a bum or a bag-lady, the matinée, you sit on one seat and your shopping bag sits on the seat next to you and then you go home to fry a lamb chop for supper. But a man should be out working. I'm worried what the people behind me might think, strangers, who in any case went to the matinée themselves, but I can't rest easy until the house-lights go down.

As if they cared a goody goddamn. As if they are back there whispering "See the guy in front, healthy-looking man? You suppose he is a drinker, a rummy? Why ain't he working? You think he could be an escaped convict or what?" I know they don't notice me, or care who I am, and still I can feel them there. There is a trick I have yet to master: to be myself and leave myself be, without all the agony.


I put in a solid day's work on Adam Bede and that's it for me and the Classics. Meanwhile I have noticed I get no mail here, not a single piece, so I took action to rectify this.

Sent away for a few brochures (a folding boat) and sub-
scribed to magazines, Look and one other. I almost went
through with this joke: send a letter to Australia with
insufficient postage, so that it comes right back like a
boomerang.

A man needs some mail. You don't have to be like
Johnson who needs a wheelbarrow to bring his inside, but
it doesn't look right never to get a single piece. I should be
like the fat man—fixes his hat in the foyer, takes his letter
from the box, and strolls away with a casual glance at the
contents. The man-about-town.

With time on my hands this a.m. I had one other crazy
notion—to follow the fat man on his morning rounds,
shadow him like a private eye. Where does the fat man go?
And for that matter, how's about my bare girl in the
window? I could pick up her trail easy enough, I am
familiar with her entire wardrobe. In fact I saw a young
lady yesterday near the City Hall, on Newspaper Row
there, who I had a strong feeling was her. Why not trail her
back?

It's what Hearn does at the racetrack with his boy Mikey.
They call it trailing, I call it a waste of time. But you pick
up the scent of a trainer, sometimes even a swipe, and
follow him from the paddock to the mutuel window, see
what he thinks the score will be. (On the theory that they
know something you don't, of course.) But trailing is a lot
of work for a little information—what Billy the Roof calls
"Miss Information, that naughty girl we know so well."
Yet Hearn is not the only one who will contort himself like
a pretzel to accomplish this dubious mission.

I could hire Mikey Hearn to trail the fat man. Track him
all the way up to the Horn and Hardart for a pie, down to
the Water Street barber to upkeep his cheeks, and then over
to Fanny Farmer for a mouthful of chocolates. I'll get the
inside scoop on this guy in no time.

Knowing what to do with your time is a skill. Or maybe an instinct, since a kid will always have it where a grown man has more trouble. I was reminded of the vacation we took at Lake Hopatcong in Jersey, myself and a little circle of friends from downtown Brooklyn. Years ago, before Tanya. One fellow worked with me at Sid's, the other two were employed at The Brooklyn Eagle, nearby, and we would generally take our lunch together in the delicatessen on Montague Street, talk things over. And once we got going on the subject of summers in the country. All of us had been upstate to summer camp as teenagers—in those days you worked your way—and we decided to pool our money and take a cottage on the lake.

Now you think of Jersey and you forget how much of it is still farms and shore. Back then, in 1932, it was all cows and ponds, even just a few miles from the city. We went in Allen Gersten's yellow Moon, I remember, and found ourselves with a charming cottage, white with blue shutters, a big screen porch with rockers and a soft couch, and we looked it over with great pleasure, parked our satchels and went to acquire a little ice for the harborside gin and gingerale we brought. A nice evening spent listening to the crickets and contemplating what a fine time we would be having, and then after that we didn't know what to do with ourselves—we didn't have the clue to enjoyment.

Because at summer camp you worked. A ten-hour day, a sixty-hour week, nothing but dishes morning to night and if you got an afternoon swim and a Saturday night in the village it was enough to fill the time. Once or twice you might climb up on the back of a horse, or hit a tennis ball, but my idea of summer fun was the sixty-hour week.

At Hopatcong we did not have to wash pots all day, or scrub cabin floors, we were free. So that each hour was an eternity. None of us was a fisherman. When we rented a leaky rowboat, the mosquitoes drove us back off the water in a hurry. Some bugs! No one wanted to sit in the sun and cook, no one was a birdwatcher like Widmer. We just waited for the opportunity to go back into the city and work again.

How to live a vacation is no different from how to live your life. Whose fault is it if you can't use the time God gave you to use? People complain frequently that they are working too hard, they need time off. But for what? They don't know. A vacation can be scary, you have to cope with the time.

Who holds the secret always is a kid. The secret of fun. A kid doesn't require a schedule of events or a big stack of fancy equipment. Put him down in any corner of the world and he will make it rich enough. Put him down by the shores of Lake Hopatcong and it will be a big new world of magic for him, a realm of treasures. Even New York City. They say Mayor Wagner owns this town, you hear it all the time, but I beg to differ. Who owns this town is Jimmy Myers, age nine. He has got friends in low places.


There was already plenty of trouble in Europe when I married my wife. Mussolini went waltzing into Ethiopia and not long after his pal Hitler was taking over real estate in the Rhineland, Poland, everywhere. Tanya had a brother still in Poland, plus all the aunts and uncles. Right then she declared the world no fit place to raise a child, and who could disagree? I wasn't even thinking about a child, what was a child to me? I expected *her* to want one.

But she never did. In 1945 when I was nearly forty years old the U.S.A. exploded atoms on Japan and she said the world was more unfit than ever. By then I was thinking, and we had talked, maybe after the War—but that was it, we never again discussed the matter. If the world ever got safe enough, I knew it would also be too late, so I got us a puppy—named Igor after my father's father and also short for Igor Beaver, but the poor creature died before he was even house-broke.

It was not meant to be, yet I like children and I admire them. It is true they have the secret of fun. Jimmy Myers comes into my house and makes himself comfortable, and meanwhile his father and I still just nod and touch our hats. He gets around, my little friend, covers a lot of territory. A runt, nine years old and a real toothpick too, yet so very sure of his own mind. Opinions!

The roar of his parents can not distract him from his higher purposes in life, which are to acquire gum, chocolate, money, Hopalong Cassidy trading-cards (in particular a rare silver-colored kind he calls a Silver Hoppy), and cancelled stamps. Other purposes include to protect his little sister Beatrice from the person named Gerry who kicked her last month and still looms large, and to overrun the city with his buddies, exploring and pretending. Also to pitch stones at the cats who have taken over the alley behind the house. His control is very sharp, much better in fact than Branca or Billy Loes, God forbid Rex Barney. And still the cats are safe.

He also likes to chat, so I told him come up anytime his folks say it's all right. Next day he comes and I ask him,

"Did your folks say you could visit?" (Because I do not wish to be the cause of any of that yelling that goes on.)

"They don't care."

"They do. They might at least—just to know your whereabouts." And this runt advises me:

"Don't worry about them so much."

I make him cocoa and we look over the Hialeah Form together. Today I let him in on my latest system, which is back all Hartack's mounts. Very sophisticated. It's not like me but listen, he rode seven winners in nine trips on the weekend and has been doing it like this every day. Hartack is so hot he could win without a horse underneath him and I have made myself a bundle from the easy chair.

"So why don't they all bet on him?" says young Mr. Myers, smart as a whip and travels straight to the heart of the matter.

"Slow learners. By the time they bet him he'll be losing. He'll go fifty races without a winner."

"How come *you* know?"

"Because I know. What else?"


Winter is really settling in now—ice in the sky, some ice chips in the harbor. Kramer is not accepting any more of my Hartack bets. "I've got a family to support!" he cries. Do I cry when he keeps my money?

I'm making resolutions. One, I am going to take myself on a trip, though as yet I have not the faintest idea to where. But why not something along these lines? I'm a free agent. I could get married in the morning if I felt up to it, or sail for Constantinople, or maybe spend an evening on Old Cape Cod. Who's to stop me? There is no need to justify and that's good since I have no justifications, only the determination to do it.

Next resolution, I will install a curtain on my window to give my bare girl back her privacy. Since she will not see to this matter, I will have to take it on. I gave it a try last night, banking on just self-discipline. Easy to stop looking, I figured, you simply close your eyes.

But I discovered that it may require the hanging of a curtain to accomplish.


I was in the Battery Park early today, stretching my legs when who should I see throwing stones but Jimmy Myers and a couple more his size. Ten o'clock on the morning of a school day this is, however, so he ducks his head and pretends not to spot me. I would never corner him when he was among his pals, and in any case he led the expedition out of there in a hurry. But in the afternoon, here, I gave him a little tickle on the issue.

"You don't like school?"

"Sure I do."

"Not enough to go there. What's your favorite subject?"

"What do you mean?"

"You like to read?"

"Oh sure, I like all my subjects."

"That's why you play hooky. Don't you want to get smarter everyday?"

"Like you, you mean. You can get rich just knowing which horse to bet on. You don't need to know anything else."

I disabused him of this, and preached hard work and education over a hot cup of cocoa. Nevertheless I was feeling flattered that he looks up to me—Oscar the intellect, so rich and smart and makes the best cocoa too—and then I figured his angle. The little weasel flatters me to shut me up, so I don't inform the parents where I saw him at ten a.m.

I would never, he should know. I like him and I don't like them, so where would my loyalties be? But I would also like him to take his schooling more seriously. He has got a lot of natural smarts, but that ain't enough. Natural smarts *I* got, and so does Benny Herz. But if you don't hang in there at school you won't be President.

Uncovered yet another lunatic in this tenement, up on the fourth floor. The trash goes out Thursday morning on this block, they come and empty the cans in the alleyway. If you place your trash in the cans the night before, the cats will naturally empty them first. They roam the streets with a Sanitation Department schedule in their pockets and they know how to make a terrific mess. Whatever you ate, put it out early and it's cat food. The gutters are lined with swill.

So I am down there at the last possible moment putting my own contribution into the can, and picking up loose ends, when suddenly comes garbage flying past my head. From on high. Two shopping bags crash on the pavement, bottles breaking, and out spills the works—rotten tunafish, chicken bones, apple-core, you name it. Everywhere. You might as well flip this stuff out the window piece by piece and save on bags, because it comes to the same thing.

And up there in the fourth floor window I spy a little man with a beard, leaning out, getting set to launch one more bag!

"Keep it!" I shout, and start to explain the flaw in his method. Too late, it's en route. Crash, rip, splat—the same results of course, and the little fellow is up there laughing. It's a big joke, this sea of swill around me.

"Are you crazy?" I ask and for an answer he laughs at me, as though we are sharing this joke together. It's a nice friendly chuckle we are having. And who knows, maybe I am the crazy one. Maybe I should feel lucky the bags didn't land a direct hit on me, because Jesus H. Johnson downstairs was not as lucky with the fat man's bathwater.

That was a while back, a month or more, although Johnson has yet to bestow his Christian forgiveness. The fat man took a bath one morning and his tub wasn't draining properly. He can't be bothered with such things, of course, so he snaps his brim and out the door he goes, leaving the old mother to bail it out with a rusty bucket.

She loads one up, sets it on the windowsill, and gives it a tilt. Meantime, unbeknowst to her, Johnson is down there praising the Lord when the dirty bathwater descends right on the top of his shiny head. Bullseye.

To this day Johnson swears she did it to him on purpose, not knowing that this was the first chore she attempted in her life without assistance. He grossly overestimates her abilities. The poor old girl could never do anything on purpose, it would never work out.

I am signed up as of today for an excursion to the North. A travel agent's package that includes a Rangers game up in the Montreal Forum (best seats in the house), two nights in a hotel with a continental breakfast, transport both ways, plus sundry features—tourist stuff. The cost is less than I won in a single day with Hartack at Hialeah, and pennies from heaven like those are pennies you should spend on a good time.

Anyway I have to exercise my freedom—it's like a muscle, goes slack if you don't utilize it. I felt proud of myself signing on, pleased to be moving around in my new identity. I am finally convinced I did it, like the Brinks Boys up in Boston, I got off scot-free. But why shouldn't I? Either you have a right or you don't, and I believe you must.

Take the case of Flitcraft. Maybe he is the slave of Mrs. Flit, a prisoner of the marriage contract with no rights at all. But if he has any rights at all—if he is a free man and not a slave—then he can do anything under the sun for the flimsiest of reasons. Why? Because he cannot justify what he does. It could be a falling beam or a fallen woman, or it could be nothing more than which way the wind was blowing, as in the case of the bohemian in the boat.

One reason is as good as the next. If you give him the right to go, you relieve him of the need to explain. It could not matter less, the explanation, whatever it may be.

I'm sure that Jimmy pitches stones at the alleycats because he is getting it all the time from his mama. Pass it on, you don't have to wax philosophical to see this much. What I cannot figure is how to bring the subject up, or should I? Would it help him?

May be best to let him keep pitching. He is building up his throwing arm, the cats seem all right, and it does help keep them off the trash barrels. And if he should stop, it won't shut up the mother—that must come the other way around. If she did shut up (which she won't or she would have already) he would likewise stop throwing (according to theory) so really the answer is I should *not* talk with Jimmy about this matter but talk with the mother instead. Yet you cannot just butt in and what if I did so and she started screaming at *me*? I can't absorb it the way those little ones can.

Not to mention she will then go after him louder than before and furthermore forbid him from visiting such a dirty old man. How else would she feature me, and what is the kid going to say in my defense? "Oh no, Oscar's real nice, he shows me how to play the ponies down in Florida." Terrific. A good reference. So best let him keep pitching and build up his arm.

Purchased a union-suit plus wool stockings for the nights in Canada. Also picked up a new notebook—who could guess I would fill one up?*

I am a little hesitant about traveling out of town, however—I remembered I don't like hockey. But the truth is I'm socked in here pretty good, rooted, and I'm nervous to abandon the nest. Two whole days gone! And so I must worry who will feed hot cocoa to Jimmy Myers in my

*Oscar wrote in those small notebooks that say Composition Book on the front, pale green pages between cardboard covers with a black marbled design. In all he filled four of them.

—Walter Ford, Jr.

absence? Who will bring in my mail, as if it mattered? And who will keep an eye on my girl in the window? It's a good thing I ain't got a plant to water or I would never step outside at all.

Now Jimmy has his feelings hurt because the old man reads a bedtime story to sister Bea. Not that he can't hear it too but he knows it is aimed elsewhere and he has his pride. And Jimmy never got these stories in the past either, he says, never the big bad wolf or the three little pigs. The schneid for Jimmy.

Myers is a nice man, just locked out at night. Why would he discriminate between his own two children? He made an assumption (and I would assume the same) that Jimmy doesn't go in for a fairy tale but that the little girl does. I'm sure this is the explanation and I told him as much. Maybe he bought it, too.

For the hell of it, I brought something home from the library and tried out my own voice, reading aloud in my chair, and I was happy to have no one in earshot. It's not so easy out loud. You must pronounce certain words that you are familiar with yet never have spoken, and so naturally you might pronounce it wrong. Then the throat weakens, the tongue dries up, and you make chopped liver of a few nice lines. You should be hamming it up a little, give it a little english, and this I am too shy to attempt even *without* an audience.

But I believe it's true Jimmy wouldn't like it. He knows too much and plus which he knew it from birth. Why else did Myers never read him? Look at the Beanstalk. Up and down the pole they go until it's all settled—splat goes the giant. Jack is safe with mama, they come by a little cash, and that's The End. But it's a phony, clearing off this giant who wasn't even there in the first place when they went down the road to sell the cow. It's not The End, it's The

Beginning. Nice to have some money, sure, but it tells you nothing. The mother might want a husband and something to do with her time, and Jack must go to school or work, life for him is just barely underway.

Or take the other one. Jimmy is also aware you don't marry a princess, you marry human. (Or subhuman.) In life on earth you get two people yelling at each other through a door, that's what he knows. You get hot sticky summers and cold slooshy winters. It's a long haul, and 10 Battersea Street is no place for a fairy story.

Big excitement, I am filing my first dispatch from foreign soil. I am sitting in the Dominion of Canada, where I must nevertheless record that the streets are filled with cars, and people, and a cup of coffee tastes just like itself. I expected the Yukon, not this fancy city, don't ask me why. I expected I would be seeing wolves and frozen rivers with penguins walking over the ice.

It did have a different look coming in. Like Siberia or something, flat and bleak and empty. We came on a bus and I slept a lot of the way, till they pulled us off at the border and frisked us, then I got back on and lit a cigar. The sweetest Havana money can buy and the pair behind me said put it out. These two are smoking the whole time, popping cigarettes like after-dinner mints one by one into the mouth, and they have the nerve to protest a Gonzales! I will if you will, I informed them. So we both did, and now they despise me. Figure it.

Anyway the travel people gave us one half-hour to clean up in our rooms, then shoved us right back on the bus to tour the city. I should have had the brains to say No Thanks—or the guts—but naturally I didn't so we went off to visit a big cross on a hill and shopped in the souvenir stand up there. (Picked up a birchbark canoe for Jimmy.)

Then we took in a few churches, Notre Dames, in the old part of town.

We're a mixed bag, with couples, some younger, a little club of old men in red hats, and the single men and women. One of the women came over to say hello to me. Wearing Rangers' sweater number 9 (because she is president of Bathgate Fan Club, Yonkers branch) and assures me Bathgate will score a goal for her in tomorrow night's game. Fine, fine, here's hoping. She greeted everyone else with the same prophecy, by the way, and also the same offer—to join up, Yonkers branch.

I was shy with this crowd and wanted all day to take a nap. So I am happy to retreat back here at last, unload a few thoughts on my dear diary, and hit the lights.

Begin the new day with our Continental Breakfast, which is French for a roll and a coffee. It sounded fancy so I was looking for them to waltz in with dead birds lined up under a silver dome and some frilly eggs, cheese on toast. In comes a roll and a coffee.

Yet they are trying hard, these travel people, they want to give good weight, so they put us back on the bus once more and stand us to a day of skiing. A few could do it and a few, including the old men in the hats, did not want to give it a crack. Everyone else stumbled around and called it fun. You got to get your money's worth—if you paid for two broken legs, you must go break them. So I tried.

A very nice girl sat with me by the fireplace inside, named Linda, from Jersey. I discovered that I have lost the knack of conversation. Nothing that passed through my brain seemed worth saying out loud, so I didn't, and then soon enough I couldn't. Linda is shy too, however, and I can tell she doesn't hold it against me. In fact the reverse—pretends that my most asinine remarks are of great interest to her, helps me along. A Good Samaritan crosses my path. She even asked can she sit with me tonight at the restaurant.

And I wanted to ask right back, Am I so bad off? Am I such a charity case, Linda from Jersey, that you are inspired to nurse me through life? What shows? What is so terrible about Oscar Fish?

Back here I checked in the mirror, to see how the world at large might see me, and there's nothing obvious. No warts on the tip of my nose, no gray hairs—I'm fit for my age. Many people have thought I was nice-looking, by which they meant that they liked me, a nice *person*. Only Tanya thought I was handsome (talking about my beautiful eyes) but there is no law that says you must be handsome.

To nobody's surprise excepting Our Lady of the Andy Bathgate, Rangers took it on the chin tonight. 5 to 1, and they were lucky to get the one, a Harry Howell squib that hit someone's foot and bumped into the goal.

Number 9 got a goal all right, but Number 9 for Montreal, Rocket Richard. This was a play worth seeing. He crashes through the two Ranger defensemen like a madman breaking down a door and when he finds himself on the other side, extricates himself from the debris, locates the puck at his feet, and shovels it past the goaltender while still spinning sideways. They say he does this regularly but I thought the noise would bring down the roof of the building on us.

It did not have far to fall, either, because the "best seats in the house" were way upstairs right under the pigeons' perch. Same as with the "Continental Breakfast" but we have no complaints. A closer score we might have hoped for, otherwise no problem—we exit in nice high spirits into a nice clear frosty night and all at once I become a leader among men. I have learned to hate the bus, so I announce I will stroll back up St. Catherine's Street to the hotel, at my leisure with a Gonzales. And though I never meant it as an invitation it sounds good to all concerned, or most, and we stroll together beneath the winking stars.

Not far from the hotel some of us elect to have a night-cap, in a lively looking spot with copper pots and greenery in the front window. I try a belt of rye while Linda drinks two glasses of red wine, sufficient so that she takes my arm on the last leg home. I can actually smell her youth, a sweet smell like a child. She is not drunk or propping herself up on me, just letting me know we are friends in this group.

"Is Peterson watching?" she says.

"Who's that?"

"Number 9, in the hockey shirt."

"Oh her. Bathgate. Yes I think so, she's looking right at you. Better let go. I'll tell her you're my niece."

"That's nice, your niece. Let's tell her that." And now she is getting loud enough for the others to hear. "Tell Peterson I'm your niece!"

Maybe she is a little tipsy. I fear she will be embarrassed in the morning, when we all board the bus for New York and cannot smoke a cigar, so I untangle her arm from mine—gently so she knows I would never answer her kindness with anything less—and send her up in the elevator.

So I had the lobby to myself, to sit and blow smoke and to ponder the fact I was sitting in Canada. Also thought about my friend Linda Stanley from Fort Lee, a school-teacher as it happens, smart girl and not bad looking. Hazel eyes with long dark lashes and a nice clean face, pretty smile. Doesn't overdo the makeup, the way the women do up here. (Worse than in the City. They wear masks, fright-faces, they roll down the block like Indians on the warpath at eight a.m. This is scary stuff.) Linda dresses simple: green coat, green dress, a few tiny pearls around her neck.

And that was it. Big oldfashioned frilly couches in the lobby, and flowerpots, but also brass spittoons all around the room, as though they are expecting Queen Victoria and Leo Durocher both on the same day. No one shows up, however, neither Durocher nor the Old Lady, so I polish off my Gonzales and ascend to my room to record these very words and now snooze.

Saturday. Back here, and time to say that was not that, dear diary, I did not snooze after all. Let's get the rest of it into the record, better late than never.

I put on my robe and pajamas and looked out the window (what else?) at St. Catherine's Street—nightclubs blinking lights, the people hustling into taxicabs, the party still going strong down there and I'm feeling restless myself. So maybe get dressed and join them for another nightcapper. It's not me, I am never a drinker, and yet there is a principle here too: you're thirsty, then drink. Why not? Because Mrs. Bathgate might catch you at it?

And just then comes a knock on my door. Right away I know what's up, that this isn't the chambermaid with an armload of sheets, or someone looking for his lost dog. I know it is going to be Linda Stanley. It is and it is not a surprise to me.

Put it this way—until it occurred I would never dream it, but the second I heard the knock I knew what it was. That's my natural smarts, I guess, because I never heard such a knock before. And my initial instinct was go hide in the bathroom and wait for it to go away. Open up the door? Never. And that's where my smarts leave off.

She had a glass of wine in each hand. One for me. And I am always the practical man, so I had the presence of mind to ask her,

"How did you manage to knock?"

She lifted up her leg to demonstrate the knock-knee and says, "I thought you might come visit me."

"I wouldn't presume—" said I, the gallant one.

"I thought that too, so here I am. May I enter your chambers?"

I am not such a big fool as I may sometimes pretend. That night in Montreal I had no idea why it was the case, yet I knew this girl was after me, I knew she wanted to play around. I will also make note of the fact that we did so, nor am I feeling any remorse. Maybe she was tipsy and maybe not, but in any case I was the one who got raped.

After which we were lying in bed like old folks and talking.

"I'm so glad you were on that bus."

"Me too, believe it. But you didn't see me on the bus. I didn't see you."

"I did, though. I watched you for hours."

"What?"

"While you were sleeping."

"What?" (Still lacking the knack of conversation!)

"You snored like crazy. Everyone was laughing about it, and I thought it was just so sweet."

"You must be joking. I never snore. And I would certainly never snore in public."

"I bet you'll be snoring twenty minutes from now, as a matter of fact. Want to bet?"

"I'm not a gambling man," I told her and that's true, gambling and handicapping are two different matters. I am making talk at any rate, that's all it amounts to. How should I know if I snore? Tanya never mentioned it.

"That's why I wanted to know you better. Because you snored for two hours and didn't give a hoot. You were so comfortable with yourself." She knows me better all right, but not so well as she seems to imagine.

"But not at all! Not at all comfortable. If I thought I was

snoring on that bus I would die on the spot. I never dreamed it, and that's the truth."

"Of course you didn't—you were sound asleep!" And this memory, of Fish in his slumbers, inspires her to emotional heights, whereupon she covers my face with baby kisses.

We talked some more and we finished out the night, and then next morning we played the part of strangers, or friends, on the return journey. A long quiet ride, snowing all the while. I walked up to my room here and filled the tub with hot water and thought to myself, Okay, not too bad. And that was that. I should take a trip more often.

Cleaned the bathroom (a first) and added a chair to my collection here, just to tone up for Linda Stanley who comes by tomorrow for "dinner and a movie and your place after." It's a new idea, my first date in over two decades and the funny thing is nothing changes—I will visit the barbershop in honor of the occasion, and worry if my clothes look well, etc. Of course I know that a girl who professes to like me because I sleep in a rumpled suit and snore in public is not going to care about such matters. It doesn't come from the other person, the bay rum behind the ears. It comes from yourself, as part of getting ready.

Meanwhile had the opportunity to present James Myers Esq. with a Canada birchbark canoe made by redskin Indians and found the courage to try a story out on him. (I am still a leader among men until further notice.) And I had a couple of surprises from this sterling effort. One, I made it through clean as a whistle—*better* than my private reading—and two, the kid ate it up. He loved it. And this was the Beanstalk, aimed at a younger child I would think, yet it was the one he requested first.

He sweated it out, worried for Jack, fretted over the poor mother, hated the slimy giant—and insisted that if

Jack was half sharp he would just poison him (easily accomplished in several ways he pointed out for me) and in The End enjoyed every kind of joy and relief. All according to form! He knows it ain't life, it's a story, that's all. Just what he wanted.


Linda Stanley departed at the witching hour last night, and drove herself back to Jersey in the snow. I invited her to stay but both preferred otherwise because (I believe) you want your breakfast in peace. No roll and a coffee here, either. When I eat in, it's Pep and raisins, and the coffee is instant.

What else to conclude but that I have got myself a girlfriend? She's nice, I'm nice, and we have a nice time doing what comes naturally. Maybe she takes too much wine but that's her business. I won't keep up with her. After a few glasses it makes me pee and I don't want to need a pee at the wrong moment.

One other possibility occurred to me. The thought came after we had completed the act and she wanted to move my new curtain and watch the snow falling past the street lights. (A bad moment, until I recalled this was a Saturday and my bare girl would be elsewhere, praise the Lord.) She watched and I agreed it was a pretty sight, yet she appeared withdrawn and maybe even sad at a time when I thought we were riding pretty high. Could be her red wine settling to the bottom but the other thought occurred to me it could also be this: she is doing this to get back at somebody she loves, someone who has made her jealous, and so she takes me on. And I am a harmless slob who can't complain when discarded (when her point is made) since after all I got mine.

A hunch, that's all, yet one from the master of hunches, Carnovsky, so it cannot be ignored. This is not something I would mention, of course, with no evidence and no desire to spoil it, whatever it is. Instead I'm primed for a little flirting.

"Linda means pretty girl in Spanish, am I wrong?"

"It means pretty."

"Not girl?"

"No. What does Oscar mean?" (Now I have got her grinning.)

"Oscar means fool, in Yiddish."

"You're kidding."

"Yes of course I'm kidding. Really it means bossman, the top dog, in Russian."

"You're still kidding."

"Now you're on to me. You cracked the code."

Oh yes I am the great kidder. So far as I know, Oscar means absolutely nothing. And Linda I looked up at the library so I could flirt pre-meditated.


Jimmy at Bulkitis' today after school, spending his bottle money on the quest for Silver Hoppies and picking out the latest funnybooks. And the nervy midget has the gall to give me a needle!

"My ma says you got a girlfriend."

"What? She says?"

"Yeah, a blondie."

"Yes? I didn't know your mama knew me, that she noticed."

"She noticed the blondie," says Mr. Worldly-Wise and who can argue the point, she did obviously notice. Just one time Linda Stanley comes through the front door, one time she goes back out (and this at the witching hour) yet Mrs. Myers stops her screaming long enough to register these events. Sharp tongue, sharp eyes.

And do I mind? Am I supposed to be ashamed, a lawbreaker? The truth is I'm happy she noticed. Oscar's got a blondie! Her noticing makes it real, to me too, and incidentally earned a new respect on the spot from Bulkitis, the family man.


Today (Friday the 16th of December, 1955) I walked the length of the Brooklyn Bridge—halfway across and then the same distance back. No temptation to go further, although I confess I felt a little frisky being invisible up there. Really I just wanted to be out over the water, and high as possible. I like the feeling, even on the bridge of the ferry-boats or on a long wharf in Erie Basin.


One more interesting point concerning Linda. In a houseful of good Jews, I will always feel I am not one of them; in a restaurant with this one shiksa, I feel I am. Linda is the All-American Goy and her brother I'm sure is the All-American Boy. What else? Blonde hair, a nice pale skin—greeneyed Protestants from across the Hudson. We were thrown together and do we fit? Well yes we do. Not to marry of course, but to talk, to share a few things, why not?

She prefers not to talk too personally, however. Likes to ask the questions, but not to answer them. It's a school-teacher's trick I guess, knowing how to duck a question and send it back. For example—

"Tell me, Linda, what decided you on the trip to Canada?" And she replies with,

"Fate. It was fated I go, to meet you there. What about you, Oscar?"

I can see the technique very clearly as I sit here and scribble it down. At the time, however, she gets the best of me. Has me going on with all my own muddled reasons for choosing to travel out, and I never did hear a single word about hers. Linda is very slick, very good at dodge-ball. But I am on the case.

With the slooshy weather it isn't so easy navigating the streets, plus which you better bundle up good or spend a fortune in the cafeterias thawing out. Hard for me to imagine Lewis and Clark, or someone like that in the old days—no cup of coffee on the road up ahead for those guys, and no road either! Just the wet woods.

But I go out on my excursions nevertheless, it's what I want to be doing, and it's enjoyable to me. I have invested a whole philosophy of life in this wet cold walking I do every day, up the Hudson side to the garment district, up the East River all the way to Kip's Bay.

1. You see the world up close. The faces of people.
2. Nothing stops you—no dead battery. You get where you are going every time.
3. It's exercise, keeps you trim and healthy in the winter.
4. It's free, costs you not one penny.
5. Uses the time just right.
6. Gives you a good appetite. This is true. It enhances the flavor of food.
7. It relaxes you, where red lights and traffic, park and unpark will drive you crazy.

So it clears the mind for thinking. You must enjoy your own company when you walk and I'm sure this is the reason I never did much before. My longest stroll was around the corner from home, to the car. Then I would drive the car everywhere, even if I was only going a few blocks. It's a wonder my heart muscle still functions. Not to mention the brain.

You cannot do any thinking under the wheel of an automobile. If you do, for half a second, you'll be dead. So you watch like a hawk and hope they don't kill you anyway. But walk and they cannot get at you so easily. At a nice safe distance from the traffic, see what you see and think what you think.

Of course there is such a thing as too far, and here you might take a train. I will be riding the railroad myself in April, to Jamaica. Still, you can walk to the train, walk from the train: let the train be a bridge between walks.


Every week Linda sets up the exact same plan. It's the easiest, she says, since she has the car and likes coming in to the city.

"This is the city? We could go someplace."

"You mean some fancy club?"

"Doesn't have to be fancy. Radio City, whatever. You name it. We could take in the Rangers and Andy Bathgate if you want, for old lang syne."

"All right, let's. But sometime when we're bored. Not yet."

Nice to hear my girlfriend isn't bored yet. Sometimes I get the feeling she will suddenly wake from her dream and say, What am I doing in this dump, but so far she doesn't notice. Maybe because she doesn't meet the neighbors, or see the neighborhood when it's light outside.

Each week we watch a movie and afterwards discuss the movie while we munch our dinner in a restaurant. We offer our ideas and beliefs, our sympathies, in this unusual way—as they apply to a moving picture, rather than to ourselves. But this is what she likes, along with the fact that she also likes sex, so why should I complain? Isn't that what I wanted?

I felt something along these lines could occur with Giselle, who is always kidding me, "Oscar come on, take me to the sun, I've earned a vacation." What she would say God knows if I should just once have replied, Okay pack a bag, let's go Mexico. Call her bluff.

We both have a little twinge of attraction now and then, as in the springtime when she blows in with a cotton jersey, and no stockings on her legs. We chat over Ryker's foul brew on a few subjects beside the bookkeeping, and maybe we flirt. I see the legs, I note the form—but no action from Oscar. Temptation you must expect, it's natural, yet action you are responsible for and can control.

Happy Chanukah, Merry Xmas. I got Jimmy a trinket, nothing big—crystal radio kit. Who knows if he'll enjoy such a thing? You take a stab in the dark at this time of year and figure they know it's the thought that counts. But I took on a little guilt, shopping, wrapping, giving. Guilt that I had nothing to give dear Walter and not to mention my dear wife. The only thing in this world more useless than guilt is yesterday's garbage, and still we all collect it.

I bought Linda Stanley a fancy bottle of perfume, the aroma of which I am sure will soon be visited on my unwilling nostrils. What the hell, I never had a good imagination for such gifts and how long can you wander around a department store without losing your marbles?

Bulkitis, my other recipient, I had just right—a box of Coronas set his Giant heart at peace for the holiday season.

"Will you be with your people?" says Linda to me. That one came home, I'll admit. How little she knows me, how little I know her. And how few are my people. Stand up and let me count you!

They have no school for the week, so I get a good dose of Jimmy each day. I make a point therefore to do my walking early and then settle in, listen to the radio and look at the papers and live the life of Riley till he arrives. Always soaked with snow, to the skin, so I dress him down and pour in the hot cocoa to restore his color. A bottomless well this one, he is hollow—one, two, three big mugs of the stuff will disappear.

Yesterday I had to rescue him from Jesus H. Johnson in the foyer. I caught the Holy Man with a handful of my friend's neck, and shaking him like a broken bird, wagging fingers in his face. The little guy didn't shut the front door quick enough and as a result a cold breeze came in under the Holy Door.

I let him have it nice and gentle, tapping on his silly plaque with the Christianity scribble. "And do you think, my friend Johnson, that your Jesus Christ would shake a child by the neck? Not to mention that it's a crime."

None of them care for me now. I try to be nice, as always, yet how nice can you be. Such awful people. I'm sure that the bearded fiend upstairs is *aiming* his garbage— he always fires away when someone is at the barrels. And then someone else stuffed a cat into one of those cans, and slammed the lid on tight, so when I pried it off I nearly lost my face. Out springs kitty—but a jack-in-the-box with claws. Someone's idea of humor.

"He shouldn't grab you like that," I tell Jimmy.

"He does."

"No. Tell your folks. He should never touch you. Does he grab your sister?"

"Sure. He gave her a shove once, for spilling on the steps."

"You're kidding me. A hard shove?"

"Ask her."

She never visits me, and is very shy out on the street as well. I don't know her. Six years old, so naturally she stays closer to mama, but I wonder. She could think I am someone to be avoided, someone who might shake her, like the Holy Man. A meanie, not to be trusted. I tell Jimmy to bring her up but he doesn't. I am a resource to him, a little gold-mine of cocoa and lifesavers and sports talk plus now storybooks, and he wants it all to himself.

An error, with Jimmy. It came from wanting to please him but can only wound in the end, and I can't think how to get the bullet back now that it's out of the gun.

He is a Dodger man, like me, a Snider man in particular,
yet has never once seen the ballpark. I was surprised, since
the father is also a fan (they see the games on television)
and in any event this frail midget seems to get where he
wants to go, all on his own. Turns out, however, that to
him Ebbets Field is not a short jaunt across the Bridge, it's
a distant shrine, like the Wailing Wall.

And I put my foot in it. In the summertime, says good
old Oscar, we will have an outing—two seats behind
Snider in the centerfield bleachers and all the frankfurters
you can eat. This is Oscar the great resource talking. Of
course I now realize it cannot be done. I can't go on
Flatbush Avenue where two thousand people know me.
And who is to say I won't meet the two Walters inside the
ballpark? They go now and then, my brother-in-law and
my nephew—Hey look, there's Oscar sunning himself in
the bleachers!


Linda still holds back on me, answers questions with
questions, not answers. She too had no school all week and
it seemed a time to vary our pattern, if only on principle.
Get together sometime during the week. But I do not have
her home address or telephone and can't get it. Even
sneaking up on her, I come up empty. Does she live alone
or with a friend, I say, nonchalant.

"Why do you want to know?"

"Are you crazy? We're in bed together and I shouldn't
want to know you?"

"Don't you like it?"

"Oh yes I like it, that's why I want to know. It seems to
me quite natural that I should want to know, but you keep
it a dark secret. Your address."

"Not at all."

"What's your address?" (Must be very direct.)

"Look it up in the phone-book if you really want to

know." She giggles and distracts me with hanky-panky. And she has another trick of acting hurt when you do not respond in kind to the hanky-pank, so there you are.

However I did look it up in the book and it ain't there. In Fort Lee or anyplace nearby there is no one under Linda, Lynn, L., nothing. Except under Liar. This is my girlfriend and I can't ring her up, can't drop her a line. We set up a date for the next Saturdays always, a week away, and what if I should happen to choke on a chickenbone Thursday? Suppose I die and have to cancel?

My new theory is no boyfriend, or maybe not. Forget the jealousy angle, this girl is a Walkaway. She left in the dust three small babies, triplets, and a loving husband, and she left them no forwarding address. She's not Stanley any more than I am Fish. I'm company for her, but she holds a hatful of secrets notwithstanding.

Not that I have a right to complain about secrets. I don't refer to Tanya either. Of course I am not married anymore. I could go off in the morning and marry with someone new, and so could Tanya, so long as we don't invite one another to the wedding breakfast. I will tell Linda NotStanley who I am and I will not hesitate to mention my wife with pride. And I will do these things as soon as she releases to me her address.


Just about now I can see the top of the bottom of the money-barrel. I am already cutting back, as on Saturday night I was oh so casual to Linda, "How's about a pizza for a change?"

And it will get worse. Not yet dire, just say I will be wanting an income in a month or two.


Carnovsky's thought for the day. We are like two boats in the basin, Linda and myself, floating, jostled by the waters around us, and not connected to anything including each other. Boats have an anchor, but only to haul out and drift where the current is flowing.

A very small sampling of the level of profundity I can produce when my feet are wet and the walking bumps my brain. Fed up with delicatessen lunches, so I made myself a soup last night, enough to heat and eat until the Ides of March, if you can stand the taste.

Mrs. K. at the library: "Mr. Fish! We haven't seen you in some time. As a matter of fact I've been holding something for you."

A dear lady. Again she has been doing my work for me, and waited weeks to let me know the search goes on. This one concerns a priest who vanished one evening from a pilgrim retreat—he retreated further. This was a man who was "always cheerful" and was just as cheerful when last seen wishing the others in his party a good night's slumber and heading off to his cabin in the woods.

At sun-up, however, his bungalow was empty, and lacking any other explanation of this fact, they concluded he was eaten up by an animal in the neighborhood. Possible, of course, but without leaving a trace? Imagine it. Doesn't even cross their mind that he could use his feet and walk away, yet they will believe he was digested whole by a grizzly bear. And that was the official version. They ransacked the woods and fields—police and family and the newspapers—and in the end concluded the animal had taken this priest along to his cave to eat him, thus leaving behind no evidence of what was obvious.

But years afterward, one hundred miles away in western Massachusetts, the fellow turned up again, in one piece and still wearing the hair-suit! He was making jelly with a crowd of monks in some other neck of the woods. So he was told, We thought the bears ate you, and he told them, No I am safe.

That's it? No bears, no scarlet woman, not even a spiritual crisis to relate? No, said the priest who had been making jelly, I am safe.

Of course who is to say what really happened on the night he retreated. Not him. He isn't even in this tale, which is in a collection of letters between another priest and a childhood buddy of his who went into politics. These two exchanged mail back and forth all their lives— the officeholder to show his friend how not all politics is crooked and the priest to prove that his chosen life can be a little interesting, or funny.

My personal guess would be that he came a little unwound that night, the jelly priest. Heading off into the woods to pray makes him suspect to begin with and then it sounds like he was behaving strangely when they caught up to him over in Massachusetts. People will excuse a crazy guy if he loves God—they give him the benefit of the doubt—but when you think about it such a fellow never had reality under his feet to begin with.

In any event I know what I know, about my own case now. Widmer had his reason for going (the usual reason, I'm sure) and Flitcraft with his beam thought he had come up with a good one too. Maybe he did, that's not the point. The point is that I did it for no reason at all. This is what I know. If I was going for a reason I would have said so. Any reason—even crashing girders or grape jelly. But what I could not say was this: "There is no reason." If I said that, then Tanya would never let me leave.

No mystery. For me, in my case, to walk away was the only way to go at all.

"Tanya I am not happy with the food here."

"Tanya I am in love with Mrs. Getz."

"Tanya I am off to make jelly now, in a hair-suit."

No. Anything I could give her to go on, I would gladly have given. But "Tanya I have no good reason to go yet I am going anyway and never coming back"—that she wouldn't buy. Not a chance. She would say, "Tough luck, Oscar, you aren't going anywhere and don't be so silly."

She would talk me out of it and with ease. Everything she had to say on the subject would be correct and nothing I had to say would make one grain of common sense, I know that. So I had no choice but to go that way, without seeking permission, and now of course here I am.

# II

## The Oriental Advantage

### Winter 1955–56—

A sexual disaster last night. My luck in this field of endeavor ran out and it happened just as I dreaded it might when Linda made the change to Sunday for this week. I did everything in my power to alter the timing, but Linda is the social director here, she sets the schedule of events, and she is also the interior decorator of our love life—in charge of sound effects and lighting. She likes the music on and the lights off, and the "starlight" must be coming through the window to bless our efforts.

So of course it was the absolute worst time for Linda, doing her rag doll routine on me and getting ready for the fireworks when I suddenly became unable. No help for it, the air just went out of me and when I struggled to come back it only got worse. Even with my eyes shut I knew that my bare girl was over there plumping up her pillows, advertising her assets in the window-frame. At first Linda in her transports did not notice. Then she could not help but notice, first me and then the spectacle next door.

Thus Carnovsky, who managed forty-eight years on the planet earth with a single naked lady in his life, has now got himself two at once without even trying. They are coming out of the woodwork. Surrounded by them, literally, my life is suddenly filling up with naked ladies and I can't cope. It should not be so shocking. After all nakedness is everywhere all of the time—it's behind every door, inside each outfit you see on the street, every suit and smock. So how can it be shocking?

Linda Stanley is shocked, that one is for sure. Even in

our homegrown starlight-dreamlight I could see her go pale on me, like a wet white flower. To her I am guilty of an infidelity. And the funny part is that at the same time I was feeling some of the guilt of infidelity to my bare girl in the window, who had me to herself until tonight. Even stranger, another page in my education on these matters, I had for the first time a guilt toward Tanya that I never bothered with before. It took two of them, an orgy, to wake me up to the fact I might be living badly, like a Roman Emperor, corrupt.

"I'm sorry."

"It was seeing that woman, wasn't it?"

"Yes of course it was. I'm sorry."

"Do you know her?"

"No, no, not a bit. How could I know her. I don't know a soul around here except the little boy in One-B."

"Oscar—"

"It's the truth. What do you suppose, that I know all the ladies in New York just because one of them forgot to lower her shade tonight?"

"No of course you don't. I was just upset, that's all."

"I understand. And I'm sorry. Maybe later."

"It's late already, though. Remember, it's not Saturday. I have to be at work in the morning."

"Oh yes? At what school again? Is this near your apartment-house? What about the phone number there—" (Trying to cheer her up with the Inquisition, a big joke between us these days.)

"Oscar—"

"Come on, give. Small studio apartment? A mansion on the hill? Cave inside the rocks? Tell me the details—is it true you grew up among the wolves?"

"She was awfully well-built, wasn't she?"

"I didn't get a good look, I'm afraid."

"She was a lot better built than I am."

"Don't get crazy. She was just a stranger, without a head."

"I thought you didn't see her."

"I saw she had no head."

"Then you saw what she had two of as well!"

"Big deal."

"I'll say it was."

"Linda, get ready, because I am changing the subject. Ready? Now. It's changed."

"What's the new subject."

"You are. We are going to talk about you. *You* are going to talk, to me, about you. Go."

"You know all about me." (I have got her smiling by now.)

"From eight to three I know a little. I hear about the schoolchildren, and the evil principal Gannon, and the nice friend Betty Robinson who teaches First Grade, and the lunches that are inedible, and the coffeemaker in the Teacher's Room that produces mud, silt. What else do I know, let me see—"

"Oscar—"

"You see? I make a speech, I raise a little hell, and all you say is Oscar. You always say Oscar. Tell me instead your telephone, right now."

"464-6111." (Or something.)

"What, really? You made it up, it's your license plate."

"Oscar I'm late, let me get dressed. I'll tell you my phone number next time. Promise. I'll tell you anything you want. Maybe."

This part is okay. We are having a little fun, maybe moreso than usual as a matter of fact. My nerves are settled, my bare girl is gone, and we have let go of our inhibitions for a change. All for the best. And now in the dark (where she is not so self-conscious) Linda bends down to pick up her things, and I find myself with an unusual view. Her head, upside down, framed between two haunches—a funny beautiful sight, a waterfall of hair, that makes me laugh. And she's straight up, hands on hips.

"You're laughing at me."

"Not at all. You are lovely to see."

"You were laughing. What was so funny?"

She approaches the bed and starts poking me in the belly, tickles me, and slugs me with a pillow. There only is one, so I must disarm her to go on the attack and as we wrestle over the pillow something happens that very soon we are wrestling with each other instead, and I am back in business. She's on, like a cowgirl whooping it up at the rodeo, and soon her little squeals are heard, and nothing could go smoother, or feel nicer to us.

All fixed up, no more disaster, no guilt, jealousy, nothing. Where did it all go? Beats me. I only know some funny events took place here and we shared them, and that put us at our ease. For a historical first, she stayed the night, which meant no sleep for me. It's a small bunk plus she got the pillow. And I was also nervous that Jimmy might duck in early, before school, as he does occasionally if there is something to report. The big news of the day sometimes comes out of his cereal box in the a.m.

No further incident, however. "Continental Breakfast" here (bagel and coffee, instant) after which she took the tunnel to Jersey and I put my face in the pillow for an hour.

Tuesday. Hauled in my biggest bundle of mail to date. Two magazines, two advertisements for more magazines, one contest, a reply from Gross at The Post to my inquiry about Benny Leonard, and a letter from my girlfriend. Some haul! I took it along to the diner with me and ate the fish breakfast for an hour, poking my important pile of mail.

It's not a letter so much as a note from Linda. These few

words—"Oscar, you are completely right. I *will* tell all. Much love, Linda."

Too bad. It was only last evening I decided it best to go along with her. I stopped wanting to know. A displaced person can't hold down a job in a school, so I was wrong to peg her for a Walkaway. And so what then but a married woman (very obvious to anyone except myself?) who likes to play around, but on a tight schedule. The husband is busy with his business, goes on trips—and maybe he plays around too. People do things this way, you hear about it every week. So she slips off the ring and slides on a wig—not Linda but some others I'm sure—and goes after a little hanky-pank. Then of course the big rush back home, into the apron, on with the ring, before the bubble breaks.

Not only is she therefore not a Walkaway, she is the exact reverse: one who is staying. (On her terms.) I could verify this, every bit, by putting my detective's hat on my head and trailing her to Fort Lee, or wherever she really goes. But I do not want to know. I decided, why force this girl to talk? She was right, it's better left unknown. I don't love this person and so I don't care if she has a husband in the bushes. I don't need any sad stories, nor do I fancy gazing upon the snapshots of husband and little children if any.

Leave me in the dark, I concluded—just last night—so of course she drops me a line this morning to announce she is ready to spill.


Wednesday. With Linda it is exactly what it might have been with Giselle. A game, and nobody's heart is breaking. It's something nice with nothing nasty. There would be no one making waves and no one worrying about the weather from one minute to the next, the way it goes in real love. An attractive girl, make no mistake—to like but not to love.

I don't know much but I do know the difference. I had

the other kind, the genuine article, where every ten seconds you perk up and ask, What's up, something the matter? Tell me, please, I detect a slight change in your face—

Tanya, of course. 1931, summer, Coney Island. That was love. She came with me, to Feltman's, Effie's Tea-Room, yes even out to Jamaica Racetrack and I came with her too, to that folk dancing of hers—Carnovsky, with two cement blocks for feet. My head was spinning for years!

She was a beauty, universal knowledge on Grand Avenue in Brooklyn and she knew it too. That was the thing. She put a little english on every move she made, to let the world know she was perfectly aware. Arrogant. She made you love her, she squeezed your heart, and believe it I was not the only one.

Friday Night. We got a nice break today in the weather. Bright blue skies and the temperature shot up to forty so I made an all-day job of it, clear up to Central Park and back, using hot pretzels for fuel.

Lovely in the park. Ice-skaters, pretty mothers talking among themselves, babies bundled up like a fragile package with just the eyes showing. Two dogs tree a squirrel. All the trees had a skim coat of ice that catches the sun and makes a glitter—a rock-candy world.

I took it in from a comfortable bench and worked my way through a couple of Rafael Gonzales Coronas, indulging the life of leisure while trying my best not to worry about my state of impending poverty. Most of my worrying I prefer to get done at night, when there's nothing else to do.

Do my money worries show on my sleeve? Last night

Linda foots the bill! Says, Why should you always pay. It isn't like I have a big family to support, I have money too. And so forth.

Did she peek in my cookie-jar or merely read my mind? I didn't ask questions (in keeping with my new policy), I just accepted. The truth is I can eat for the week on what I saved last night, what with the two bottles of vino and all. That's where the cost comes in, getting into bed with a lush. Not with a talker, however—The Serious Talk, as she calls it, must be postponed. Tonight we will have our fun, she announces, and on Wednesday (after work, no less) she will trot over here to spill the beans.

So now I cannot be so sure of my theory. The way she said about having no family to support, she wasn't lying to me. Yet if there is no husband, there must yet be something else. One possibility, she is a sleeparound. She likes it in bed and is ashamed to like it so much, only not so ashamed she'll miss out. So she takes it on the sly, here and there, keeping a few different men on ice around town and keeping them apart from her true life, which remains the teaching of kids.

I don't believe this new explanation, I don't get it from her—even if once or twice she talked a sailor's talk in bed—I am only bound to take it into account.

Likewise I must take into account the possibility that it is all very simple. She got herself a Jew and can't show him to her friends. I don't credit this one either, however. For one thing, this is a good girl in my opinion and for another, if it was anti-semitism she would not be coming here to confess on Wednesday. That's a crime *no* one confesses to anymore.

To better address the problem of my financial worries, I took a longshot at Hialeah with Kramer. With two bullet works since a good fourth, and dropping down five hundred, I figured this horse was worth a twenty dollar investment (against profits of 250 if he should happen to get home).

A gamble, a longshot who ate dust for seven furlongs and then made a late move—back to the barn. Not for nothing did they make Hubba Bubba 11–1. A horse must be hungry to win, says my colleague Hearn, however I don't think he means hungry for lunch.

When I am on, I feel like a genius. I can see between the lines, even from a thousand miles to the north. When I'm not hitting I feel like every other jerk in the grandstand, sticking pins in dolls, working the voodoo shift. Every instinct I have is wrong, until by magic it snaps back lucky. No such luck with my friend Hubba Bubba.

Tonight Linda comes to "tell the truth." Last night I had a shock already from my other one, Our Lady of the Rear Window. I was only half-attending the show, the other half asleep, when suddenly it grew very bright over there—as though someone threw on a spotlight—and she did the amazing deed. Pulled off her panties. Yanked them down and put her round backside up on the windowsill for me.

And there it sat like a pair of soft white melons for a long time and finally she turned around and showed me her face too, which was enormous, the size of a hot-air balloon and just as smooth. No eyes or nose, only a tongue sticking out at me.

I froze on the guilty seat and could find no way to escape. My muscles would not budge to flee, so I had to sweat it out while she let me have it. Caught at last and my face felt red as a radish. It never crossed my mind this could be a dream because it never can when you are dreaming. That's what makes it rough, that within a dream there can be nowhere to hide. So I gazed upon this terrible face, a balloon filling up the window-frame, and I was positive it was her, it was real.

To tell the truth I still think so, I think I really saw the bottom half of her. If she did it tonight, dropped her drawers and sat like Humpty Dumpty on the ledge, wouldn't it look exactly as it looked in my dream? There it was, after all, and what else could it look like?

Linda sets up shop as The Answer Man. Ask me anything you want, she says, and I will give the answer. So naturally question number one from me was,

"*Why* are you going to answer whatever I want to ask?"

"Good question. Cause I want to. I like you and I want to be fair with you."

"Tell me your phone number."

"That isn't a question, it's a command. I like you, Oscar, but I won't obey your commands."

"Fair is fair. So please then, madam, just for my records, what might your telephone be?"

"WI 4-1517."

"Bingo."

"You aren't writing it down."

"I can remember. So what made it a secret—that the wrong person might pick up?"

"Correct. Two wrong persons, my mom and dad."

"Your folks?"

"I live with my parents in a six-room house in Fort Lee. I've lived there since I was eleven, except for a few years in my early twenties. My brother moved out at eighteen like a normal human being."

"What's normal. You must get along with them nicely."

"Of course, I love them very much. And it makes life very affordable for all of us. But it is not The American Way, Oscar, not for a thirty-one-year-old woman."

"I'm forty-eight."

"You are not living with your parents."

"A good thing, where they are—underground."

"So you're not appalled. That's nice. I knew if anyone

wouldn't laugh at me it would be you, Oscar. You really are a nice man."

"Thank you. And you are a nice lady. So that's it? That's the big secret?"

"Hardly. The worst is yet to come."

"You robbed a bank. Took a traffic ticket. What?"

"I seduced you."

"That I'm aware. I notice such things sometimes."

"I mean I seduced you on purpose, it was premeditated. It was—oh Oscar it was such a big mess I don't even know how to explain it to you."

"You did already, remember? It was my snoring that got to you."

"It really *was*, in a way. This is so awful! I know you think I'm attractive, maybe even a little sexy? Would you believe that in my entire life I have been out on about six dates? Or that for the last four years I never went out once?"

"No I wouldn't believe it unless you told me so. Why shouldn't you be popular with the men?"

"I never was, that's all. And now there aren't any men. In the past there were lots, they just never saw me. But now I only see two men besides my father: Bill Gannon, the principal, who is both horrible *and* married, and Mr. Ahearn, a nice man who drinks whiskey in the boiler-room—he's the school super—and who has snakes and lobsters tattoed on both arms."

"Lobsters?"

"I think so, yes."

"All right then, lobsters it is. So you were lonely. That's no crime, Linda, and it's no crime to try and change it."

"Six months ago I went in for a check-up with our family doctor, who presented me with a clean bill of health and a free lecture. Or not a lecture, a bit of fatherly advice that no father would give."

"Seduce?"

"You guessed it. He said, You're over thirty, your life is going along, and you are a virgin. And he said I might wish to remain a virgin but that it was his opinion as a physician that a love affair would be very good for me, for my *health* mind you. No need to marry anybody, just go to bed with a man, he said."

"He had himself in mind?"

"Oh no, nothing like that. He really believed in the idea. Of course I didn't have a man to go to bed with. I didn't even have one to go to a movie with, except Dad. So Doctor Barnhill said, I know that, go find yourself one. Half the people in the world are men. Make a conscious effort, join groups, take a course, go out hunting. So I went out hunting, like a leopard stalking her prey. I went to parties without an invitation, I joined an acting class, I took a boat ride last August on the Great Lakes—spent a lot of time and money, looking for a man to seduce! And then, as you know dear Oscar, I went to a hockey game in Quebec."

"I am surprised you didn't find one sooner. On the boat? Did they all hide from you again?"

"Beats me. I was looking. But when I saw you asleep on the bus, snoring like an old dog in the sun, I knew you were the man for me."

"Very funny."

"I'm perfectly serious, though. I could see it with you. I wasn't afraid of you—you were nice and it showed. And you were handsome—"

"For an old dog in the sun."

"Well maybe a little at first, I thought that. But I chose you, hunted you down, and even then I had to drink myself under the bed to come down the hall after you. *You* were no help."

"Linda I never dreamed. I wouldn't have presumed—"

"So you said, literally. So I did presume. And so I still do. But it has been such a nasty trick on you."

"Have you been hearing complaints?"

"You didn't know the truth. How could you know how arbitrary it was, that it might have been someone else, any face in the crowd."

"I disagree with you. You found no one at the parties or on the Great Lakes, so it was not so arbitrary as you think. More arbitrary in a way for me—you knocked and I let you in."

"Well we both were ready, I guess."

"That's it. Plus we both were lucky. Believe it, I could go twenty years without the courage to fill that prescription he gave you. You did better."

"But you have to mind. Being Doctor Barnhill's pills—for medicinal purposes only. Don't you think we have to stop now that you know it's once-a-week Spinster Therapy we are having?"

It was at this juncture in our discussion that I came close to uttering a lie. I was close to telling her, No it's more than that, what we have now. I bit my tongue in time, however, and I'm glad. Maybe this does end us, and maybe it just ends her taking too much wine to get herself primed on Saturday. Who knows, maybe changes nothing at all.

But we both should know what it is and what it isn't. Sex therapy, for each, not only for her. (Once a week, like with Tanya as a matter of fact, and in between times we go about our business.) I'm happy I let the truth stand, as that was the purpose of this special Wednesday night talk, the truth. All I said was,

"No I don't mind. It's therapy for me too. That's one smart doctor in my opinion, I only hope they don't lock him up for this kind of stuff."


Today for some reason I recalled my late brother-in-law Louis Schecter, who is a long time gone, dead nineteen years. A sweet kid, gentle man, and not thirty years old when he went, an unbelievable thing to us all. Maybe it was going through the neighborhood this morning—Attorney Street, Seward Park—because Louis always took The Forward.

He was helpless, and I recall going to his parents' house many times, fixing water-pipes when they burst, putting a lock on the door after they got robbed. Louis and Florence were married only two years, give or take, but they were always a couple. When we were living on Avenue P. he would show up for her on his rollerskates and they would skate up Gravesend together, under the El, to the moviehouse on Church Street. Childhood sweeties, like a brother and sister I thought, good buddies. Louis was like a brother of mine too—always around, and friendly, and in need of help. And I had none of my own, so an open spot on the roster.

What a shame for both of them. I had a love for him and today felt his absence for the first time in how long, a decade? And it is odd how I can miss the dead and yet not miss the living. I was halfway to the land of the dead today, they were as real to me as anyone still breathing—Louis and also my late parents, of whom I thought. Maybe I really am a ghost, a dead man, a wisp with no fire inside.


So long to the month of February. Jimmy brought the dead back to life this after—a head in the doorway can do it—came up to protest sister Beatrice getting top cut again. They give her what she wants while him they only scold. And of course he does not *care* that they love her and hate him (this he must insist) but merely prefers to see justice done.

"What makes you think this?"

"A million things. Everything."

"Give me one or two. Give me one good one."

"She's a girl, that's why."

"She's a little shrimp and you are a big strong fellow who can take care of himself pretty well. So naturally they would worry less."

"My dad took her to work with him and he knows I wanted to. I ask all the time and he always says sure thing, real soon. Then he takes her instead. And he didn't even tell me they were going."

"So what can I do to cure your hurt feelings?"

"I don't have any hurt feelings. I don't care."

"Of course you don't, I know that."

"Do you like my dad?"

A sudden shift in the wind! I was hard at work on the first topic (and making very little headway) when bango he changes over to another toughie. Because what kind of answer would he like to hear?

"You know, I never had a chance to talk with him much. I don't know him well. But he must be a good father to have such a fine son." And I give him a nudge, a friendly poke, and see he prefers to keep the glum face on. Did Myers say something nasty about me? I wonder. Then Jimmy is at me again.

"Do you have any kids?"

"You see any? You think I have a few underneath the bed? In the closet?"

"You don't."

"No I don't."

"Are you going to marry the blondie?"

It's the Spanish Inquisition now. Jimmy will ask these questions, one after another. He is not nosy especially, but let something pop into his mind and he says it, what the hell.

"Do you like her?"

"She's probably okay," he shrugs for me. "How should *I* know?"

Nothing resolved, yet we both feel one hundred percent better nonetheless. Finished off the cocoa dust.

I look in the classified without even knowing what I might be looking *for*. It's a very discouraging list. Not that they don't have jobs—they can cover two and a half pages with their jobs. But you read the information and suddenly the job isn't there anymore, it's gone, like smoke.

Who's going to pilot a baby-food truck through the Bronx? Or check-out groceries in mid-town like a pimply kid? They have nothing for a person like me, it's either too big or too small, takes a Ph.D. or a certified moron.

I'm not in the mood for these jobs, that's sure. If I had a few more cookies in the cookie-jar I would not even bother opening this page. And doing so is not going to solve my problem in any event, so I have my nervous moments. What happens if I get down to the bottom of the barrel, and don't have the cost of my daily bread, and still can't budge off the mark? Is that who goes to the bank and borrows?

No, that's who they won't loan. And they won't loan me anyway if I'm Fish. They don't hand money over to a ghost, you must have some collateral, plus all the paperwork. I don't exist at a bank.


Whoops, I don't exist in bed anymore either.

The problem I had once before came back. Linda was nice about it. Maybe you had too much to drink, she said. No that was you, I said. I understand, she said, you're angry, frustrated. I don't feel angry, frustrated, I said.

What do you feel then? she said. Do you hate me for Wednesday? Not at all, I said, I figured we were better for Wednesday.

What, then?

And I don't know what. Maybe it was worry, and trouble with sleep. I aired it all out, my situation, concluding with the present financial picture, and again she was very nice. Talked and was very sympathetic. We used the time and we stayed good friends. But we did not solve my problem, or hers.

Monday. I asked around for work. Asked Bulkitis if he knew of anything, asked at the ferryboat exchange, person to person. The classified is like ether, it leaves you motionless. You might find something small, asking person to person, yet solid.

Asked at the Wing Wang and received the same response as always from him: no problem. He hammers his head once (never twice) like he's butting an imaginary insect a few inches in front of him, and spits out his favorite syllables—no prob lem. Terrific, glad to hear it I'm sure. Mr. Wing Wang has got The Oriental Advantage over everyone else—he knows what he thinks, but he's the only one who does.

Also asked Kramer, with slight embarrassment. A lot of embarrassment, to be truthful. I have been betting twelve or thirteen years in Kramer's shop and if I ever had a problem in life he never felt it. I need his confidence and I need my privacy, so for me too it has sometimes been "No problem." But Kramer knows a lot of people and he might know a situation.

Certainly, Oscar, he says, I'll look into it forthwith. He is a busy man, he reminds me, but he will shake the branches and see what tumbles down. I'll hear from him on it. So I place my well-being in the hands of a book-maker (salt of the earth he is not) and the fact is I'm cheered up. Because yesterday it was in my own hands, a far worse prospect!

Kramer tells me they are going to remake Aqueduct, shut it down and shine it up to the tune of millions. I never liked the place myself and I'm sure I will like it less shined up. All racing dates will split between Belmont and Jamaica while the work goes on and then they are talking close Jamaica for good. That I would hate to see. I went there first, my father took me, and maybe that's why I like it best. True it's a shanty alongside Belmont Park, but some men a shanty might suit.

Jimmy Myers ran away from home. Just as I say, all kids will do it. And he decided to do it alone because he couldn't trust his sister. He could trust me, however, and stepped inside to say a goodbye.

"I'll miss you, Oscar." (Sometimes acts like he's in a movie.)

In the getaway kit he had stowed a bottle of Hires Rootbeer, a waxpaper deck of Ritz crackers, the baseball cards and the Hopalong Cassidys all completely organized, and a few more items—all crumpled into the corners of an A & P bag with handles. Looked not unlike my own luggage when I went, as a matter of fact.

"If you find yourself close by, you could drop in and visit."

"Under cover of night?"

"Whenever."

"You keep an eye out for Bee-Bee, okay. She's all right."

"Listen, Jimmy—you have cash? For food and so forth?"

"I can get it."

This he can. Takes in more than me, at present, about one dollar a day from empties in the park plus an occasional strike from his subway-fishing. He combs the gutters and grates, comes up with a dime, a quarter, it all adds up. I won't put a figure on his income but he always has plenty. In fact I was going to offer him a modest loan and thought better to ask for one instead.

I was very sad when he took off, though not because I ever dreamed he was really going. I knew he would be

back in time for supper and his favorite television pro-
grams, and he was, no problem. It just hit me that way—I
got a little emotional—when I saw his back.


Prior to today I never got one word beyond Hello with
Timothy Myers, the father, and so I was very surprised to
find him at my door. And I thought if he's here it's for no
good reason—maybe to nix my visits with his son. But I
was wrong. A neighborly call, to thank me for being kind
to Jimmy and furthermore invite me for spaghetti dinner
next week.

No way to slip the noose. He knows I'm here and puts
it, Pick your best night, so stuck is stuck and I'll go eat
with them. And now he reassures me it will be all right, he
will see to it "that Mary stays sober." At this I might have
fainted in his arms.

For months now I had this man pegged as a drunkard.
Not like Linda Stanley, taking a nip of Mother Courage
now and then, but a guzzler, a falldown lush, and it's true
that he stands in the foyer bellowing "Let me in, let me in,
it's my house too!" And he skips in later than the average
man. But in his version it is the mother who does the
drinking for them—and he thought everyone knows it,
that it's obvious to all the world.

I take his testimony at face value and I do not. She could
march herself up here and tell a different story, I would not
be taken aback a second time. I'm removing my judicial
robes, finishing my stint as judge and jury. Let them be
loud and let whoever is right, if any, be right. Fine by me.
I'm a reformed character and won't consign anyone down
to hell unless they purchase their own tickets, and sign all
appropriate papers.

I told Myers, however, that if he ever finds himself
locked out in the cold he can sleep on my rug. He said he
might take me up on it too, so I was obliged to let him in

on the rumor about my snoring, and we parted the greatest of friends.

A definite losing streak in my love life and there is nothing funny about this even if you must treat it humorously. A situation like this one you can talk over once and have a nice time talking. But not twice.

Maybe Linda was right, that her confession signals the end. I was positive it couldn't make a difference, not to me at any rate, and yet it is to me the difference has occurred. It comes like a short-circuit, a buzzing in the head and then the power goes out. I know I am sound yet I am unsound at post-time, when we are ready to run.

And like any losing streak it gets you down, gets worse before it gets better. Now we are both *expecting* it to happen, so that Linda has her troubles too. Because her body does not wish to commit and then be disappointed. There is a trick or two besides the usual that I would be happy to try, but these she wants no part of.

"This wouldn't have happened if I'd kept my mouth shut, Oscar. I know it wouldn't."

"A good question," I admit, this time around, because it makes no sense to me, yet coincides.

Friday. Four consecutive days of this icy drizzle, in the midst of which I survived Mrs. Myers' spaghetti, just barely. I would have put it into the record if not poisoned and confined to my bed all day. No desire to scribble this week in any case, and so I didn't. The author's prerogative. (sp.)*

*My guess is that Oscar meant to check his spelling of the word prerogative. I don't blame him, I checked it too, and wondered if he kept a dictionary in his flat. Very few words in the daybooks *are* misspelled, insofar as I can discover, whereas a fair number have been lined out and corrected.

—Walter Ford, Jr.

I can't tell if it's this weather, or my losing streak in the sheets, or my empty coffers that's getting me down. With this many woes you are hard pressed to weigh them out separately and rank them. Jimmy hasn't checked in all week himself—why visit the dead?

Took a crack at the library yesterday a.m. and found even Mrs. K. with a cold in her nose. Plenty of my fellow scholars were in there tanning themselves by the radiator. They have to make it through the winter too—not needing a book, just needing a coat from the cold.

You see all the magazines with ads to travel out, Get Away Today! Flee To The Sun! Like Giselle, let's go Mexico, but I can't see it. If I could see it, I still couldn't pay for it. A trip like that might cost thousands and just to see a foreign church, some castle in the rain. I can't talk French or Italian and we got plenty of nice buildings to look at right here—which of course no one looks at, unless they are from out of town.

To please Mrs. K. I took along a couple of titles, both by Melville, a long and a short. I remember liking this guy in high school. He was a traveler too, she says—she surmised I was planning a trip from my attention to the ads—who ended up near here, in lower Manhattan, because he went to work at the Customs House. Truly, she assures me. The best writer in American History working for a paycheck around the block from here.

That's a story for you, I said, like the Queen of England going to work in a bank, or punching tickets at a mutuel window.

And she says, what kind of window was that, Mr. Fish?


Eating our pizza pie we both pretended not to be thinking about the main event later on. When it got later, both pretended not to be pessimists. All this pretending did nothing to alter the outcome—no action from Oscar, all bets off again.

By then I didn't even care. I wasn't going to worry it to extremes so long as it went home and left me alone. I did not wish to be sympathized with further, or analyzed more deeply. Let me just take the loss.

Yet Linda stayed put, would not budge from my bed. So the two of us were in there with our pizza breath chained together side by side. And I really believed I would strangle to death when she says, Tell me a joke. It takes all kinds.

"A joke! Nothing's funny." All right, some things are funny, even to me—but never a joke.

"I'll tell a joke, and *then* you tell one."

"I don't know any joke, Linda."

"Okay here's mine. Who is bigger? Mr. Bigger, or Mr. Bigger's baby?"

"Get serious."

"You have to guess."

Her face promised to add to my misery with a bucket of tears any second if I didn't take a shot at it, so I replied,

"Mr. Bigger is bigger, naturally."

"Nope. Mr. Bigger's baby is a little Bigger. Get it?"

"I'm sure in your line of work you hear a lot of jokes. I don't hear any. I never cared for them anyway."

"Make one up, it's your turn."

"Fat chance. The only one I remember is the same one everyone knows, the Great High Lama."

"I don't know it."

"You don't want to, then. It can go on all day."

"Go ahead and start. I'm ready."

My Uncle Julius loved this story and would always begin it in the same way: "Would you like the one-hour version or the twenty-four?" He never told it the same way twice. And of course it really cannot be funny if you don't make it long, endless, so I gave her at least twenty minutes of the fellow searching out the meaning of life uptown, downtown, way out west, to the North Pole, down into the basement of the Kremlin and so on, following a lot of crazy clues. It got him to Tibet in half an hour flat, out to the Himalaya Mountain Range, past the Low Lama and the Middle Lama and the High Lama's mama and then I had him waiting—one day, two days, a week—for his first audience with the Great High Lama.

And so on. Until on the third audience (because it was always the third one with Julius) the Lama finally opens both eyes and hears the man's question, What is the Meaning of Life, and closes them for an hour, opens them again, first one and then the other, and in the end pronounces that "Life is a fountain."

By this time I was enjoying myself a little, nostalgic, and she was too because she really didn't know the story and was eager to see how it comes out. It was news to her, this ancient joke, that's how it is with the goyim. So I put on the mustard and relish and gave it the works, where the truth-seeker is confused and disappointed having come all this way at such great personal expense to hear such a silly pronouncement, and asks incredulously "What? Life is a *fountain?*"

And the Great High Lama replies at once in the voice of a Delancey Street tailor, "You mean it's *not* a fountain?"

Not a bad performance, if I don't say so. You must get fully into the spirit of this terrible joke and I did my best, which was good enough to put Linda into hysterics. A tiny smile at first and then it sinks in and the laughter starts up. In the end she was rolling on the floor in a laughing fit. (I'm sure the red wine contributes to this result. Like that comic used to say, You don't think I'm funny, then have another drink.)

So she forgot herself. Forgot to be shy and forgot to be nervous and so did I therefore. And when we lost track of our problems our problems lost track of us too and we started up the engine with no difficulties and continued in like fashion. We took our therapy after all, because life is a fountain.

"Tell the truth," I said after. "Did Doctor What's-It give you this solution? Swap jokes and forget your troubles?"

"Nope, I thought of it myself. And it worked too."

"Yes it worked. But Linda, I'm serious—it really is the only joke I know."


One day cured by the Great High Lama and the very next day the sun takes up its spot in the sky. Officially it has been Spring but now the weather agrees, and the benches in Battery Park are warm and dry.

A horseplayer knows best what everyone knows—when you're hot you're hot—so I was not surprised to also discover it is not my fate to starve. Kramer, the son of a bee, comes through. (And damn near neglected to mention the news to me!) I went in to bet a lousy five bucks, all I could risk, and I am on my way right back out the door when he wakes up and remembers—lifts his nose out of his book and plants the eyeglasses in his hair (such as it is) and remembers who the hell he's talking to. "Oscar. By the way—"

He thought it wasn't good enough, that I'd pass, but I am not passing this week. I need an income. Yes I am too old to work for tips and yes, much to smart to work menial I'm sure. I have been too this and too that all month in the newspaper and now it's time to take what shows. Who am I anyway? It isn't like they are rolling out the red rug for me in front of the brass doors at Waldorf-Astoria. I'm not royalty.

And the truth is I think I may like this job. Free food, short hours, and it puts me at the racetrack, right where I want to be. So what's not good enough about that? If I can pocket two incomes at once, in the course of half a day?

In Kramer's eyes I am dropping down the class ladder. Bulkitis only says he's happy if I'm happy. Confesses: "I was really worried when you bought White Owls last week, Oscar. That's not you." Absolutely correct, that's water seeking its own level.

As for Jimmy Myers, whom the cat dragged in here this morning before school, he is stunned to learn I must soil my hands with work of any kind. He had the conviction I was sitting on a nest-egg.

"A millionaire! Where did you get that?"

"My mother says you got plenty."

"It's news to me."

"She says you don't have to work for a living."

"I hate to disappoint, but I'm low man. I don't even have burying-money, like 2B. Or the price of Havanas."

"What about Hartack?"

"Good while it lasted. Money has a way of getting itself spent sometimes, to sustain a belly. You need something steady coming in, like the bottle business."

It's tough preaching hard work and responsibility to this kid when all he sees here is a horseplayer at his leisure, a millionaire on sabbatical.

I caught a beautiful sunny morning on which to travel out and receive my official indoctrination from a little gentleman named Wiley, a thousand-year-old man who is captain of the waiters there. I can see this job just fine, I like it already, except there is one slight obstacle they put in—clubhouse employees may wager as much as they wish, only never in the club where the customers can see you. And naturally they have a rule against leaving the room during working hours.

Wally Wiley has a direct line to one of the clerks, who holds his money by prior arrangement—"my broker" he calls him. John the salad man in the kitchen has his own kid running relay races to a buddy in the grandstand. There are other ways—for example the busboys can shake free more easily and they could have some of your money in tow—yet everything I heard was to no avail. You can bet with such tricks, you just can't win money. Because you can not handicap in a rush. The tote must be allowed to settle. Sometimes a late move is dictated. So yes you can get your money down, but no way to be smart with it. A challenge, that's all.

One other possible snafu, they expect Fish to have a Social Security Card and join the union. Can he do such things? He will have to look into the matter very soon. But they treat Fish like a brand new man, a neophyte starting out in life, and it is true I had this job, waiting on table, at the age of seventeen. Which is not to argue it is easy work, or work unworthy of respect. Watch out here for my colleague Wiley!

I respect everyone, that's the truth, I even respect a man who doesn't work at all—face it, I was that guy two days ago. Wiley (installed in the clubhouse here when Man O' War was standing on shaky legs) puts it like this: more people in the world are working as waiters than any other job, including factory. So anybody looks down on a waiter is only looking down on himself.

Rests his case, I'm sure. There are no kids doing the job in this room, and no dopes either. Even the busboys have some age on them. My opening came about, in fact, when a man named Fortini passed away from old age, over the winter. To which Wiley adds with a perfect straight face, "He didn't go in harness but we thought we should bury him in style anyway—laid him out on a bed of lettuce, gave him the whole treatment. Fortini liked a touch of pomp."

April and sunny and I am sitting on the Jamaica train
with a Gonzales in one hand, The Telegraph in another,
and a pencil tucked in behind my ear, and guess what? I'm
on my way to work! Who could predict it? And yet the
feeling is the same as always, like the feeling a kid gets
when he pulls his catching mitt out of the mothballs. The
heart gives a jump. It's a brand new season, so let's go.

I noted that the racetrack is crawling with security in
plain clothes, some of whom eat in here and one who
stands all day. His outpost. (You must keep an eye on the
uppercrust too.) He gave me an itch at first, the way you
itch when a cop puts in an appearance in your rear-view
mirror. You did nothing wrong but he doesn't know that,
and he's a *cop*, so you feel him on the back of your neck as
you drive along most innocent.

One of these blue-suits could have been on my case—say
a night cop from Brooklyn doubling down here days, or
someone who last summer was working the missing persons shift. But I was over my worry in a hurry, simply
because I know I am not someone they need. It isn't as if
the whole nation has been turning over every stick and
stone because the gross national product slipped in my
absence.

They looked for a few days, Tanya made them do so I'm
sure. But after that why bother? What would they do if
they found me? It's a free country, America, you can be
missing here and still not be a crook.

All the cops in the world can't change it now. I am the
Invisible Mensch, that's all, your friendly waiter, and
happy to bring out a nice slice of the cherry cheesecake—
very good today, yes—and something to drink with it
perhaps? No problem. And anyway the one in here, Ed-
mundson, has no desire to make an arrest. Too much like
work, he testifies, content to have another club sandwich
on the plate in front of him, compliments of the house.

As a general rule people do not look down on waiters. A few of course, but then a few will also look up. Most respect you if you give good service, for which they are after all paying good money. I give it without exception and enjoy a nice relationship with my customers. And the place runs smooth from the kitchen out, a veteran team, very well organized.

My goal in any case is getting by, so none of it concerns me too much. I pick up my tip and put it in my pocket. The money I make is small change compared to the sums I have been making since the War at Carnovsky's but I am in a position to appreciate it nonetheless. Admit it, dollars are real. Yesterday I swept up $1.10—I had to untuck it from an ashtray filled with lipstick filters—and I got a kick from it, just like a mousie picking cheese crumbs from the dust. You cash a bet at any price, because the money is real and everyone can use it.

Another of my crazy notions: every time I pick up a one-dollar tip from the debris I am tempted to pack it straight into an envelope and ship it off to Walter. No message, just the bill. I would always give him a dollar in the past, to watch his headlights shine. So naturally he would know the source and being a smart boy he would also know enough to keep it mum. Every kid loves a secret and Walter always loved that dollar—so I would be sending him a daily double out of the blue.

Too risky, of course, You cannot play games. Play fair— if you're gone you're gone. Yet it can be fun to dream things up and in any case thinking is not a crime anymore. Since they got rid of Joe McCarthy, no one puts you in jail for what you think now.


A new outlook on the races from on high. It's a far cry from my usual, what Hearn calls my office—I like to set up shop right along the rail by the sixteenth pole where you can see them parade just before the post, check the jockey's face and the horse's ass at the same time, and then a few minutes later you catch the finish in the same spot. I like being in the pit when the mud flies up. It still has got a beauty to it from the clubhouse but of a very different kind. You miss the sharp flavor. Watching them go from on high is like watching fish in a tank, where they float around and make no noise.

Include Linda Stanley among the ones who look down on waiters. In fact she has begun to look down on me in general, now that we have shared all the secrets. Now she knows who it is she visits on Saturday night and she also sees where, and so now we find ourselves disagreeing. We do not have a fight, we simply "disagree." Because now I am from a "different generation" where I was not from any particular generation last month, or it didn't matter if I was. And she looks down on waiters:

"Oscar what you need is a challenge."

How can she know what I need, if I don't know myself? I'm happy with my job, and it's enough of a challenge getting my money to the window on time.

"You are a highly intelligent man, that's all I mean. That's why you left the old job, because it wasn't enough of a challenge for you."

"I liked my old job. And I was making a living, not looking for a challenge. I had no complaints with my situation at all. And Linda, really and truly, I'm sorry if you are not impressed but I have no complaints with this one either."

"That's just because you don't complain. You don't believe in complaining. But you can still feel the cause."

"You don't complain either and do I tell you your job stinks?"

"I didn't say that, Oscar. I said you needed more."
"Such as what? What does 'more' look like? Should I be running for President against Ike?"
"Oh Oscar."
This is how it's done, to disagree without a fight. We are getting expert at it, the two of us. Linda does complain, however—she complains about me. Though for my own sake, I'm sure.

Linda Stanley may not accredit it but waiting table is an education in itself. It's people on parade. Today we had a pair in who insisted on changing tables twice (and of course they landed on mine) and then staged a wrestling match over the menu.
"I told you, Meg, I'll take care of this."
"Oh great—like you did last night!"
I wanted to ask her what he did last night—forget to hold the mayonnaise? But he must be the one in charge and she makes it her aim to embarrass him. They behave like snakes and in the meantime you must be nothing but charming in response if you value your percentage.
"It's a volatile situation," says Captain Wiley of my guests. "With this kind it can go either way. He's a psycho. So you look for two percent or twenty-five. With a psycho, it's never fifteen."
But does Wiley look down on customers? I will remember to ask him one of these days.
I never wrestled Tanya for a bill or a menu. She ordered hers and I ordered mine, less confusion that way. We don't bother one another in general because you have to see it as a partnership, not a romance only. And you have to get along. Starts *out* with a romance (or else forget it) and it ends up one of two ways: a partnership or a battle-royal. It depends upon respect.

Wally Wiley is a philosopher, a sachem, always happy to impart his wisdom. He was a jockey once, about 150 years ago, and he is still a wire-haired terrier. If there are great waiters (and why not?) the way there are great rocket-scientists and great shortstops, then Wiley is among the elite. I take pleasure in watching him work the floor, the old pro, but best I like his gems of wisdom.

"Horse, man, and money," he says, one of his favorites. "That's life, Oscar—horse, man, and money. The part you are, the part you aren't, and the part you can't control. Think about it."

I like it a lot, it's perfect. When I *think* about it, however, I can't make horseshit out of it. It'll come to me, I'm sure.

THE PART YOU ARE

THE PART YOU AREN'T?

THE PART YOU CAN'T CONTROL?

But whenever we witness an oddity, if a customer stiffs a waiter or conversely leaves a twenty-dollar bill ("likeness of Jackson") on the table, or if we see one of the married track officials waltz in here with a girl-chick on his arm in broad daylight—anything of the slightest departure—Wiley is apt to shake his head and pronounce,

"Horse, man, and money, Oscar. The part you are and the part you aren't."

And the part you can't control, don't forget. When he abbreviates, I finish it off for him in my head. It's like a singing jingle for candy bars or tutti-frutti, and makes about the same sense to me, just a little music.

I once took up drawing on Saturdays at the Cooper-Union. I couldn't do it then and I can't do it now—least of all horse man and money. Maybe I can draw a car or something like that, but no muscles and nothing wrinkled.

Spotted Hearn this morning by the walking-ring.

"You look the same," I told him.

"Glad to hear it. That's all I ask. And yourself as well, Oscar. Where have you been keeping yourself?"

"Right here every day they ran."

"No sir."

"Every day. I'm staff. Working up in the clubhouse—waiting table."

"Tell me another."

"It's gospel, Hearn. I got a fresh start in life. Come in today and see for yourself. I'll discount you."

"A fresh start at the bottom! What for? What the hell for, Oscar? You can do better than that."

"Sure I can. I can also do worse. But I enjoy it, Hearn, really it's all right with me."

"Jesus, Oscar."

Add him to the list, he looks down on waiters. I will have to report him to Wiley. And what does he do himself, Hearn? I think nothing. Stubbed his toe in the War and receives a monthly check in the mail. It's enough to keep his suits smelling fresh dry-cleaned and his leather shoes polished. Who knows, he might have a sideline in the numbers or deliver Chinese food on the midnight shift. Maybe sends out a fleet of women to walk the streets, and skims off his 75%.

But Hearn is okay. Like Linda, he is just concerned for me—he means to be nice. I won't report him. Seeing Hearn with his boy Mikey gave me a bright idea, though, that may solve my problem with Jimmy Myers. He is turning up the heat on our Ebbets Field plan but now I'm working I can beg off and maybe substitute a day at the races, even up.

His folks won't mind because after all I am the gentleman who brought a bottle of wine to dinner. Upperclass Oscar, gets fed spaghetti from a can and he brings a nice wine to go with it! So I'm gentry.

And Jimmy's eyes would pop at a real racehorse. He could pick a few winners, maybe get lucky with a longshot and clean up—and he can run my bets to Silva in the grandstand. I'll buy him his unlimited hot dogs here, at cost.


The day after Linda I am always of two minds about it. A split person. I believe that if we "disagree" and if we don't choose to stroll out on a Sunday in the park—if we are not at least a little bit in love—then we should not be rooting around like animals on Saturday night. No one's fault. I'm no less guilty for this than she is—a couple of weak links on the same chain, that's all.

However I can also believe the exact opposite: why not

this sort of attachment? Who does it harm? We both know the score and take our therapy where we find it. You can't get a sex life anywhere like a bottle of milk, it can be hard to come by. You can do without of course, and many will, but if every citizen had a nice neat schedule like ours, a schedule you can count on, I'm sure a lot of sad sacks would cheer up fast, the shy and those who lack confidence would perk up right away, and all the phonies would die of honesty.

It tides you over. Leaves room for the world's work to get done—cure diseases, new inventions, etcetera—and no one jumps off the stoop in despair. If by accident you have a baby it could present a problem, but at least you have the baby and that's something.

Linda sees to this aspect for us and I'm sure she does a good job, with help from our friend the Doctor. A slip-up is always possible (the part you can't control, boys and girls) and if we slip up we have to own it. If we slip, I become Fish officially and she has no choice but to drag me out to Jersey, introduce me around. And I hand out cigars, White Owls for the goyim.


The horsemen eat in here from time to time, and the higher-up the more likely. Wiley puts it this way: if his hands are clean we'll see him for lunch. If he has touched a horse lately, he'll be eating in his trailer or in the back-stretch kitchen. When I remarked to him that he maybe looked down on owners, my friend's reply was, "Truth is a defense, Oscar, watch and see."

Not unusual to see owners claiming each other's stock over a glass of whiskey. One young one is in soaking up doubles all afternoon and never shows the effects. His stomach is lined with tin. Drinks up ten or a dozen and still walks nice, talks nice, and remains considerate of others.

He is what Wiley calls a twenty-percenter. But the man doesn't even pee. He's a liquor-closet, a camel, storing it in his tin-lined gut.

It is worth listening if trainers munch together. You never take anything at face value out here, but these guys know their own stock and have the kind of information that can give an edge maybe one race a week. Who but the trainer knows a two-year-old maiden starter?

Sometimes you get the same edge browsing on the backstretch, where anyone can ask a question and everyone will have an answer. You don't need to be a turf-writer to say, How's Two Ton Tony going this week, or why was Bamboozle held out last Wednesday? You will always get an opinion down there and none valid without the signature of our founder.

You can also see with your own eyes. You will see a horse with bad mange, or a case of the runs (in which case he won't) and sometimes the word will leak out that a stable is getting ready to plunge on some concealed goods. That can be money in the bank, though if you know how to look you can see it between the numbers on the tote board.

About one year ago at Belmont Park I was going in pretty big on a horse named Charming Filly. I figure if they make a late change from a bug boy to Ted Atkinson it's because they need that much more to move up in the winner's circle. Then they parade past my office and we all detect in Charming Filly a strange gait—a limp to be accurate. Was this horse rank? It goes both ways (you always have the paddock slouch who gets up at the gate) but this time I lost my confidence, held onto my hundred bucks, and watched the race as a spectator. Good thing. The horse broke late, fell back early, and faded deeper into the sunset at every point of call.

Now that animal looked good to a lot of people, she was

bet down from 5–1 to 8–5 following the jockey change, and so naturally you heard the whole house groan when the nag could not go with them. Fix! they screamed. Ted, they screamed, dammit, why'd you pull the horse? They always do. No one pulled the horse. The horse was hurting and should have been scratched. Why she wasn't is another matter and no one out here knows it all. An allowance race, so they were not looking to unload. Possible they really hoped she would come around and get a check for them. And yes they may have had some dough on another horse—not pulling their own, just knowing she couldn't go and utilizing the knowledge to milk a nice mutuel.

If I spend a little time on the backstretch these days, it is not in quest of an edge on the day's handicapping. Just a nice way to pass an hour before I pull on my zoot-suit—it's sunny and quiet and I enjoy the atmosphere, like backstage at the circus. You might see a trainer's kid getting trained, and maybe a girl or two, the owner's daughter. People in half costumes, dirty silks and blue jeans, horses in blankets, the saddling and unsaddling, plus all the shit being shovelled.

Fifteen hundred horses is no joke. It's enough horse-plop every day to fill Carnegie Hall, and they cart it off direct by train to the farmers on Long Island. It's a big business, really, worth thousands a month to someone.

I am what Wiley calls a democrat. Not a Democratic, like Truman and Roosevelt (though I am also one of those)—to Wiley a democrat is anyone who only looks down on the higher-ups. A garbageman you must respect and I do. I can see it takes knowhow to dispose of six thousand pounds of swill. Technique and experience, like anything else. These guys know the score, and some people would be surprised to interview a Bowery bum or a South Street pier rat sometime. They follow politics and they know the score too.

I like to strike up conversations when I walk, making my rounds, and that's Oscar the democrat, enjoys a word with anyone. Truthfully I always preferred talking with a total stranger than with my close associates back in Brooklyn. You know a friend, you know what he has to say on the issues of the day, give or take ten percent. With a total stranger just off the boat or up from the swamps of Florida, you never can tell. They might supply you with an original slant.

An example of this. They have a girl here who handles a few horses for Farr Brothers, a young woman with a lovely appearance, who quietly goes her way, keeps her own counsel. But she looks intelligent and anyway I'll trust the judgment of the horses—they go for her.

A girl like this, though, someone unexpected (working the stalls and a real beauty too) isn't she more likely to have something interesting to say than the Queen of England? What can the Queen of England possibly have to say?

I took this matter to my sachem, to garner his opinion. What would the Queen of England say?

"A bit of watercress with a nice hot cupper. And plenty of lemon!"

"That's what she'd say?"

"More or less."

"What about at home or with her buddies?"

"Bloody awful weather we're having, eh wot?"

"That's it?"

"That's it, my friend. You think she spouts Shakespeare in the afternoon or something. Oh that this too too solid tortoni would melt!"

"I don't know Shakespeare. I'm not a reader."

"As you like it," says Wiley the sharp one. Even I know it's a line from Shakespeare he turns to.

Bumped into Timothy Myers at the grocer's just now and we visited on the street coming home.

"I feel badly not to return your hospitality. I want to feed you soon—it's just I am not a cook."

"We know that. That's why Mary had a dinner for you. She figures we ought to feed a bachelor in the building. You don't worry about it."

"Still, I'll get around to it," I told him. But it is not the cooking. I could cook better than Mary Myers with frost-bite in eight fingers and a blindfold over both eyes. What I dread is the social side. You can hash over Jimmy and Beatrice, but that will only make the poor kids squirm. You can discuss the spaghetti dinner even as you are choking on it—from a can!—praise the spaghetti, and then what else? Let them know how much you admire the photo of Ike, in uniform, framed, upon the wall in the dining area, though it orders a halt to conversation and digestion as well. And anyway Mary Myers is not out to feed the lonely bachelors of this world, she's just nosing around for a little gossip.

With cocoa season over and the Great High Resource gainfully employed, I see less of my pal Jimmy. When I'm around, and he comes around, I now provide him lemonade. It's lemonade season. Results are the same, same intake. He swallows half a gallon of the stuff without blinking. Enough lemonade to flush a toilet and this kid won't even burp for me.

He's got a new collection going, Indian chiefs in the cereal. So he has me buying Post Toasties and urges me to eat up fast, have a second bowl each day, lots of vitamins— so I can buy more boxes with the Indian chiefs. These people know how to sell their cereal!

At his house it's the same routine I'm sure, forcefeeding little sister and dumping the stuff dry into the trash—rakes a page of the Mirror over the top to conceal his crime? He can be slippery that way, a real go-getter. I heard a terrible groan issue from him, like he took an arrow in the chest, when I opened the new Post Toasties and it was Sitting Bull inside. Sticks his mitt in there right up to the bony elbow and fishes for the card, then lets out with this groan. He was looking for Cochise or Osceola. He has already three Sitting Bull, two Crazy Horse, two Geronimo. (These are statistics I keep abreast of.)

"Trade with your pals," I advise.

"But no one's got Cochise or Osceola. It's always Sitting Bull."

"You got Chief Joseph of the Nez Perce," I remind him.

"I know it! I'm the only one who does."

He wants to have them all plus he wants to be the only one so blessed. A touch of madness of course and yet I can understand. Or sympathize at least—he's got me emotionally involved, if only because I like to see him happy. So I open the Post Toasties with the same emotion I have watching an underlay stagger to the wire with my money in his saddle-bags. Come on you Cochise, come on Cochise baby, get up!


A big race, stakes race, is the toughest to handicap because for one thing with the shippers you are asked to compare apples and oranges. In addition to that, there is always too much talk and a lot of strange money going around, so my general principle is leave it alone, let the suckers play this one.

However a handicapper is a handicapper only if he is willing to reconsider his own rules, and yesterday I had a strong feeling for Son of Erin—went for him big at a decent price, and he got it. We had a nice tight finish, a photo, with Erin bobbing up on the last jump with a helpful whip-tickle from underneath by Boland. In a photo, it is often the best pose that wins.

"Come on Son of Erin, come on Son of Bitch—get up!"

I was worked up watching the stretch run and I think my rich lady got a shock when I ran down along the big window to the wire, the way I do on the rail, to keep my horse company. Bert didn't see it but my rich lady had a surprise and she was laughing. She likes me. She keeps telling me this, as though I stand around wondering does she like me.

"I like you, Oscar, really I do." But all the time. She is in every day, always my tables, and she approves of me. Gives thanks for anything I bring her, including the bill, and tells me she likes me, she likes me.

"Oscar, I didn't know you played the race."

"Sometimes, you know."

"I gather you had the Son of Erin."

"I had him, Mrs. Whitman. A nice investment."

"Good. I had him too. Let's celebrate together, shall we? I don't suppose you are allowed to join me?"

"No I don't suppose. But you enjoy it and I'll be enjoying it too. I'm not a drinker anyway."

"Not a son of Erin, I guess! Well, I'll have to tipple for two, that's all. Here's to Willie Boland, who can sit still in the eye of the hurricane."

"Wiley says you could serve drinks off that guy's back."

"But Oscar, you can't mean you don't take a single drink, ever?"

"An occasional bottle of beer. I prefer soda."

"No! What then, was your old man a soak? Is this related to some childhood trauma?"

"Nothing like that, It's just the taste—I prefer something sweet."

"Have a sloe gin, then, I'll treat you sometime after hours."

I can just picture it, me and my rich lady tippling after hours. Not that she scares me with all her furs and money. She's people and I'd put her at my age or maybe plus five years. A lovely speaking voice but a face like an unbaked loaf, soft and soggy. She was never a beauty, just tries to show herself a good time. The Duke of Kent tells me she is divorced and had a son killed in the War, so now she buys horses and chats with her waiters. The Duke had her in the past and made a living on her tips.

"She gets tired of you and changes over. I had her two meetings last year, we've all had her. You're the new blood, so enjoy it while it lasts." (The Duke speaking.)

Wiley adds, "Some people like Mrs. W. go through husbands, she goes through waiters."

"Much easier I'm sure."

"Oh yes, and cheaper too. But that dame knows horseflesh. The hell with her table change—you watch what she does with her money at the window."

"They say the rich get richer."

"And do they. but this old girl will never skip a race. Like a dummy, gets her bets down early on every race they card—but *sharp*, Oscar, she will never miss twice in a row."


We closed up late tonight. No one was rushing off so we sat and looked at the news on television. Once Bert goes home we own the room, it's our clubhouse and we form a nice little club. The Duke of Kent (really named Mickey Klutz, but he likes to put on airs) will hold forth on the day's events, with Wiley setting him straight from time to time. Sid polishes his glasses, wipes down the bottles, etc. He's a fiddler, can't keep his hands still without a pair of handcuffs. And I will furnish myself and Captain Wiley with cigars, settle up the tips (plus any side-bets), and sip my lemon soda.

Everyone concurs Ike is looking old. (He should treat himself to Morris' pep pill doctor on Joralemon.) But he is running and will hold himself together long enough to gather in the vote—*then* he'll slump down in his chair. That's the fear. We will all survive if he hangs in there, we proved that already the last four years. But if he goes out in harness, better duck, because then you get the Vice-President Nixon. A phony. He's the one who gave everyone a hot-foot over communism. A dangerous character, a joker playing serious games. Even Bert, our resident Republican, is afraid of this guy.

So we have agreed to organize Jewish Mothers For Ike on nationwide basis, to insure he gets nice hot chicken soup everywhere he goes until 1960.


Today on the main dirt track I watched the young woman Caddy Moore (her name compliments of the Duke, who knows it all) working a half mile at top speed on Farr brothers' Criterion. You see her in their barn where she rakes, swipes, handles the tack, and you see her walking hots but never on the main track before and this girl can ride. Very poised. Criterion threw in a 48 flat running on the new cushion and that horse was really dancing.

Women could be your natural jockeys. In this country, how many bantamweight fighters will you see, or flyweights? We eat too well and we are a tall people too, so a jockey is hard to find. He can't be a midget—he should be lanky, an athlete and yet a tiny fellow. A boy hasn't got the strength, plus he will naturally grow out of it just when he has the know-how. But why not a woman?

Easy: prejudice. It is true many of them are weak and unathletic—a few are allergic too I'm sure. But there would always be a supply. In every one hundred men in this country you might find one the right size. In every one hundred women you will find forty or fifty and in a field that large there will be plenty with the potential.

This Caddy Moore is the proof in the pudding. She is a worker and she is knowledgeable with horses. She talks to them but can also ride them, turning in a 48 flat half-mile in blue jeans and a sweater—no silks, no whip. Nice muscles in her arms. And that isn't Nashua she's sitting on either, the horse must make a contribution too.


I must have had Walter on my mind when my rich lady inquired "Do you have any children, Oscar?"

"No, Mrs. W., I got a nephew, that's all. Three of them, actually, and three of nieces as well. All my sisters have kids and that's it for me."

I expect she intended for me to ask right back, And what about you, Mrs. W? The Duke of Kent had forewarned me, however, that she likes to do this—get rolling on the subject of her son she lost at sea, and refuse to return you your arm until you both have dropped a few salty tears in her gin tonic.

So I declined the invitation, as the Duke would say. It's easy to hide behind a class difference—rich lady poor waiter—if you wish to avoid a personal remark. There are ways I know to show in your face, without a word spoken, that you respect the class difference and will therefore answer a question but never ask one. I was brilliant in this role and shut her off like a water-tap. But for what?

Why not let the lady cry if she needs to do it? Why not lend her a sympathetic ear—what does it cost me that I can't afford? This might be too big an imposition on Mickey Klutz but I can take it. I'm not in such a great hurry and here's this nice lady lost her only child. She likes me, and I like her, and I would just as soon hear anything she wishes to say about her son. And if she ever takes another crack at it, I'll be happy to so conspire, maybe even grease the skids.


Early this a.m. we experienced a small fire at 10 Battersea. The whole asylum emptied out into the street, like kids in the schoolyard—a fire drill, except wearing bathrobes. Mary Myers came disguised as Frankenstein's Bride, very convincing in her pink curlers.

All this thanks to Jesus H. Johnson who was so busy Praising the Lord that he set fire to his muffins. Of course he panics—starts howling the Savior's name, knocks over the toaster, and manages to ignite a bag of newspapers on the floor. You might think something like this can't happen, that no one is that stupid, but think again. It happens once every eleven minutes. (New York Post.)

And there appeared in the street, in among the known commodities, a pleasant soul I had never glimpsed before. Mrs. Vickers, a widow with two grown daughters on the Island. She has inhabited the asylum twenty-four years, up on the fourth floor with Lopat, our junkball pitcher, and she never shows her face. A sweetie, however, kind and cheerful old dame. She was the one who called in the hook-and-ladder boys, while the Holy Rollers were too busy making things go from bad to worse.

A person could feel foolish standing on the sidewalk in his bathrobe and bare feet, yet not so much when everyone is in the same boat. We all live in a hole in the wall, like rodents nesting, and learn to fear the light of day. Then something like this occurs and you get together—someone's got a bag of crackers and the morning news and soon it's not a disaster, it's a party. And I'm sure that's what Johnson had in mind, bringing the inmates together under the good fellowship of God.

No serious damage, but the hallways were smoky, so I offered to take Myers along with me to the fish breakfast. A couple of uniform cops in there that he knew to say hello, and they asked after his family. Myers shows a handsome smile (thirty-two perfect teeth he has been keeping in cold storage) when he gets away from his house. I grabbed the check, to help even our social score. Now if I treat the Bride to lunch at the Horn & Hardart we'll be even-steven.

Wiley got started tonight. It was an item on the news that did the job—a couple of cars collide on Bruckner Boulevard and out jump the drivers, mad as two roosters, and they go at it until they notice the truth. And the truth is they are brothers, who never got along and had not spoken in eight years, and so they meet again. Fate takes a hand!

Everyone had his own version of this. To Sidney it was all a matter of fault. Whose fault? He knows the intersection, a very tricky spot he assures, and diagrams it for us on a placemat. But to the Duke of Kent it is a simple question of compiling damages, because he has a brother in the body-shop racket. And if you ask my opinion the whole business is funny stuff, vaudeville, it's the Marx Brothers on Bruckner Boulevard.

But to Wiley, our sachem, it is Life itself and he must dress it up with the pearls of wisdom. How I love this man.

"I don't see why anyone's surprised," he starts in.

"No one's surprised, Wally," says Sid.

"We're *not* surprised," adds the Duke.

"What's so surprising?" says Wiley. "This was no accident, I can tell you that much. There is no such thing as an accident."

"Here he goes," says Sid.

"Go on, Wiley," adds the Duke, "tell us about the shitting ducks."

"It's only the truth," says Wiley. "Oscar did you ever stop to think about all those tiny ponds way back in the woods where no one lives, no one even hunts? There's fish in those pools, thousands of fish. Millions."

"Helluva number of fish," says Sid.

"Tell it!" says the Duke.

"No one stocks those pools, Oscar, and so how do you suppose a fish arrives there? You think he hitch-hikes up, or rides the bus? I'll tell you. Those pools are stocked by wild ducks flying over the whole of New York State and excreting their dinner."

"He means shitting."

"Duck soup."

"It's only the truth. That's how they get there. An accident, gentlemen, and then again no accident atall. Something else entirely. Oscar, did I ever tell you the story of how I met my wife Sylvia?"

"No, Wiley, you didn't."

I can tell from the others that this story is old and familiar like the shitting ducks, and it must be, since Wiley got married sometime back in the sixteenth century. But I don't mind an old story and anyway—it's like Linda and the Lama—if I haven't heard it yet, then it's news to me.

"I'm chasing this goddamn cat down the block, trying to scare him off because the ugly beast has been jumping in my window all week. And this young lady steps right in my pathway, stands fast with her bundle of groceries in her arms, and yells Halt. Whereupon she starts in with a big lecture about cruelty to animals right then and there on 33rd Street. That was almost fifty years ago, forty-six to be precise, and that was her, my friend, and I say that was no accident. Something else entirely. I still hate a goddamn cat after forty-four years of living with them in my house."

"Hear hear," says the Duke.

But Wiley is no dope. He put a son and daughter through law school, a couple of legal eagles under his wing. This wife, with the bag of groceries and the lecture on 33rd Street, also had a father in the fur business—an only child, Sylvia.

The show moves over to Belmont Park, like a traveling circus, the whole operation—lock, stock, and a barrel of oats. I prefer Jamaica because I'm a homebody and it's more like home. Over here we have the Grandeur of Thoroughbred Racing, translated to mean they are quicker to locate a can of paint and stock a few more flowers. But I'll admit it's a major league operation. The oval here is so big that you are out of town without your Teddy Roosevelt binoculars, and the backyard is like old times in Kentucky.

And of course the big horses ship in, the top of the crop, and they carry the big-name riders. Even the sea-gulls look bigger, though they have the same routine. They hit the air when the gate rolls out and float down on the infield while the race is run—then back on the track for twenty minutes of treasure-hunt.

The young lady Caddy Moore came over with the caravan. By now we know each other's faces, so we have smiled and nodded like friends—but silent friends. All my information on her comes from the Duke of Kent, always a close observer of the ladies. He makes her nineteen years of age, college, and says she owns a horse, though only a pet horse somewhere on the Island. He reports she has a reputation as a snob, which I doubt it. (She has a kind face and owns the easy affection of the horses. She wouldn't be here if she was a snob.) I figure she is quiet, she is shy, and they are the snobs for snubbing the rich.

Nonetheless, with Wiley spawning attorneys and this cute hot-walker attending college somewhere, I am beginning to think I don't have enough education for the racetrack. Pretty soon it will take a Ph.D. to steer the garbage-barge down the East River and I can't even read the House of 7 Gables—I quit after 2 gables! Now I read Pioneers and Indians to a nine-year-old, that's more my speed.


Day off. Took a haircut and ducked in on Kramer. I'm in your debt, I told him, meaning the job he got me. There is no such thing as being in debt to Kramer for money, it's pay as you go, one strike and you're out.

What the hell, he said, you're no good to me broke, are you? So I gave him a little action.

Linda wrote to say she must miss this week. Guests coming to her home and she can't get away. Fine, I will utilize the free time. I'll bring in delicatessen, take a night boat while it cools, and listen to the ballgame. I'll burn two Coronas and Newcombe will burn up the Braves. That's my plan unless I get an engraved invitation to the White House for dinner in the interim.


A few days back I happened to take a peek in the alley and saw some young people loading a station-wagon, marching in file with cartons and crates and pieces of furniture, a lamp, a chair, and I thought of course somebody is moving out. Figure it's the month of June so here goes probably a teacher, or a student, safe bet.

Then I noticed a familiar shirt, oxford cloth shirt in a quiet shade of purple you don't generally see, lavender call it, and inside this garment is a young lady who fits the description. Dark hair cut short, well-developed, early twenties. Just a female with nothing distinctive except the nose by Durante. I never bothered to take a closer look.

It was her, however. Next two nights the back window stayed black at half-past-ten and then on Saturday, always her night out on the town, the lights came on and I found myself gazing upon a new blue curtain. Orange flowers blooming on a piece of blue cloth. So that's that. My bare girl has walked away, this miracle of regularity is ended, and I am minus both a temptation and an entertainment. The longest running show off Broadway has closed down.

The spectacle of this girl undressing for me was as much to be relied upon as the sun in the morning, darkness at night, the trash-man on Thursday. What can you count on? Death, taxes, and my bare girl in the window.

Now the field gets smaller. I scratched taxes already—now scratch my bare girl and what does it leave!

Sitting in Battery Park with Jimmy Myers, inhaling the salt water and listening to it too, in between the honks and sirens. Smoke a Corona. Statue of Liberty right there, growing up in the basin like a big green plant. Jimmy informs me there are rats in the Statue. (Eating the crumbs of tourists I'm sure, like half the world.)

"Living there?" I said. He overheard a sailor's joke most likely, or a pair of drunks trading rumors. But I took the question up with my sachem anyway. I like to give Wiley first crack at a problem.

"Wiley, what do you know about the rats living inside the Statue of Liberty?"

"Everything there is to know," he says. "There's three of them."

"Not the way I heard it," chimes in the Duke of Kent.

"Three precisely, named Athos, Bathos, and Pathos. Sid, let me have two vodka gimlets, please. Why, Oscar? You like to borrow my kittycat?"

He won't take it seriously, of course, and I can laugh too. But there could easily be rats living in the Statue when you stop to think about it. They are in the East River, they are in the Hudson, and they are all over the boats in the basin. A certain number could climb out of the water and move into the Statue like immigrants. They got no quota on a rat.

To me it's worth knowing, like any fact. To the rest it doesn't make a difference, rats or not rats, three or three thousand. Very matter of fact on the subject, until you put them in a room with Mr. Rat himself.

If Caddy Moore the exercise girl is nineteen years old (as Mickey Klutz declares) then she was eight when the War ended—bouncing a pink rubber ball and jumping hopscotch squares. I was sitting behind a desk in Brooklyn when the War ended and I was *thirty*-eight. Paperwork in the War Office downtown Brooklyn—sorting the dead was my department. Dead or Alive Division we called it, because if you use a little subtraction you can also determine who is *not* dead. That was my real job, to check up on Daniel each week. Tanya's brother was still in Poland, a Polish citizen, but I had access to that too and every week I checked to see if Daniel was dead, then subtracted so I could report to my wife he was still alive.

The War ended and we stayed put. Reports kept coming—there was still plenty of paperwork after the footsoldiers went home—but never a word that Daniel was among the dead, and he wasn't. He made it. But a letter came to the house instead, to Tanya. Daniel didn't write it, one of the aunts did. He made it, yes, but they slaughtered his family. Wife and the two little children, age nine and seven, gassed by the fucking Nazis.

Daniel made it. He escaped Auschwitz, a miracle. Laying on his face in a latrine forty-eight hours, hiding from vicious dogs in a cold river-bed overnight, freezing and starving for weeks. He crossed Europe on foot and later he came to America. A true story that is hard to believe in 1956, even for me and I know what went on over there. Someone like Caddy Moore, age eight at the time, could never believe such a thing, walking her pretty horses in the morning sun.


That letter—Daniel's life—is distant past and still it seems very fresh, shocking to me. My blood can still boil and my heart aches for him and his loved ones. So what

138

about him, Daniel himself, now here? With the blue numbers branded on his forearm that like a fool I once asked
him, Can they be removed? "What for, Oscar," he said to
me. "So I can forget the past?"

Sarah's husband Ralph is a great kidder. One of his lines:
"You know how the Catholics expiate their guilt? By mak-
ing all those nice Jewish boys into Cardinals—Cardinal
Newman, Cardinal Spellman . . ." Not funny, of course,
Ralph earns a living but not from his comedy routines.
He's trying—as in the old vaudeville joke, God is he try-
ing. But once when Ralph gave us the line about the Jewish
Cardinals, Tanya started up.

"We ought to be running that country now, instead of
helping them out. That country should not *exist* by now."

"Tanya," I explained her, "He is talking about the
Catholics, not about the Germans, and besides it's only a
joke."

"Catholics, Germans, they're all the same. It's not a joke
to me."

Naturally Tanya and Daniel have no sense of humor
about Hitler. Count me in, how could you? But even an
intelligent person, when angry, can allow her mind to
wander. Plenty of anti-semites around I'm sure, and yet it
is also possible for a Jew to hold a prejudice. Don't tell that
to my wife, however.


Needles returned 3.30 winning the Belmont Stakes. I
left it alone, the short odds. Yet far from the shortest, as we
were recalling. Citation never made anyone rich, except
his owner. He paid ten cents on the dollar running in Triple
Crown races. Or Native Dancer who went off at 1–20 in
the Preakness—against the same horse, Dark Star, who
had just beat him in the Derby—and fully justified it. More
than once, according to Wiley, the price on Man O' War

went 1 to 100. Imagine taking the action. Side bet on the margin of victory, maybe.

This Needles is okay but for a payoff that small he better be a sure thing. He came from the back of the pack and then barely hung on at the wire, and that's not my idea of fun. Some people believe a handicapper likes to suffer, that he revels in the sweaty palm. A gambler maybe, but not a handicapper. He wants to be right, and win the dough.

A nice quiet night in the Park and back here with Jimmy, following a couple of major league shocks earlier in the day.

One. Maglie is a Dodger. Of course I thought Bulkitis was kidding when he said it, and then there it was in The Post, black and white. Trading Sal Maglie to Brooklyn is like trading Ike to the Communists—you don't do it. Maglie is the enemy, a New York Giant of the very worst kind, the kind that is tough on right-hand hitters. He can not become a Dodger just by changing his clothes. Bulkitis also screaming about this deal: he says it means the pennant for Brooklyn absolutely, because the guy can still pitch and he will.

Two. Mrs. W. my rich lady has thrown herself at me, makes me an offer I can't refuse, except that I do. I like you, she says, with frequency, and I give it no weight. It's only her manner of speaking. Sure she can appreciate the man who carries in her food and drink, in the right way at the right time and never without a pleasant word. It's her style, the others tell me, and she liked them too.

But she never requested the pleasure of their company, whereas I got myself invited for a weekend at the Saratoga meeting in August, all expenses paid! No sleeping arrangements I'm sure, just keep her company at the table, take her arm at a concert, things they have going on up there. A companion, to share the fun of playing the races.

"A grand time, Oscar, don't miss it—let it be my treat."

I wish I could let it. I would love to get there, and believe it I also know what it took a lady like that to put the question to a man and then hear "No thanks." Mrs. W. does not look down on waiters. The reverse in fact: she looks up. To her the waiter is the true aristocrat—we wear our linen well up here in the clubhouse, we walk a nice graceful line and speak a nice English, and so she requests the pleasure of our company.

"No, Mrs. W., I can't say yes. I'm sure I would enjoy the time, but I would feel wrong using your money—"

"Why, Oscar? I've *got* the money."

"I know. It's me that hasn't got it."

"Exactly. If you had it, then you would be the generous spender. We'll share the money for a week or so, for the fun of it."

"I can't. Call it pride."

"Call it *stubborn* pride then. Oscar, we are friends. Why should friends be silly about a little money, about pieces of paper?"

"A good question. No reason." Of course she doesn't know she is conversing with the man who does things for "no reason" and doesn't mind saying so. "It's always in the gut. You understand."

"I do. Yes, of course."

"But listen, maybe I'll get a big win and make it upstate on my own. Then I'll take you to dinner and treat you to a day of racing. Or better, we'll take each other, Dutch treat. That I would go for."

"Oscar, you know I like you very much. So I won't mention it again."

Mention it, mention it, maybe you'll convince me the next time around! I could weaken if given half a chance, because really I would love to get up to Saratoga and really I cannot pay my own way just yet.

But leave the old girl a little dignity, Fish, see it her way. A ladies' man such as myself has got to use a little consideration, and not take unfair advantages of the weaker sex. You cannot reject them and then hope they come crawling back to try again.

THE DUKE: So did Mrs. W. request the pleasure of your hand in marriage?
OSCAR FISH: What makes you ask? Is this part of her famous modus operandi?
THE DUKE: No no, you'd be the first for that. We just saw the two of you hobnobbing and it looked more serious than the usual.
OSCAR FISH: Yes well she offered me her hand in marriage and half her millions but I told her I was unable to make it that day.
THE DUKE: Too tight a schedule.
OSCAR FISH: I'm too young for her, Mickey.
THE DUKE: Well nothing better will come along, Oscar. Count on that.


They say the horsemen are tight-lipped and maybe they are in a way. Maybe it's true they have nothing to say to the Six O'clock News or to the stockholders of a horse. But they talk easily among their own, so it is interesting that they do not talk to Caddy Moore.

To me she is a distraction, you notice her. This pretty girl always takes her coffee alone, undoes her thermos and leans on the walking-ring rail like a lone cowhand from the Rio Grande—in blue jeans so old that the blue wore off, and the red windbreaker from the stable. With light brown hair and dark blue eyes, she is some attraction and yet not a soul will notice her. What makes this girl invisible to them?

They have a checker-game, card-game, dominoes, and they form their little huddles just punching at the past performances with the back of their hand. They will talk Maglie, and Needles and the eight of clubs, but they don't talk to this lovely girl, shining in the sun right before their eyes.

They don't see her, but I think that she must see everything, with eyes like that. She is awake. So does she see me in among the furniture on the backstretch, does she see an interloper from the kitchen patrol? I would say not except that I am in such demand—the ladies' man. Everyone wants to snap me up all of a sudden, Linda who could not resist the beautiful music of my breathing on the bus to Canada and yesterday my rich lady Mrs. Whitman put in her application too. (Yes I admit it. I reject the application yet accept the flattery.)

And why not the exercise girl? How can she resist what others are craving? Of course it's a joke and I understand the difference. Still, I am getting regular on the backstretch just in case she decided to take the plunge. It's a wild idea and I won't hold my breath waiting, yet when we are both alone down there with our coffees I can feel the possibility. I'm in range.


I'm in range and I am also crazy. Or at least will scribble crazy things late at night when I'm past my bedtime. Now I'm further past it—can't sleep. What exactly do I think I am in range *for?* Can I picture myself strolling arm-in-arm down the boulevard with this young lovely? I can not.

Furthermore, how can you like someone you never even met? It's stupid. She could be Nazi, or at the very least Republican. I resent the fact she is keeping me awake.

On a dark day at the racetrack I am apt to fall back on old habits—a few words with Bulkitis, two or three more with Mrs. Kearney as I select a new volume for Jimmy, and of course make use of my feet. (Either my pants are too tight these days or my belly is too loose, I'm not sure which.)

Also for a nickel I can grab a boat-ride, travel out over the water to Staten Island and back. The briny deep, and deep it is I'm sure, one helluva bathtub. Miles down and three thousand miles across to Europe—when you are on it it's so much water you could almost believe in God.

So I live it up like a kid on his summer vacation, except without any pals. A lot of kids have no pals on vacation, however. It was for that reason Walter always hated vacation-times, an only child and he had no pals. (In school yes, but not to ask over. Like my pals at the racetrack. There are friends and there are friends.)

Kids can be lonely too, which people underestimate. Caddy Moore can handle whatever the world sends her way, and Walter will too I'm sure. She is young, however, and it might surprise the snobs at Belmont Park to know that this girl could use a friend. Democracy is a two-way street.

Tested out my hypothetical question on Wiley tonight: how young is too young for a woman to be, if a man is fifty years old give or take. Because there must be a line somewhere in particular and it isn't forty-two, it isn't thirty-seven, so where is it? And I am rewarded with the following answer,

"It takes two to tango, Oscar, but it only takes one to waltz."

What more could a pilgrim wish for? It sounds exactly like an answer should sound, so I brought it home to play with. Anything that sounds that much like an answer must

144

be one. (Unless my wise man is just a wise guy.) So far this one is over my head.

I know this much. If I said the things that guy says I would seem like a fool. The trick is in *how* you say it, like hitting a cue-ball.

Mail from Linda Stanley. She is among the missing for three weeks and now comes a letter saying, "We must talk." Not we must do the therapeutic deed, but we must talk. All right so let's talk—I'm curious what we'll say.

"Yesterday," I told Jimmy, "I won a million dollars in the eighth at Belmont."

"Bull shit," he told me.

"That's a nice mouth, squirt. If you don't believe me, say so."

"I said so. Tell the truth, Oscar."

"Why should I? Is the truth worth more than a lie?"

"Sure it is. You don't lie to a friend. If you do he isn't your friend anymore."

"A code he has, to live by! And I agree. So then why did you tell your father I took you to Ebbets Field yesterday when it wasn't the truth?"

I had to watch the poor kid sag against the ropes and I felt like hell. A bully, that's me, smacking this poor little punching bag. Imagine a man so smart he can trick a trusting child.

"Hey Jimmy, stop it, don't cry, it's no big deal."

"I know what it is."

"It's a stupid joke, that's all. I'm sorry, Jimmy, please accept an apology. I thought I was cute, making my point. I was only worried where you really went off to yesterday—what you were covering up."

"I didn't cover anything. I was at the city pool all day."

"So why?"

But I knew. I figured it out for myself the minute I pulled the string on him, and saw his expression. He must have told his old man for months, ever since I promised him, about Ebbets Field. I'm going, Oscar is taking me, it's true it's true. So he was losing face and all my fault. I didn't come through and instead today I bungle much worse by sandbagging him, a real cute set-up.

So I tried to do some salvage work by setting a definite date for Belmont Park early next week and this I can do, show him around the racetrack, no problem. But Jimmy will believe it when he sees it and who could blame his attitude? Head down, sullen, he says, "Thanks, Oscar, thanks a lot, that sounds like real fun."

You cannot horse around when you are dealing with children. I never had one and yet I always knew it. They are the most serious of people and also the most vulnerable. So you do it right or don't do it at all.


It's the truth about lying and yet people lie all the time. No one says I just won a million and expects belief, but many will tell you, I had the Double, just to look good in your eyes. In this way the racetrack breeds a liar.

If I glance back over the nonsense I have been storing in this notebook (and I do, keeping track) I can say to myself it's at least the truth and nothing but, right on the button every time. I could put down anything, or change the names to protect the innocent, yet I record the whole truth even when I squirm to see it there. Why lie to your own diary? You can lie to yourself and hope it passes on the wind, so long as you are not *storing* it. With a diary, however, there is no point—why keep a diary if you plan on telling it lies?

Unless of course you are out in the spotlight. Never trust the diary of a public person, movie-stars, office-seekers, etc. That isn't a diary—not when they trot it out in the feature section of Saturday's Post. They have an eye on reputation and will say whatever it serves them to say.

I could get famous overnight. Just write in my diary how I spent Christmas Eve with Marilyn Monroe one time, when Dimag wasn't looking, and then lose the page on a car of the Long Island Railroad. A week later I'd be talking on television, a celebrity.

Wiley has friends everywhere, including the town of Saratoga Springs, New York. Now he says he can get me a night job there for the month of August, at a steak joint near the racecourse. A new deal, and why not? Sounds good, I told him—nights to work, days at the track, and still my mornings free to lounge like royalty—sign me up.

And that's when I realized I have a crush on the girl. My very next thought was will Caddy Moore travel upstate with the circus or stay put in the city. If she travels, so much the better. If she stays, I'm out of range—and maybe never see her again. What's that but a crush? Old enough for the glue factory and I'm coming down with a crush on the teenage queen!

What the hell, these days I've got a crush on life. After the long sloppy winter cooped up with my many worries (not to mention all those crazy-eights at 10 Battersea) I love every summer morning. I come out earlier and earlier and it's always the same: a soft blue sky, nice low sun on the tin shedroofs, the rainbow of flowers along the course. And yes, Caddy Moore is part of it too. If I spotted her on the train car coming out she might look like less—just another traveler—whereas here she is part of the scenery, adds a little spice to it and vice-versa I'm sure.

You can see men freeze before your eyes on the Bowery in March yet riding cross Ozone Park in July you can understand a hobo who lies out the cornfield with a friend, or with a jug of his favorite pain-killer, or both. Someone who is happy putting his face up to the sun unencumbered. You can worry over all the things you meant to do, or all the money you never made (while others did), or all the people who had such big expectations of you. But you could also skip it and be just fine, like a hobo in summertime.

A dream last night, in which I am getting combed and ready for Linda, in my new shoes—a true detail, new this week—and then I hear a tread on the stair. When Linda first arrives, in real, I need a little push to get myself going and to get events underway. I feel a deadness of muscle, lack of steam, which for some reason I am not experiencing this one time, in the dream. This time I hear the tread and feel eager, excited at the prospect, like a kid skipping into Luna Park.

Because it isn't Linda. I see the chestnut-colored hair, dark blue eyes, Caddy Moore. Blood comes flooding to my face and she smiles, reaches for my hand. I look down, however, and see that my hands are full—each holding one of my old shoes—so I have none to offer her. She shrugs and smiles once more and I wake, frustrated that I couldn't free up a hand for her.

No point denying the contents of a dream. Call a spade a spade, call a crush a crush. Some dreams are a mish-mash and would baffle even the high priests on Park Avenue. This one is as clear as a ball score. Three to two. Bango.

So the worm turns: I can spare Mrs. W. but who will spare me?

Among the casualties for this week, myself and Linda Stanley. We are kaput. No surprise to anyone after a month in which we hid from each other, and neither is it the

occasion for great suffering. The vote was unanimous, two
to zero.

We concluded our business on the ferry-boat. Saw no
movie, ate no dinner, drank no wine, and did not indulge
in any last-minute therapy. Just took to the water on a very
hot night, and talked. Linda never said as much but I
would venture that something has changed in her life in
Fort Lee, something good has come up, and a young man
is the best guess. Maybe she took another junket and
turned up a younger schnorer.

If you are virginal the circumstance dominates from
inside you and yet shows to the whole world, so that you
become ineligible—they cross you off the roster. You assume no one could want you and such an assumption will
fulfill itself day to day till it seems impossible to dream the
reverse. But break it down, change it by *doing* and suddenly you are surrounded by possibilities. Suddenly the
impossible becomes a leadpipe cinch.

It's funny, Oscar the ladies' man, and yet a woman *could*
find me now. I'm sure it's the same with Linda. A brand
new man appears on the scene, one who never met the
virgin, the wallflower, and he sees a different sight altogether. Sees it and feels it that here is a woman, for him.
This new man in Fort Lee—the gym teacher, biologist, the
butcher's boy—can provide her the therapy without the
commute.

And I'm nothing but happy for her. I only hope she will
agree to see the butcher's boy on a Wednesday or Thursday
sometimes, and walk out into the air on Sunday morning.
Say hello to the Butcher and Mrs. Butcher too.

"I think it was good, Oscar. And that it worked."

"Sometimes it worked!"

"No, it was good. It couldn't have been any better,
unless it was something else entirely."

"I understand."

We are both being grown-ups here, paying respects and

going for the right tone of voice. Why offend now, when we are soon to be free?

"And when I say it worked, I mean that I had a big problem when we began seeing each other and I don't have that problem anymore."

"Now you have new problems."

"No, just us—do you know what I mean?"

Yes I know. Like myself, she looks forward to our nights of pleasure with nothing but dread, so let's cancel. We went three furlongs and did all right, but try to go a mile and we will swallow more dust than a donkey. We've been losing ground.

So scratch our entry, it's for the best and is in truth already accomplished. True to form it's Linda who takes the reins—"We must talk"—but I had it on my agenda too. My feeling for Caddy Moore makes a break necessary, makes me ashamed of bed with Linda, past present or future, ashamed every which way.

Someone in the old days, Alfie Wohl it was, came up with a good trick for meeting the girls. He bought himself a mutt, put the mutt on a string, took the string in his fist, and took his feet to Prospect Park. Every day this mutt would make him new friends, because alone in the park you are a stranger, a threat, but hold an animal on a string and the world comes falling at your feet. A nice lesson for the confidence-man. Wheel a baby will get the same results, if you can get the use of a bambino.

I can see Alfie shrug—"They are just looking for an excuse to speak too. They want what you want. The trick is to make it happen."

Don't I know it. I have been gazing at Caddy Moore for weeks and I never said a mumbling word, though I have come *close* once or twice and always aimed at inventing a means, however idiotic, for broadcasting the word hello. I never thought of Alfie Wohl and his mutt on a string until I got out here with one of my own—Jimmy Myers, unpremeditated. But a free ticket. With the little boy in tow, I'm in like Flynn the Irishman.

She was working on False Alarm, big bay sprinter, and I'm nearby giving pointers to the squirt—this one is a nice chestnut filly, look at the markings, etc.—very smartass I'm sure and playing the Nice Guy who tows a kid. Then Jimmy, this little operator, has an instant eye for the pretty face and strikes up the band: "How about that big guy, Oscar, is he going today?" This he puts on the P.A. system, loud and clear, so the girl cannot miss picking up his signal.

"Would you like to say hello to him?" she says.

And that's all it takes! A mutt. She has already a smile for me, to squeeze the heart, and a carrot for Jimmy, to feed the horse. "You can give this to him. But let him take it. Yeah."

"Jesus, Oscar, he's huge!"

"He's just a lad like you," she says. "He's three years old."

"I'm ten." (He rounds off for her.)

"So that makes you two about the same." (She explains him the age of a horse.)

She has nothing as yet to say to me, so I stick in a little horse talk—False Alarm moving up to 5500 despite slow works etc.—and she responds in kind. She has to figure I'm the daddy (what else?) so I introduce myself, Oscar Fish and this is my young friend Jimmy Myers. (Not the daddy.) And she tells us her first name only, Caddy.

"You know how to ride a horse," I tell her. "I've noticed."

"I know."

Just like that, a kick in the shins. Because it's not to say Yes I know I can ride, it is to say Yes I know you have noticed. So I went red as a hardboiled lobster, and tried to slip the noose by saying, "You know how it goes on the backstretch, a person keeps both eyes open."

"Absolutely. I keep mine open everywhere I go."

And with this I get one more smile that says: I kicked you in the shins, old man, but just for fun. I don't mind you looked at me, not half so much as I might mind you *not* looking. It is not flirtation, this sharp talk and the smile, it's a statement—I'm not the nervous type, so why not relax about everything. No time to relax, however. Jimmy sees it and quickly inserts the needle.

"Oscar," he says—calls me that, speaks to me like a colleague—"It's time to get to work, I think."

What does he know about time? He's got no wristwatch. It's the bull. But we made the introduction and enough is enough, New York City wasn't built in a day. I told her where I worked, I'm not ashamed, and got a feeling she knew it already, though of course that is this girl's style, knowing. Maybe, though, she took the trouble to find it out. I was asking questions about her, she could have done the same about me.

Dreamer. What could she care? Who would she ask? More likely she spotted me up there one day in my shiny brass buttons at a time when I was busy with a twist of lime and didn't see her too.


There are times when I'm sitting in my chair with the radio on and hope Jimmy won't come up and disturb the peace. I could be tired or grouchy, or just not in the right mood for a visit. Not that I will send him away if he comes at such a time, but he will be extra baggage to tote.

If someone is baggage long enough, however, there grows up a bond, of comfort and trust. (Not to mention of course the times are rare, and usually I am delighted to see his face.)

It was riding the train back I realized what pals we have

become, such that we can sit in silence and watch the light
seep away and a hundred street corners flying past. No
need to speak, both of us tired and contented. And at last
he slumps. A head on my shoulder as we come back into
the city, and I note my mutt is dozing.


On the Belmont Special I always take a window and
watch the scenery roll by even though it is nothing to see,
nothing lovely. Queens shows its back to you if you ride
the train—a net of trolley lines, back windows and
trashcans, piles of scrap behind the body-shops. Why
look?
What you never see is a person, a human being. They are
all inside or out front, I guess, and so are the trees and
flowers, if any. If I look, and like it, I am looking at the
morning light itself—light in the sky, light on the bricks,
whatever. Maybe because I love the daytime more and
more, and have not much use for the night.


Found Caddy at her station, face up to the sun. (She is
like me?) Her hair has become quite fair, and new freckles
sit across the bridge of her nose like a little saddle. I love to
look at this girl's face and today I was free to give it some
study, as her eyes were shut tight. I also took my opening
from this—determined to keep the ball rolling even though
flirtation is like rolling it uphill in mud.
"Excuse me."
"Oh, hello. How are you today?"
"Wonderful! And yourself?"
Too strong, to say Wonderful so loud, yet I could not
muzzle it any more than stop a sneeze. She smiled and
nodded, looking sleepy and speaking without words: I'm
wonderful too, in a quiet way, though I don't mind your
noise.

"Your eyes were closed." (The Opening.)
"Pardon me?"
"I was sorry to disturb you, but I thought you might want to know, after what you said the other day."
"Tell me what I said. I forget."
"That you make a point always to keep your eyes open." Oh I am a silly fool, pushing my luck. Intoxicated, is what. And yet she is determined to let me get away with it.
"Oh yes, I do," she says, as though my stupidity is not in the least bit stupid. "It's just there are times you have to shut your eyes in order to really *see*."
"Go on, you were asleep at the wheel."
Yes I can flirt. A pigeon can walk too, only not very fast. Caddy has nothing but good will, however, and a laugh like soft music. No interest in exacting a price. I did not have my next line ready, so I elected to rest on my laurels and left her the way I found her, sunbathing.


Bad luck this afternoon at Belmont Park—my ship came in and I couldn't climb on board. I got shut out on a winning quinella that paid 63.50 and I would have had it ten times. I was set to go with it, using Benny the shoeshine boy outside, who is my last-minute system, working no commission on a lose versus two bucks against a win. Time was very tight, however, and I had a family with Captain Fingersnapper at the helm, an ice-water drunkard.
I took my exercise for the day pouring water for these five. The little ones must have been dumping it in the rubbertree every time I hit the kitchen so when I reappeared on the floor he could instantly demand a refill, like a birthright. I'm leaning on the door with Jackson's portrait in my fist, ready to grab Benny and buy my action, when I hear his fingers snapping, the King of Siam. Snap snap. Snap.
Of course I should have kept on going, through the

door. You can always pretend not to hear a jerk, but I allowed myself to hesitate so he knew and then it was Waiter Waiter! Snap Snap! Curtains for my winning quinella.

Why not shoot such people? An empty glass to this man is a call to arms—let it stand empty for sixty seconds and surely the earth will tilt off its axis. But granting the guy his foibles, the water, there is no excuse for manners like that. Even the children looked guilt-stricken, embarrassed by the pushy father and not the least bit thirsty.

Mrs. Fingersnapper had on a very low-cut business, with her boobies served up like fruit on a tray. Midget weightlifters inside there, one on each side. It is something for a mother of three to look like that and at the end— knowing that with everything I did and all the dough this guy had cost me already he would still leave mouse-cheese for a tip—I had a sore temptation to drop a load of cubes into her cleavage. Wake up the weightlifters.

I was leaning from one side with the pitcher and she was leaning from the other side with her dress wide open and the two balloons floating onto the table and for one second I thought I not only had the guts to make it happen but that in fact I could do nothing to prevent my hand from freezing her frontage.

Again I should not have thought. Chickened out, natu- rally. Gave a little cough to choke back my laughter, ex- cused myself politely for the cough, then filled up her glass and not her navel. A missed opportunity on a day of missed opportunities. Too bad. The first time I hated a customer, because I let myself get stuck. There are plenty of bad apples and nasties in here, but I ignore them and do my job. Why let them get to you?

It's the curse of the Jews, I think. A Jew is a good boy. He knows what it takes to be bad, knows how it is done— just not how to do it. It's something the other guy can be counted on to do, while the Jew must do the right thing.

He is living inside a strait-jacket from birth, even a profligate like Carnovsky.

Rough morning all around. Began at Bulkitis' where I found no one at home. My friend sells the numbers, of course, so once in a blue moon they make him stroll up the courthouse and genuflect. It could be that, because he was in the pink yesterday and it's not the time of year for a nose cold. But no Telegraph.

I accept this defeat and cross over to Wing Wang, where I present my slip of paper and instead of bowing me my nice brown package he says to me, "No shirts."

"You mean No problem."

"No shirts," he repeats, clear as a parrot.

"*Three* shirts," I come back, jabbing my receipt at him.

"No shirts."

Very firm is my friend, and happy with his new syllable too. Rests his case. I gave him my side of it, but as soon talk Greek to a Negro baby. This little fellow doesn't make mistakes. He takes it in, washes and folds, adds it up right. He doesn't speak the language but he knows his business and the result is he gets me wondering. Did I give him those shirts? I thought so, and here is the receipt, yet if he says No shirts then it must be somehow my mistake.

And that is where our discussion ended up. All I could say by way of winding up negotiations, still wishing to part on good terms, was, "Okay, no problem." It's the low common denominator, I am dragged down to it, and shirtless to boot.

I caught a gimpy train-car out which stopped to catch its breath three times in the middle of nowhere, till all the hard-knockers were using body english to push it home. The morning was gone and it was raining, much worse out there than in Manhattan. I never got down to see Caddy Moore and then had to take it on the chin from Bert for wearing a wrinkled shirt. So much for No problem, Wing Wang.

The goddamn shirt does not even show, of course, once you are in full house livery. Bert sees the manager's job this way: if a man does something correctly, no need to notice, or praise, since he is only doing his job. But if he does it wrong, right down to his manicured pinkie, spot it every time on the basement radar. He will never pass up a chance to fan the winds of criticism.

Wiley puts this one to rest. Cruises past with a big wink and says, "You two ironing out your difficulties?" and that gets it done. It adds up to this. When you need the manager, he is "not available." When you are hoping he's out of range, because you just broke a plate, forget it—he watched the thing crack on radar and will arrive in time to witness the burial.

Another big approach. The ladies' man swings into action with a line I dreamed up and rehearsed like Shakespeare. My stage debut, I trained for, but very casual the stance and very casual the voice—

"Will you be traveling up to Saratoga Springs next week?"

"Hello. No, I'm afraid I won't. How about you?"

The girl is such a beauty that the blue sky, the universe, is just a background for viewing her lovely face. The more I see it, the more I want to see it, the way eating one piece of candy makes you eat another. And this time she will talk. Discusses the ins and outs of waiting on table as though the fate of the economy turns on it: she is aiming to be a democrat too. And makes mention of Jimmy Myers. We are small-talking. You will be back at Belmont in September? Yes, but only for a couple of weeks. I bet you go to college. You win the bet.

She blushes at the college, dislikes confessing to intelligence. She would prefer to be the tomboy who can pop a bicep, the stockyard hand, workingclass hero. And she is for the rights of women. "I'm always glad to see a kid come around the stables. They are the only ones who aren't surprised to find me there. They don't know enough to be prejudiced yet." "I agree. They should run the country, for that very reason."

She studies me now, closely and without the least embarrassment, studies my eyes until my face heats up. Something is coming. "You weren't always a waiter." "At your age I was. In between I took thirty years off for good behavior." "And then misbehaved? But during the thirty years, what did you do then?" "What would you guess?" "Something interesting. You have a look, like you're wanted by the F.B.I. or something." "No. Nobody wants me." "No, really. Who did you kill?"

She has the nerve, and the personality, to sass me. "No one you know." "Spill the beans." And she is grinning at me. She is curious after all, just as I am. Put a priest and a prostitute together in the elevator and they will be the same way too—human. But give credit where it's due, she sees something and it is the truth I have a mystery. It just doesn't happen to be very interesting. It's only myself I killed, I am the skeleton in my own closet, although even that much might be interesting to a co-ed.

Mainly she is teasing me, I understand this. She's being friendly. Feeling sorry for the old guy with the crush, instead of afraid, and so she cheers him along. This much I know: I am a few generations her senior yet am willing to rely upon her wisdom and experience.

"No Caddy," I say and she looks up startled to hear her name issue from my lips. "I'm no one special, believe me. It is my great self-discovery, in fact, I'm Oscar Every-man."

"No you're not," she tells me, and that's flat. She isn't laughing or crying about anything, just has an idea in her head about me, God knows what it could be. She thinks I'm Pretty Boy Floyd or someone.


It is a danger just to live in this world, where you can get your brains beat out for nothing. You go stand around the stables looking out for a horse with diarrhea and what happens but you fall in love. The stone in the belly.

A couple of weeks back I rejoiced to be heading north. Let's beat the heat, grab a vacation, and enjoy the show-place of thoroughbred racing in America. Etc. etc. Now Saratoga is only a place she will not be.

The bug has bitten Jimmy too. Imagine not being safe at the age of nine! It is since the day we went to Belmont that he has acted funny, however, ever since the very day I scribbled down how close we were. And now we aren't. Now he is polite to me, that's the word for it.

"Thanks, Oscar, that's nice, but I'm busy," he tells me, after I journeyed all the way to the library and back for Tarzan and the Jewels of Opar—at *his* request. The cold shoulder, and though nothing is spoken I conclude from the timing that it has to do with Caddy Moore. Jimmy's lovesick too.


It is the same as with Tanya. I thought it was impossible to feel such a way at my age, that I did not because I could not. But I can. It is convincing, this business, an emotion like this erases everything else. Here is my theory:

For each man in this world there are a few women he can not resist. That he will go for in spite of anything, perhaps even if it was criminal to do so. You might find them and you might not. You know right away if you do. What happens if you meet two such on the same day? What then? I don't know the answer. It might not be possible, especially if chemicals are the cause. And I'm sure you stand a better chance of meeting none in your entire life than two on the same day.

For me it will be a woman who belongs very much to herself. She is strong and calm within her skin. Pretty yes, but something larger than looks with the irresistibles—a woman who owns herself and might let you have a part. You cannot earn it or win it by an effort, cannot deserve it: she will either give it to you or she won't, your heart is in her hands. Tough luck.

Of course with Tanya I knew I had a shot. It was her decision and yet I expected her to make it in my favor. I knew she liked me, I fit the bill, plus we had friends in common, a background. Whereas with this young one I am a case she might study me in college. She thinks I don't sound like a waiter. So what does a waiter sound like? And if I sound like someone else, then who? She is just out to solve a riddle, have a little fun in life.

She could truly believe I am a killer, or stole the crown jewels. Crime might seem romantic to a silver-spoon girl. Wiley says "You can love an outlaw more easily than an in-law" because from your own set you might rebel. That's what she's doing down here in the first place. To be debutante of the backstretch makes her special, something different from her friends at school. Which is not to say she lacks a sincere talent with the horses, or that she shouldn't indulge. On the contrary, may she own it.

If she is slumming, though, muckraking the streets, she might guess I am slumming too. And if such is the case she will be disappointed to know me better—there's nothing much to know.

Getaway day at Belmont Park. A hard warm rain since morning, that is still coming down now (eight p.m.). I had a speech rehearsed and might have delivered it, might not have. No opportunity to find out what I would do, since Caddy stayed away, just as the sunshine did—and these events seemed to me connected. No Caddy, no sun, no speech. Just a sinking sunken emotion, stone in the belly.

The backstretch was a ghost-town, with most already gone north yesterday or very early today. Smallest handle of the meet, between the wet and the funeral feeling. See You in September, Wiley sings me in his nice baritone. I'll miss him too.

Some packing to do yet, here tonight, and a little cleaning up. Note the purchase of three brand new shirts. A goodbye to Bulkitis. Made another attempt to patch up with Jimmy but the squirt was having none.

Stubborn, but *why?* What is he stubborn *about?* I don't know why or what. I know that Jewels of Opar must wait, however, as I am gone bright and early tomorrow, placing my life in the hands of Mickey Klutz who according to Wiley is the Pete Reiser of driving. Early Pete or late Pete, I say, wondering if he's on the ball or off the wall. Both, says my sachem.

I would never have dragged myself to the bus station, I was ready to kiss my chains and stay, broil the rest of the month in Battersea Street. What I felt was, Don't send me summer-camp I'm too young to leave home. But I'm sent, because Mickey Klutz was counting on me for half the gas money.

Not until the last possible second, of course, does Wiley

make mention how tough it is finding an accommodation in the town of Saratoga. The place is over-run, he tells me, what did you think? I think he put in the fix, why not? He's my sugarplum fairy, ain't he, on the job around the clock. I was not good company, sitting next to Mickey as silent as a heap of beans. Dazed I was, a displaced person. To me (yesterday morning in the drizzle) the Taconic State was nothing but a long gray river floating me farther and farther in the wrong direction—like a slave sold downstream. Soon as we docked I was obliged to set Mickey free. (He's up here for fun and I am existing in a state of bereavement.) But then the rain came down in sheets. You couldn't see through it and I'm going door to door like the old boll weevil.

I could hear my feet squeak every step of the way and my suitcase was putting on weight like a sponge. I went through a pocketful of coins in the telephone—hotel, motel, 22.50, 32.50, 42.50, the sky's the limit. Or else, Nothing till the Fall, sorry no vacancy, sorry sorry sorry. I'm sorry too. I can't muster thirty bucks a night just to put my head on a pillow. All I'm assured is fourteen dollars a day (plus tips of course, but *assured*) and I don't even start until the weekend. So what do you do? You drop down, go a peg lower on the ladder and curl up for the night in the Greyhound terminus. Talk about dignity. You camp out on a grimy bench, dine on candy bars and tapwater coffee from a rusty gizmo, and you room with strays, bad characters. You get a stiff neck to end all stiff necks and a tongue like pressed shoddy, and you learn what it's like to visit the bottom. It's why you work.

But I awoke a new man, Oscar the optimist, who welcomes the dawn with a positive attitude—thirty bucks to the good, having saved on rent. Sunshine is the trick. The same streets I waded down last night look lovely to me from a restaurant window this morning. You discover oil in every puddle, the rainbow after the storm. Wasn't twenty minutes after I put a big tip on the table and walked outside, that I found myself choosing new lodgings off a list at the Chamber of Commerce. A room in someone's house, family of three, at a good location off Circular Street.

The hotels up here have no sense of shame. To them it's a simple case of supply and demand, but these are people. They advertise "By the Week Only, $50" and yet when I took it for the month they lowered the weekly rate by ten dollars. Discourages the riff-raff, they relate—we are happy to have you and don't intend to squeeze you dry. Nice to know I'm not riff-raff, also nice they don't look down on Jews.

I have my own private entry off the back porch, cherry trees and a white picket fence, plus a big window in which the moon is rising right this minute. Couldn't be better if they put me on the cover of the Saturday Evening Post. Convenient to everything—to the downtown, the racetrack, the Wagon Wheel on South Broadway—and by convenient I mean a perfect distance for someone addicted to foot-travel, exactly one mile from anything you can name. I got to stay in shape now, I can't afford a new wardrobe.

For a few bucks extra I can also join them at breakfast, instead of munch a doughnut in my room. Pleasant people. A factory man who drives to Glens Falls (north of here) and cuts dies, and his Mrs., plump smiling housekeeper. Plus one daughter, sixteen, whom I have yet to meet.

This a.m. I met the daughter at the breakfast table and I can't be dining with this daughter. An astonishing sight, her mouth. It won't close and there are metal braces, scrambled egg, and chewing gum inside it. Don't ask me how she manages to swallow her egg and retain the gum, it's just a talent, as is her ability to prevent the whole package from falling out the front window. But a terrifying experience. I'm sure it is a small matter, the business of table manners, yet we all must draw the line somewhere. Incredible to me also that this vulgar infant can be so close in age to my golden girl of the walking-ring. The calendar gives you even less information than the newspapers, that's all I can conclude.

Explored the village on foot, including a duck-in hello at my place of employment. Groundskeepers are at work on the turf course and hammering away on the concession stands and turnstiles. An impressive set-up here, with the backstretch spilling across the street in a world unto itself, outside the grounds. The horses cross the road, stroll right in through the main gate, then saddle up under the big trees before entering the paddock ring. They've got the space and all the graces.

In the afternoon I sought out the Duke of Kent to show him I am not a corpse, contrary to what he saw with his own eyes. He was on the town, so I left greetings for him at the Van Dam desk. Had a glass of beer to celebrate my being alive and then made the mistake of sampling the famous waters in Congress Park. That's a chaser for you. The mineral springs started it all here of course and they still have the reputation. (Not only that but they give it away free, the fabled elixir, at fountains in the park and one on the saddling lawn over at the racecourse.) So Oscar the adventurer had to take a taste and discover for himself he was tasting sewerage. The stuff is poisonous. You could never get down an entire cupful without throwing up on your shoes. At least I found out why it's free, since what it's worth is less than nothing.

Never made it out to the Spa (on the other side of town) and they closed the Casino a few years back, but I will have plenty of time to explore in weeks to come. As it was I walked till my shoes came loose, and enough is enough. A pleasant day in a nice place and if I thought of Caddy as I walked then my thoughts were not the least bit gloomy. The opposite in fact, though I miss seeing her.

Not gloomy until dark, in my little room here, where the exact same thoughts—just mental pictures, really—make me lonely. It is not being alone that makes you lonely either, in my opinion, what does it is love unreturned. If you do not happen to be in love, you will be doing just fine on your own. Why not? Everything comes easily and the pressure is off. But if your heart aches for a girl it spreads through your system and won't leave you alone, and nights are the toughest.

The Wagon Wheel Restaurant. Consists of three big rooms—The Ranch, The Barn, and The Bunkhouse. I am stationed in The Bunkhouse but no one is snoozing in there, believe me, just munching. Same exact menu in all three rooms, steak and baked potato, but they help to break up the hall. This is for more "intimate dining," as in the Times-Union advertisement. So instead of three hundred sitting to chew, you have only one hundred in The Bunk. Which is still a fair-sized herd grazing, and makes a substantial racket, chewing through the tougher cuts like a chorus.

Takes five of us to serve them all. Myself, a swish named Owen, and three old ladies who lick their pencils and dye their hair—two blue, one gold. The triplets, Owen calls them. Tips are on the low side, percentage-wise, but we make out because the bill is so high, plus we turn over three full seatings, sometimes four. The people begin chewing right after the last post and are still at it when doors close at ten, so even at ten percent it adds up. First night I took home $40 in cash and of course you eat a free meal of roast chicken and vegetables etc. No steak for the help, fine by me.

It's hard work. It's a factory compared to our little club at Belmont, and it never slows down, but there is a cameraderie in the kitchen and right this week it suits me to be working hard. I expect it to be my great salvation. Work the track from breakfast through the eighth race, then hustle down South Broadway and work The Bunk until eleven. That ought to do it.

Something I discovered. When you miss a girl and want to see her again, you get the impression you are thinking about her constantly. In truth she is very little in your thoughts. These are not thoughts, or even pictures in your mind. She is absorbed deeper, somewhere in your blood. Like a germ that saps your strength. Your thoughts might form an occasional picture, a snapshot, but the bulk of it is in the gut.


Blue Tuesday. Begin it with scrambled egg and Wrigley's Spearmint, and then too much mooning in my room. Had no urge to stroll, no impetus to go in motion, and the schedule cannot save me until tomorrow when they run for the money.

And a slow night at the Bunkhouse. Total of $27 along with a customer who swore he would take his case to the management. All I need is litigation. Slowest service in his life, he testifies. "I can't serve your cow raw," I told him. "I am waiting for the man to finish cooking it." Nonsense, I ordered it ten minutes ago, it *must* be cooked.

Recalls the story they used to tell on Arcaro at Belmont. Some hotshot trainer sends him off with careful instructions—bring the horse to the top of the stretch just off the pace and then turn him loose, he will do the rest. Of course the nag does nothing—a still life—and of course the trainer rushes down to pin the blame on his rider.

"I thought I told you to move up on the straightaway!"

"Without the horse?" says Arcaro.

They are off and running at the Showplace of Thoroughbred Racing in America. (Very proud they are, of themselves.) It is a gorgeous place, if you like gorgeous. I have to confess a taste for low-life. To me, you don't stage a cockfight at the White House, or race greyhounds across the lawn at Buckingham Palace. It's everything in its place and a place for everything. This joint is aimed for the uppercrust and a person could feel uncombed here, even in the grandstand. It takes a cashmere sweater, tied around your waist.

But the quality stock comes here and the best race riders. Atkinson and Boland checked in, Arcaro and Hartack en route. The pro's pros, though at the mutuel windows it is strictly amateur hour. First of all there are the guessers, an army of them, playing merry hell with the tote. Tourists on tap, strewing dumb money. You walk through the grandstand or out on the lawn and most of them don't even consult the Form—they play the house selections, or the morning line in the newspaper. Or worse, they bet their seventh cousin twice removed to the third power and win a bundle. Dumb money, dumb luck.

Right in front of me a hefty gal from the city, up here on a bus of them, wins two hundred bucks on the Double. No one with a brain could have won it, because neither race approximated form. She won it playing Uncle Harry's birthday both times and then played him again in the third race and was outraged she didn't win more! To her it's a giant giveaway, she's never heard a word about past performances.

Then they throw a lot of two-year-old maidens at you, unraced babies by the gross, so everyone is left betting on mommy and daddy while the stable makes a killing. In the 7th race today I had a little bet down on a Chicago horse with plenty of class in the bloodline and watched them sucker me good. Another unraced filly plummets from 12–1 to 6–1 and my pulse took itself. One big drop, that's the stable betting or else the big guys on a tip from the stable. Just before post they dumped another bag of cash and I knew it all. At 3–1 they had a perfect score, a nice price and no one gets it but them. The horse went wire to wire. On the day I went zero for four, and the hefty lady got back on the bus with her purse bulging.

My thought for the day is that love is democratic. Even a bum can fall in love with the fairy princess or the gentleman's daughter. That's how Hollywood makes money. What's to stop him from falling, except lack of opportunity? If she shows up on the wrong side of the tracks and she is irresistible, then he can't resist her either, he's human.

So she ought not to come there slumming—she should arrive with an open mind. That's thought for the day, part two. (It's my night off, so I have time to think twice.) Caddy Moore is taking a crack at it, she is willing to recognize the different kinds of quality in life. That there can be a great jockey and a great grease-monkey, as well as a great doctor lawyer.

Chatting with me is part of her democratic platform. She means only well, yet it is tough to shake off your breeding. One thing to try for an open mind, another to achieve it. And the road to hell is paved with good intentions.

After a couple of tries I still had not gotten hold of Mickey Klutz, until I bumped into him under the elms today. How's your vacation going, I say. Wonderful, says the Duke, and I have a wonderful lady I would like for you to meet. Come.

He had her sitting at a table in the clubhouse sundeck—firstclass accommodations for the Duke of Kent, he likes to make the worm turn. Meanwhile his wonderful lady may be as he says, but I make her a hired gun, a whore. She makes a point to let me know as much, as if to clarify she's on the clock—doesn't *like* my friend, oh no she can do better than that! Not a nice attitude yet what can you expect, undying devotion?

In any case The Duke is feeling no pain. It is impossible to insult his royalness, that's an order can't be filled. The boy just ain't sensitive. He is, however, in the process of divesting himself of accumulated funds (spending his money like water, is the translation—on this dame, on gambling, night spots, you name it) and adds that he does as much every year at this time.

What is money for, he asks, and he answers enjoyment. Of course different people will enjoy different things and not everyone wants a prostitute on his dance card. Nonetheless my friend will not rest until I have taken down a phone number and assured him I will give it due consideration my next lonely night. He swears by the whole stable, a lock.


Naturally there are a few famous names in town for this meeting and naturally you hear rumors that others are here when the truth is they're two thousand miles away. Everyone wants to rub shoulders with the famous, for reasons foreign to me.

At the restaurant, in the papers, at the racetrack, everywhere you overhear such whisperings. Sugar Ray Robinson was at the paddock ring today, I swear it was him. No no, that was *Jackie* Robinson! (The hell it was, he is in Cincinnati for a three-game series.) I say so what. Let these Robinsons go where they want in peace, let them breathe some oxygen too.


I let Miller know I have new morning responsibilities at my work, and so please cancel my bacon-and-eggs with thanks. A white lie—to protect his feelings and at the same time my sensitive stomach. Meanwhile I already have a new routine. With all the hubbub in the afternoon and evening, this town stays very nice and quiet in the a.m. You pay 42.50 to put your head on a pillow, I guess you want to leave it there a while. So I collect my papers—Post, Telegraph, and Times-Union—and stroll a few sunny blocks to a back-alley hash palace they call The Chicken Shack. And move in. This place has it all, the comforts of home plus terrific food at basement rates, yet they have only five or six tables occupied and consequently don't object if you spread out for a comfortable stay. In fact you do your homework in there from nine to eleven and all they do is top up your coffee at no extra charge. As a waiter myself I feel obliged to tip generous, and adding a little for the sublet I might end with a tip that's bigger than my bill, leave two bucks to cover a 95¢ tab. I can afford it. Got to work today. Cashed $35 ten times on a nice filly overlay who surprised a few at seven furlongs, and added a steeplechaser across the board at 4 to 1. So it's cookies in the cookie jar, and I had some fun. I admit I prefer making a hundred dollars handicapping the horses than make two hundred working nine-to-five reliable. A sickness I'm sure, yet to this patient feels just fine.*

Climbed aboard a sightseeing bus today, saw the sights. Saratoga Lake, white sails, red canoes, paddlewheeler for fifty cents. Then the old Casino, some polo grounds, and a

*As an investments counselor, I might say in my uncle's defense that, even setting aside the enjoyment factor, a career in informed parimutuel wagering does not strike me as "sick," fiscally. The takeout does hurt but the rate of return can certainly be comparable to a money market bond or conservative prime stock. Given Oscar's genuine expertise, I would have to declare his "portfolio" at least relatively sound.
—Walter Ford, Jr.

spooky place called Yaddo where the mosquitoes are as big as birds and everything is rotting. And at last a glimpse of the celebrated Spa, where they provide services you could never dream up on your own. They will baptize you in a bubble-bath, or tenderize your flesh from top to bottom and stick you between redhot sheets to relax. The things they have dreamed up make it hard to distinguish between luxury and torture, although in fairness I should confess to a congenital dullness. Several on the tour were ecstatic at the prospect of bubble-bath, and likewise the sauna bath after, which I have always found a ticket to suffocation. To each his own is the rule of thumb.

Dropped a postcard in the mail to Jimmy Myers and hustled over to Union Avenue in time to peg two winners at a modest profit, about the same I made on tips tonight. I do not look forward to punch in at The Bunkhouse. It's a drudge job now, the bloom is off it (didn't take long) and if I had to keep it up I'd quit. Fortunately, no problem. I am already right in the middle, between the last time I saw Caddy Moore and the next time.


Very nearly done in today by the Duke of Kent. We met (as planned) for the day's racing and he had the same companion as before, or very similar. Plus he had an extra one—for me. A redhead in a yellow dress with body by Fisher, va-va-voom style from headlights to the toe-polish. And he confides, "Oscar, it's on me. My treat."

Terrific. I took him aside and begged. "Mickey, I can't handle this girl, it's not my style."

"But she is. I hand-picked this girl for you, factory-tested and fully guaranteed. Take my word for it, she makes a very nice companion."

"I'm sure."

"You don't like her?"

"I do, I like her very much. A nice girl and very sexy. But I don't *know* her, she's a total stranger."

"Of course she is, for Christ's sake. She's a hooker. She is supposed to be a stranger, Oscar, you don't expect to see your little sister in a situation like that."

"Mickey, listen, thanks but no thanks."

"You can't do it to her. You'll permanently wound her feelings, not to mention the problem that I paid in advance. She cost me a bundle. They don't all look that good, my friend, it's like anything else on life's banquet table—you get what you pay for."

Easier, I decide, to explain myself to Vicki (the girl-chick) so I drag her downstairs in a corner where we can discuss business without the Duke's encouragement. Worse and worse, however, as Vicki takes a different meaning. She concludes I am acting impatient, hot to trot, and cuddles me up. "Shhh," she tells me when I try to protest her, "Shhh, it's okay, I understand."

The hell she does. She is all set to go! Places my hands underneath her dress, right up the sides of her legs to the top—nothing on. Hips, backside, naked. And says to me, "We can do it standing up."

No help in sight. I'm like a drowning man, dragged down by waves of confusion. And just in the nick of time I shout out loudly "No!"—loud enough to hear it echo— "Please! Don't be hurt. I can't do this, there's a misunderstanding."

"What is it? What's wrong?" She looks up worried, but keeps my hands in her nest.

"My mother. My mother died, today. Mickey didn't know about it. I can't be doing this today—"

"Your mom died today?" She loosens up. The dead mother is going to work, thank God, whatever made me think of it. Saved by the dead mother and Vicki won't be permanently hurt—only I will.

Because later on (and this is ten hours later on) I am unable to sleep. Unable to erase from my palms the silk of that girl's hips. Which is very crazy. If she walked in the room right now I would send her packing. (And then when she was gone, maybe wish she'd been able to stay.) A very crazy business, this sex. Goes beyond my understanding.

I can't blame Mickey. He theorized this was just what the doctor ordered, same doctor as places the orders for Linda Stanley. To each his own affliction and I've got mine. But what is it that makes everyone mean so well, and take such good care of me? I can take good care of myself. I'm a big boy, I do it all the time. Does it look like such a lousy job I'm doing, to turn the whole world into a goddamn samaritan?

A girl you don't want is the one who wants you. The world is full of girls and though I make this discovery late in life, it is no less the truth. This one with the red hair, and the Mickey Klutz stamp of approval, she is a girl all right, believe it, with a body to stop your heart. Yet stops your head too, this kind of arrangement. A girl you want, and have chosen not from left field but from the annals of your life, that one you cannot have. And it may be the case (I'm sure a psychiatrist would say so in The Post) it's what makes you want her.

Even with Tanya. I won her over, yes, and made her marry me, so naturally I assumed she wanted me. But she didn't. It took me years, a decade, to notice this simple fact, that she didn't want me. There was a lot of confusion in those days before I figured out, because it was not as though she wanted someone else instead. Now I only say it's bad luck for a virgin to marry a virgin.

I doubt Caddy Moore can be one. A quality you see in her—that she would enjoy sex. Not with me, of course, but with the man of her own free choice. The one she wanted.

Summer Tan came here to cop the Whitney and got an

unpleasant surprise. Four-year-old colt Dedicate broke the course record for nine furlongs—worth forty thousand to those who buy his oats.

I laid off it. Following basic principles this meet and getting the job done. You can put ten bucks on every nag in an eight-nag field if you want—Damon Runyon did this for years and the in-crowd thought the guy could talk to horses, he knew it all. And some of these will take a dozen, two dozen slips on the Daily Double and come up smiling all the time. They play the big cheeseburger, cash a lot of tickets, but you know they are getting murdered by the pool.

So you don't undercut yourself. Pick your spot and stick out your chin. I had only one play today. The steeplechasers I usually plead ignorant, as with the dogs or trotters. But I have noted up here that moreso than the flats a steeplechaser will run to form. It's a long race, and one that involves skills as well as speed and placement, so that form comes up by the time they see the wire. This horse's name was foreign to me before the morning paper came out—I just backed my own theory, went with the chalk, and took home $165. Nice work if you can get it.

And untaxed, naturally. I feel like I should send Uncle a money-order now and again, to pull my oar. The week just concluded I took on $235 at the Bunk and better than that at the Showplace and it's all cash, tax-free. I am not a taxed individual anymore. They hold back a few pennies from my wage that I may never see, but so what? They could keep back the wage too, or feed it to the monkeys.


"What's this about your sainted mother?"

"Mickey, please. Let it drop."

"When is the funeral? Hadn't you better catch a bus back to the City at your earliest?"

"You want to be reimbursed I'm more than happy."

"Christ, no, that's not the point. I got my money's

worth from the both of them before the stars fell on
Alabama. But seriously, Oscar, we are up here for some
fun in life. Don't save yourself for marriage—nobody even
wants a virgin anymore."

"I know, I know." (Having ruminated the same point.)
"What do you say to Saturday apres-midi, the selfsame
foursome? How's about it?"

"No thanks, from the bottom of my heart. But please,
let me treat you to the threesome. I'm getting rich up here
as fast as you are getting poor."

"You know, if you disapprove of Vicki you are also
disapproving of me."

"I approve—of everyone. I wish I felt the same way as
you, I just don't. It's my upbringing."

"Let me treat you to a few rounds with a psychiatrist."

"Save your dough, it's too late for me."

"Oscar, these are nice women, clean-living girls. These
girls dine out regularly with governors and senators in
Albany—creme de la creme."

"What do you think, I'm a snob? Believe me, Mickey,
it's nothing like that."

"Then what the hell is it. You're a healthy redblooded
male."

"Last time I bled."

It's over with now, he won't try me again. Nonetheless a
struggle, as the Duke is tenacious of a point. He wants his
taste approved, as though I didn't care for the dish he
served up. Far from it—a raving shiksa beauty, shoo-in for
Miss Rheingold next time around—but no percentage telling Mickey Klutz about principles, he's got his own set. To
him, if it costs a bundle it must be fun and if it is fun then it
must be good.

Not bad reasoning, so long as you remember that your
hand ends where the next man's nose begins. I have
nothing to argue in defense of strict principles, I'm not the
rabbi or the rabbi's son. It's all air to me too, just happens

to be the air I breathe. I am telling the whole truth when I say No Objections—each to his own and may he own it.

I spied Mrs. Whitman descending the clubhouse stair to the paddock area. Recalled at once my promise (to dine) and upon reflection decided we would both enjoy it. A friendly date.

My fear approaching her was she might have forgotten my promise, or her own invitation, but it never crossed my mind she might have forgot me completely. And maybe she didn't. Maybe she was blinded momentarily coming from indoors to the bright glare of the backyard, or maybe she was bearing down on her quinella selection in the 6th.

Whatever was the case, I caught up to her and was set to open discussion when I realized she was looking right past me. I was a face in the crowd to her, not in focus. Not Oscar, but Everyman. Defrocked of my livery, displaced from my station, I lost aristocrat status. So I backed off and let her pass unmolested.

It's a very different proposition to wait table in a restaurant. At the clubhouse there is much less bustle. The clients will be there four hours, the whole day of racing, so they sit back and sip. Consequently you get to know the party and the tip will generally reflect it.

At the Wagon Wheel no one has heard of relaxation. Get them in and out in forty minutes, from breadbasket and silverware to the last sip of coffee and the check, or else you will hear them moan and groan. And the tip will reflect it.

It isn't anything I can fathom personally. If it was me putting that kind of dough on the table just to top up my belly, I would take my own sweet time. I'd make it a two-cigar finale, shoot the works. Paying four dollars for a steak I would wish to keep it company for a while, savor the flavor. But not these. They prefer to keep on the move, chew and flee.

So there is a mental strain to the waitering, plus of course myself and Owen are low men on the totem-pole, the temporary help. The triplets, the Three Maidens of the Apocalypse, are the incumbents. They get the best stations, bus-boys who know the job, top cut of every steer, and a fast deal in the kitchen. If we make out on tips it is because we swim upstream all night to get there. We are the other two, put on for the month of August, and the word is out that no one undergoes this ordeal twice.

The Incumbents do not even deign to say hello. We must sit with each other and chat, before and after the rush, while they sit next door sorting out their cigarettes and piles of cash. Both of us shy, and him a swish, but we get along. Turns out we both live in the borough of Manhattan. His place is in the Village—he waits on table there too, in a spaghetti palace two blocks from his flat.


Owen is wide open, a great confider of secrets. Gets very personal once past his shyness. For example he makes no attempt to hide his condition—a real hothouse flower who blooms every time he moves or opens his mouth to speak. Yet he is very sweet, asks after everyone in the kitchen, and makes regular customers who will insist on his tables to the annoyance of certain blue-haired biddies.

Last night he confided a Walkaway story, my first in months, and he was in it, though not the leading man. His kind will sometimes stick together I learned, they can marry without papers. Cannot have a child of course, but keep house, share a life, the same as man and woman can. He personally was married twice. The first ended in a divorce, also without papers, when he was young and just as glad to watch it go. The other time was the bitter pill.

A true love match this time he says, nine years in tandem with the man of his dreams, complete with lace curtains on the window and a pair of matching parakeets. Yet the object of his devotion flew the coop and he did it by doing it—no apology, no explanation, just gone. "I knew where he was, of course. I knew he was a weakling and a coward who couldn't face me with bad news." (This he confides without an inkling who else might fit the description.)

The bad news was a love match with a fruit they knew in common on Fire Island. Owen was too hurt, too jealous to spend a nickel confirming the damage. "Oh I *knew,*" he says, punishing himself as he likes to do. "I didn't have to call anyone. If he wanted to talk he would have done it before he left."

Never crossed his mind the companion was snatched, or lost all memory in a bar uptown, or fell off the bridge and drowned. But that's what really happened, he was in the drink and floated up a week later near the Tappan Zee Bridge with his skull bashed in. Murder, and to this day unsolved.

"But I was overjoyed when I heard the report. Elated. Because it meant he loved me, do you see, he hadn't let me down after all!" Even this Owen will confess to me unsolicited. Of course there came some guilt, and a load of grief, such that he believed at forty-two his life was over. He is a dramatist, Owen, apt to say such things as that for five years he has not been alive—"just walking through my part, speaking my lines without any real feeling, do you see?"

If you can have a love story without a happy marriage at the conclusion, then why not a Walkaway story with a corpse. Leave it in the hands of the official scorer. (Wiley would say "If it doesn't curve, then it ain't a curve-ball.") A shame for Owen in any case. Emotional guy and sweet as they come, he looks half the time like Jesus with the nails in. He is crying for love and I hope he gets it.

Too bad Mickey Klutz couldn't fix something up for

him. I'm sure they have one of everything for sale up here, in a plain brown wrapper. Mickey could, in fact, but Owen couldn't accept. He's like me, wants a lover that is honestly come by. And in the meanwhile settles for the love of tourists, who crave his services and praise him twenty percent worth under the ash-tray.

Used my free night to dine in splendor and hear a little band concert in Congress Park. Corny stuff, Stars and Stripes plus a few show tunes, but it sounds nice to have some music in the sky. Made the acquaintance of two lovely young people from Virginia, Jim and Beth Long-acre, who convinced me to ride out to the lake with them for a fireworks display. They had a cottage out there and a little boat, so what the hell, we rowed out on the water and watched a few flares go up on the other shore. (Upstate they set their sights lower, spectacle-wise.) Yet I loved their hospitality (he even drove me back, five or six miles from Saratoga Lake so twice that for him) and would gladly reciprocate if they weren't here today gone tomorrow.

That accounted for my free time and otherwise the schedule protects me, as anticipated. Cannot mope or droop when you're booked solid and yet I have noticed this: my best times of the day are times alone, the witching hour when work lets out and the early hours prior to post.

I'm sure a genius of any kind needs to be left alone. Give him room and he will uncover the secrets of life, crowd him and he will just do the laundry. Your solitude is where you get some answers.

The weather also helps. Air this good can infect a person happily, just as too much rain or slush depresses. In a country like Sweden where it is dark ninety percent of the time in winter, the people start jumping out of their windows. Like frogs leaving the lily pads, one after another—a downpour of jumpers. It's just a detail yet one that matters. Look how many souls will uproot a life-history to get to Florida or California, where sunshine is fully guaranteed. (Though happiness is not, I'm sure.)

Home on the late side again tonight, and wakeful. More mental pictures of Caddy to sort through. I took a glass of beer with Owen in a place on Caroline, then a roundabout route home. Nights are cool, stars are clear, streets are wide and quiet. A soft peaceful time, with my pockets full of money and my cigar slow burning.

I didn't want to subject my hosts to a Corona. Mrs. Miller says no cigar smoke, Mr. Miller gets himself in trouble arguing for my constitutional right to puff in the privacy of my room. He sticks up for me, so I'll stick up for him, by abstaining. Or by smoking on the hoof, prior to my arrival.

Mrs. has become invisible to me. I keep strange hours, yes, but I never lay an eyeball on her anymore. Evidence that she exists—my room sparkles, sheets fresh every day. Also I have experimented along these lines: if I leave my window open, I come home and find it closed. Conversely, leave it closed and find it open. She is letting me know who is boss, that's all, so now I shut it each day upon leaving, to insure I have plenty of fresh air in the room when I return at night.

With weather this perfect and continued luck at the windows I have my optimistic days. I can reason I'm in good shape, looking well and rested, so who knows? Maybe Caddy Moore looks up and says, Hey, who is this guy, he's not so bad!

But I am not eager to test it. I am well aware that in these matters two and two don't always make four. You might look like a candidate on paper, with all the best ideas, but you are not a candidate if you cannot bring in the vote. Doesn't make a difference how good I look in my mirror, or sport a fat bankroll, or chance to make a funny remark in public. The fact remains I am ineligible for a girl like that the way a mule is ineligible for the Travers. Class tells. The $3000 horse can't look the $5000 horse in the eye, and everybody knows it.

The way I see it now, it's not so bad in Saratoga, and I'll be back in New York soon enough. I might not win her, but until I go back there I haven't lost her. And I know whatever I say or don't say, she will be gone soon after and I'll be staring at chilly weather. When the chill comes down on us, I'll be out of work again, but it's not the money now. There are other factors (Caddy, and Jimmy estranged) to make me a little nervous contemplating my second winter at 10 Battersea. Maybe Florida for me too.


They do a lot of fishing up here, tourists and locals alike, My landlord Miller goes every Saturday, never misses he relates, with some buddies from Glens Falls. And for this coming Saturday he invited me. "Come along with us if you like."

A nice gesture to make the offer. We were both glad when I told him no thanks. If I want to catch a fish, I know how: take a stroll down Fulton Street and catch it in a crate of ice. This method never fails and is a hell of a lot cheaper as well. My landlord's free dinner that he nets—when you figure in his transport plus equipment (and these fellows don't leave without first packing up the kitchen sink)— probably is costing him thirty dollars a pound amortized over life.

Of course I am not so dull I don't understand the difference. He went and got it himself, so it feels free. There are easier ways to make money than handicapping the horses too, but the sport is worth a little something, if not always measured in cash.

May be true that I have no complaints here, nor do I intend to complain. Yet I also had no complaints when I was still in Brooklyn. Complaint is not necessarily the unit of measure. Even Linda said it to me, "You don't complain." That's my policy.

In Brooklyn with Tanya I never felt the least bit unhappy. Looking back I can say this: my happiness was complete yet very small. Like a kid with electric trains, who has one perfect oval of track that the locomotive goes round and round perfectly—no tunnels or hills, or bridges, and crossovers.

You might choose a large unhappiness over a small happiness, sometimes. Maybe anything beats No Complaints. Jail, torture, death. Because No Complaints is a jail, it is torture, it is a death. To have No Complaints is to be finished, and limping home to your grave. Nothing matters.

You can convince yourself, and especially when you have No Complaints, that on the contrary everything matters. That the tiniest trivial detail is crucial to you. And so you sit at your desk and wait for the telephone to ring, because what if someone wishes to order ten cases of beer, and someone else twenty, and what if you might hit five hundred cases for the week. So don't step out, you could lose a commission. Step up onto the roof for five minutes and put your face up to the sun, inhale the saltwater, could cost you a dollar and fifty cents, watch out!

It keeps you going, but only like I say, round and round. These things do not matter as much as you think—you might be happier digging a ditch. You nurture and protect what's yours until one fine day you get a wake-up call and find you have nothing worth protecting—No Complaints.

No fault of Tanya's. I had no complaints with her and

I'm sure I love her very much, right this very minute sitting here. But I could live another thirty years on earth and the idea of all those years taken one day at a time (which is how it is usually done) with nothing to complain about—

So yes I started gambling more, and sat by the telephone a little less. The simple fact is my business kept growing. If you run away from someone—a girl, a puppydog, a client—they will chase you down the block. It's when *you* do the chasing they go the other way. To me success and failure are the same joke, exactly.


It's the Grand Finale tomorrow, scrambled egg and Spearmint at the Last Breakfast. Miller insisted and I caved in, such a nice man. I can measure up one time, as a social grace.

Meanwhile a decision—definite, maybe. It is to stop pushing Caddy from my thoughts, and stop pretending I have nothing to lose, even if I have no chance to win. Acknowledge the reverse, plenty to lose and it's time to lose it.

Forget about No Complaints, shoot the moon is the correct answer. I must let her know my feelings, let her laugh at me if she likes but get my money down with no undercutting. Shoot the moon and when I miss it, *complain*.

# III

## THE LEANING SIDE

### AUTUMN 1956–

So I traveled back to New York just as I came away one
month back, in the safekeeping of my friend the hedonist.
A livelier session from me this time, and always lively the
Duke. But the highlight is Mickey Klutz Forgives All, as
fate takes a hand. He informs,

"Oscar, you had more sense than I gave you credit for.
That Vicki gave me the clap."

So it's a social disease for the Duke of Kent! Call it the
common touch. And I said to him, Well well, we know
that the Lord He moves in mysterious ways His wonders
to perform.

"So did she, my dear fellow, so did she. It wasn't how
she moved that got me down."

But the Duke is never down. He is so pleased to be
seated at life's banquet table, as he calls it, that the truth is
he's probably happy to have a dose of the clap. It's part of
the fruit that falls from the tree of life, and the Duke wants
it all—one big picnic on the grass to him.

I honor this quality in my friend. It is the quality I wish
for myself, to risk a little something now and again. I'm no
moralist, just fogbound, an islander by background. It's
plain enough to see that the Duke's misery gives him more
to laugh about than all my virtue and my No Complaints.

"Mickey, I owe you an apology in that case."

"Yes, Oscar?"

"It wasn't Vicki's fault, the problem you are having. She
got it from me, that day beneath the grandstand."

"What! You mean it? That's wonderful, Oscar!"

I thought he would know a joke when he heard one. Instead he was tickled to hear I had mated with this mare, not to mention the idea I had mated with worse previously in order to have something communicable. He was so thrilled over his role in having helped to corrupt me after all that I had to own the truth and stop him.

"Mickey, no, it's only a joke. You know me, I never did anything with her."

"I *thought* I knew you. What's the story, Oscar? Did you or did you not partake of that jeune filly's charms?"

"I did not. Just kidding you. I was sure you'd get steamed up about it, and then I would break the news."

"Get mad? Dammee, sir! I'd happily share a germ with you anytime, so long as good sound recreation was enjoyed by all concerned. I selected that girl for you particularly, you know—I had you very specifically in mind when I enlisted her talents."

"A very pretty girl. A Miss Rheingold."

"Oh yes? She never said a word about that to me."

"Oh oh, here we go again. Not a real Miss Rheingold.* I mean that I thought of her that way—a beauty contestant. You know, a gorgeous girl."

"At least we can agree on something. The filthy bitch. She gave me some Senatorial clap, I'll bet."

"Counselors and Kings, I'm sure. The top of the line."


Tuesday after lunch. A gap to fill time-wise. No brass bands to welcome me back. Jimmy said the word hello, a nice soft cold shoulder. Bulkitis has the plywood over his wicket, and a note posted—Back After Labor Day.

---

*The Miss Rheingold Contest was a promotion run by the brewery, in which the public selected from six contestants whose smiling faces decorated the subway cars and corner stores in a six-panel black-and-white display ballot. Children did most of the voting and stuffed the ballot-box freely, but it didn't matter as the six contestants were more or less interchangeable.
—Walter Ford, Jr.

I can use the time to fix things up at home, put my affairs in order and get a shine on my trinkets. Spring cleaning on the final day of August—Bon Ami and elbow grease, a little patching plaster, and a splash or two of white paint. Don't wait for the landlord to attend to these matters, because he can wait longer, till Christmas of the year 2000.

A shopping spree, for more improvements. I picked up a two-burner hotplate to increase my culinary range plus a few pictures to decorate the walls. (A lot faster than with patching plaster.) This idea stems from The Wagon Wheel, though my scenes are French, not the Wild West. French and Dutch countryside, fifty cents apiece up near Washington Square—you shop for yourself in a big bin.

Ordered a telephone, as Fish, unlisted, and they said, Fine, we will bring it right over. Just like that.

Jimmy Myers is the mystery. He won't come up on his own and resists when I try inducements. I cornered him in the park today and put it to him: help me spruce the place up and I'll pay good wages. Some fresh paint and lemon oil, come on. Got a verbal agreement from him, but then no show. It's like he was my ten-year-old pal in July and now one month later he's sixteen, and alienated.

Best not to push it. Wait him out. After all, he wasn't at the Spa being offered bubble bath, he was down here sweltering in the streets. Could be the heat, and he needs a freshening. But it feels terrible to me. May, June, July, we were reading together, strolling in the neighborhood— now I can't imagine such a closeness.

Clubhouse reunion, as the meeting begins tomorrow. Wally Wiley passed the month up in the Adirondacks with his offspring, the legal eagles, including various dogs and grandchildren. (I lost count listening.)

"So what did you do to keep busy?"

"I did nothing, that's what. Read a magazine, have a smoke, drop a fishing line in the water. That's it. That's what they do up there."

"Nice to take it easy."

"Awful, Oscar, the worst. The whole month I had to pretend I was a sane person, that's what put the strain on me. Because I lost all my marbles the first few days. But I made a deal with Noel, my boy, and I had to keep to it."

"No Complaints?"

"No, he's after me to retire, take the rest of life off. I ask him what for and get no answer of course. But I told him I would try it to stop him badgering me—one whole month with the family. No work, just do what a retired man does. Nothing."

"It didn't work out?"

"That's putting a fine finger on it! It was hell on rusty wheels. I'm telling you, I went bonkers up there, I was ready to put dynamite under the house and run for the bus."

"How did Noel take it? Disappointed?"

"Sure he was disappointed. He wants me retired because I embarrass him. He wants to say, Meet my dad the retired gentleman. Not, meet my dad who waits on table."

"Your own kid?"

"Looks down on waiters."


Wiley's boy is afraid he will end up like Carroll Shilling.*

"I told him the story one day, that's all," he shrugs.

---

*Carroll Shilling, once a great race-rider at Belmont Park, was found dead at the entrance gate to the racetrack many years later, a derelict apparently, come home to die. O Henry might have written such a script, but this one comes from "the annals of life."

—Walter Ford, Jr.

"Noel isn't rational on the subject. And his wife thinks that Satan is the Racing Commissioner. What can I tell you?"

It's a story you don't forget. But who is to say Shilling was in the wrong place. Maybe he died with a smile in his heart. Probably not, yet maybe. And if not, he would have been no better off someplace up in the Bronx, or the suburbs of Katmandu.

A shock to see her this morning. So young—just a child. We exchanged a greeting from twenty paces but it is chaos on the backstretch this weekend and I was loathe to interfere with her work. Delighted to get the greeting accomplished and leave it at that for now.

Somehow in my memory bank I had trimmed the spread, so instead of 49 and 19 we were maybe 39 and 29, almost within reach. I never counted out the years incorrectly, just one side of my brain was fooling the other—all within the same noggin.

Possible that a mental picture weathers the same way a real picture would. Like a snapshot you take from your wallet, after sitting on it for a few months. The picture has aged a lot faster than the person pictured, like an old parchment, or a piece of leather.

Bogart's Baby, who she rubs for Farr Brothers, had a nice win on Saturday and I told her so. She looked older already, dusty and quite mature today.

"Yes we were pleased to have a first."

"She ran well in the summer."

"Two seconds. She had a string of good races, but she never even made the lead before Saturday's race."

"A professional maiden. Anyway, second pays too. You could step her down a little."

"We have, down and up, like a yoyo. She ran third at

7500, so we dropped her and she ran fifth at six thousand. Wes decided she was insulted, so he moved her back up to seventy-five and she came through."

"That's it. I hope you have the same luck with Sound the Trumpet today."

"Thanks, but don't bet your new hat on him. He hasn't been working his hardest this week."

"He'll make it at six furlongs. All summer I thought that horse wasn't designed for a route, and he could win a sprint for you—now I have to put my money where my mouth was."

"It's your money."

"So far it is—for at least a few more hours."

That got a smile from her, three seconds of happiness supplied by yours truly without even trying. When I would lie awake in Saratoga Springs and watch the moon, I would attempt to map out a conversation with Caddy. Weather, politics, the latest in the world of show business. But horses! That's the language we share in common and I don't have to drum up my lines.

A good thing, too. Because my mouth kept working but my mind was stuck on what *she* said—that she noticed the hat was new.

"Did you really back Sound the Trumpet yesterday?"

"Even better. To win, and also I put him in a quinella with Bolo Punch. So I cleaned up."

"How much did you make?"

"By the hour it was more than Henry Ford makes. Of course it was just two minutes worth."

"Well I wish I could say I gave you the hot tip."

"But you did. Because I decided you are luck."

"I guess that's a compliment."

"Sure it is. What beats luck?"

"Ask me again when I'm old and wise."

"Like me. No Caddy, you get older but not necessarily wiser. Unless you're lucky. So now I need a hot tip for tomorrow."

"We have nothing going until next week actually. But I don't handicap the horses—I don't have a clue, and when I watch them parade they all look terrific to me. Do you win a lot usually?"

"Only when I'm lucky. I win enough."

"Enough to support your family?"

"No one does that, except the high rollers who bet ten grand on a favorite to show. Anyway, I don't have a family to worry about."

"You never said what it was you did before you were a waiter. Remember I asked you?"

"A business man."

She looked surprised. Maybe because she still thought I was Pretty Boy Floyd the outlaw, or maybe because to her a business man was something much bigger than Carnovsky's Fine Liquors. Like General Motors, or whatever her daddy did to get his first two million. So I added,

"Small-time. A little business of my own. Although I made ten times the money I'm getting now."

"But you didn't like it."

"A good listener. You are a very good listener, young lady."

Except I did like it. But what the hell, conversation is an art, not a science.


We coincide and speak each day, just like that. Nothing to it but to do it. A few men on the backstretch might eye me suspiciously and maybe they say, Who is this old guy hobnobbing with the girl swipe. Because they still freeze her out by polite agreement. Well I will tell them who, it's Fish the conversationalist. Doesn't even bother to rehearse—a charmer, doing what comes naturally.

Really, such a nice girl is easy to talk to. It's no trick. The fact is this girl respects me. Because I am a track rat and she is a rookie. And because there are two kinds of young people: those who hold their elders are fools and those who hold their elders are wise men. Respect for the decrepit, she's got. I became a genius the minute I watched Citation run. The Genius of Racing Past.

"How many times did you see him?"

"Six or seven. No one was close to him, no one ever beat Cy fair in his prime. Even after he was lamed out west and lost his four-year-old season, it took a great horse to beat him."

"Who was in his class? Whirlaway?"

"No one, that I saw. Next rung down you have Whirlaway, and maybe Count Fleet, Stymie—the War hurt them both. Seabiscuit on a given day, and Armed. War Admiral. But no one you could bank on like Citation. You know, Caddy, I saw the Man O' War too, though I admit I was too young to appreciate what I was seeing. My father took me."

"What did he do, your father? Business?"

"No, work. He came here from Russia and he worked. His father, who I never met, was a newspaper man. My father spent twenty years in a print-shop, eleven hours a day, for wages."

"Low wages."

"Bupkis. Please excuse my language."

"I like it, though."

"Pardon me if I don't, in that case."

"What about Nashua. Wes says he could beat any of them head to head."

"Maybe he could. Certainly he is a head to head runner—you saw him yourself in the Grey Lag. Native Dancer was another great one, you might have seen. They both came up short in the Derby and they both won everything else. To me it says the Derby is an over-rated horse-race, too early in the year. Pretty soon they will be retiring a horse to the stud farm before he ever runs a race. The Nashua you will see here in the Gold Cup is one strong horse—a year ago May he was still a young colt."

And my golden girl marvels in disbelief that I can be such a genius, to have lived so long and seen so many horses of distinction. I have seen Presidents too, starting with the fat man Taft. I remember Wilson very well, seeing his long puss every day in the Eagle. But I don't merit a genius rating for recalling these men, only for recalling the horses.

A boon to have Wiley back in the sheepfold. My sachem, my father-confessor. I can bring my problems to him, in all his wisdom, and get some of the usual bullshit in response.

"A man my age, a girl so young—where can it lead?"

"Where it always leads. Don't worry so much, don't underrate yourself. I don't think you appreciate your own charms. You are a lovable guy, Oscar, not some wet dog with an odor. Age makes no difference at all."

"Wait, I know the line. It takes two to tango but only one to waltz."

"And what the hell is that supposed to mean?"

"Don't kid me, you're the one who said it. To me."

"I said it? Then it must be right."

Terrific. After all the time I put in on that pearl, he is disowning it. And I think to myself: It's *not* a fountain? And I say to my sachem,

"Wiley you are *such* a bullshit artist."

"Let's not talk about me. Have you heard what happened to the scholar's ass in the stable?"

"Tell me about it."

"The poor dumb beast starved to death halfway between two bales of hay—from indecision."

And he's got me again, with another Wiley wisdom. He is a bullshitter, no question, yet when I listen to the actual bullshit it always smells sweet. As Wiley says himself, What is bullshit anyway but sweet timothy hay? And if he can make it smack of truth, well figure that as the artist part.

But I am not the scholar's ass, I am on the move. Yes I could have starved to death in sight of food by playing deaf and dumb, the shy guy, but I did the job, and I am getting to know this girl. And I didn't honestly come to Wiley seeking advice, I came to show off a little. I'll advise myself.

Still it is fine to have Wiley's reassurance, because plenty of people would say that it's robbing the cradle—or else raiding the crypt!—to act on such an attraction. You read The Post and it's always the psychological rigamarole, mid-life crisis etcetera. As though it makes no difference the individuals involved. There is a mid-life crisis all right, also a begin-life and end-life. Every day it's a goddamn crisis right there at the crossroads of your own front doorstep.

You cannot always simplify it. They give it a cute name, that explains it without explaining it. People fly the coop at any time. They might go after a single night together, a month, a year, a decade. They could go all of a sudden after fifty years bliss, it has happened I know. They will not depart on a neat schedule, however, so that someone down at The Post can play Sigmund Freud and call it by a cute name that doesn't touch the truth of actual people.

Mrs. Kearney up at the library remembers me. I reported to her for duty, told her I was away but keeping up on my reading. She knew enough not to ask me for titles.

Nothing for me this time, except an apology. No more Walkaways. That's all right, I told her, I'm studying new subjects. And for today I'll be content to leaf through magazines, get reacquainted with the facilities. Novels? Maybe next time.

I returned her the Jewels of Opar, three weeks late. Rated a fine of eighteen cents. She wouldn't take a quarter for it, insisted on making the 7¢ change.


Today the subject was me. Not Citation and Whirlaway, just Oscar Fish. She caught me off base unprepared, when she asked if I happened to be a married man. I was not sure what the answer should be. If I say I am not, then it isn't the truth and if I say I am, the same will be so. And what's a Walkaway to her, if I was in the mood for lengthy explanations of my status?

"I was." The best I could manage on short notice. That I *was* married.

"Do you have children?"

"No children."

I await the next arrow, death and divorce, but her mind takes a different turn, to the subject of herself.

"I won't get married."

"Not yet, no. Maybe you can't imagine it. I understand. But don't be surprised if in a few more years you can think of nothing else."

"That's an insult, Oscar."

"Not at all, I didn't mean it that way. Just small-talk. But I remember myself at your age and believe it I had no thoughts of marrying either. A few years later I was ready to toss my hat in the ring."

"I have one friend who is getting married next June, right after this school year."

"Too young, in my opinion. But what do I know?"

"I want to go to England next spring, or summer, and ride on the steeplechase circuit."

"A pioneer. The Jackie Robinson of the girl jockeys?"

"The Sheila Wilcox, you mean."*

"And would you take it for your life's work? If you could become a jockey?"

"For a few years—till I got fat. I wouldn't do any one thing all my life. You wouldn't either."

"I *would* have, I just didn't. What else would you do?"

"All kinds of work, and travel. Read and write and everything trite. I mean, when you have never seen or done anything at all really, there must be quite a lot to see and do."

"I'm sure."

"Whereas if you get married you see the same thing every day."

"More or less you do. So then freedom is the cry for Miss Caddy Moore. For myself also, by the way. I'll tell you sometime."

"Sometime soon, I hope. I'm leaving in two weeks, you know, for a while."

"Yes I know."

We are friends. I know about her family, her house on Long Island, cottage out in Pennsylvania, and her horse The Doormat. But it made no sense to hear her remark that I was her "best friend in a way" so I argued the point on the spot.

"After The Doormat, I'm sure. But seriously, we are still getting acquainted, still strangers."

"What I mean," she said—and said as though it was all thought out beforehand—"is that you are the person I most look forward to seeing, right now."

*Sheila Wil*l*cox had stunned the British equestrian world earlier in 1956 by running second at the august Badminton Horse Trials. She was to win at Badminton the next three years in succession.

—Walter Ford, Jr.

Some category, as I told her. And some mouthful too. But if she looks forward to racing days so we can talk together, then that's nice. So do I.

"If you didn't show up, you know, I would be very disappointed. I realized that the other day." (And I realized the same thing a long time ago, on the last day of the summer meeting at Belmont, when she went AWOL.)

"Well I'm as good as clockwork, as it happens, and so are you too. You could be out shopping for school supplies one of these days, and your back-to-school dresses."

"Not a dress." But why not? A blue dress, I would choose for her, the color of laughter in her eyes.

"A coat, then, a pair of shoes."

"I did buy a sweater over the weekend. And I was trying to find a little present for you, Oscar."

"Me?"

"But I couldn't. I didn't want to get something stupid, and I couldn't think of anything nice."

"A cigar."

"You seem to have those. Besides, it's too much like Father's Day. But I haven't given up yet."

"Don't worry too much about it. But listen, we could have a cup of coffee sometime, away from Jamaica I mean. Before you go. We could have a nice civilized talk—sitting down."

"Sounds luxurious. I would like that—so long as you know how it is."

"How it is?"

"You know. That I'm not interested."

"In a cup of coffee?"

"Don't be coy. In a love affair. And not because you're older than I am, or anything like that."

"Fine. I'm not interested either. And not because you are younger than I am, or anything of the kind."

"Touché."

"As a matter of fact, Caddy, I make it a point to never become romantically involved with anyone born after the Man O' War."

"Good. In that case you might want to apply for the job of my chaperone next summer in England. I was thinking what a perfect arrangement it would be to have an older— not old, mind you, just older—man around to keep the younger wolves at bay. They would assume you were my lover and I'd be guaranteed peace and quiet."

"What do you want with peace and quiet at your age? And are you really so besieged with offers?"

"No I'm just joking. But I do like to choose my own company—it's the excruciating part of being a girl. It gives anyone the right to bother you."

"You can tell them no, of course."

"It's not that I don't. I would never go out with a boy I didn't already like. But it's not exactly fun to do either— saying no to people, I mean. Boys *are* people, aren't they?"

"That's up to the official scorer. And I don't want to bother you, but where are we in all this noise about our cup of coffee. Having or not having?"

"Having."

"Good. And you can tell me how it was you decided to chase steeples instead of eligible young men."

"And you can tell me about freedom. Remember?"

"A good listener."


I was working my way up to it, measuring out the days remaining, and now it's out in the open air. Not interested, she says, yet *she* brings it up.

Don't rush things, my father would always tell me, let it take care of itself naturally. He preached the value of patience: doesn't look good tonight? Wait and see about tomorrow morning. He had nothing special he was waiting for, just his children growing up and he didn't mind if it took plenty of time.

He wasn't getting the Nobel Prize for setting nice type fast. When I won a contest in grade school—most chin-ups and they handed me a real blue ribbon—I asked him if he won things ever. "Dirtiest fingernails," he smiled. "I win every day."

He could never get them clean, although my mother made him put in fifteen minutes on it before she let him eat. But patience I got from him. If you *take* your time, he would say, then you will *have* the time, like anything else you take. Otherwise it's gone out the window before you used it.

So panic can urge you on, and fear can hold you back, and the result is you are patient by default, with a girl. And things must take care of themselves naturally, like he said.


Likewise with Jimmy, I exercise patience. Snubbed by him again, on the staircase. Did this estrangement occur one inch at a time, during my leave of absence, or all at once for some reason I missed. Is it Snider again? I will have to ask him, as soon as the smoke clears.

Meanwhile a few more improvements. Picked up a little carpet from Monty Ward, blue with a turkish trim, and a set of coffee cups with saucers, brand new. A couple of books by big-name writers to dress up the shelf on my wall, Meyer Levin and Steinbeck.

Finished improving and fried two mackerel. Rice and salad, a nice dinner, then radio music and a Gonzales. The life of Riley, except the truth is I was waiting for the telephone to ring. Having installed it in my quarters I expect it to ring and be her. Not a chance of course, I never even forced the number on her.

But I find my "peace and quiet" disturbed by guilty

feelings. Sitting next to this silent telephone, I think of Tanya and what if she minded a great deal, more than I imagined? These emotions don't always show. Doesn't show to Caddy in the morning breeze at Jamaica Park, how much I wish for the telephone to ring at night. She couldn't guess.

Although with her, maybe she could. She reads my mind. Like making sure to announce she is "not interested" and then the assurance "it's nothing to do with age." She knows it all, this lovely girl.

She still likes a racing story best and today I recalled a good one for her, the false start that took place right over at Jamaica back in the early Thirties sometime. Rideaway battled Clock Tower from wire to wire, neck and neck all the way around, and beat him by a nostril but the race was negated. It had been called for a false start, they just could not rein in those horses, so they let them go around and then loaded them back in the gate to race again.

The second time, for the money, the same two battled it out, only this time Clock Tower prevailed by an eyelash. And it was maybe the sourest crowd in history that afternoon, the ones who thought they won the same race twice and had to tear up their tickets.

"I was there," I told her. (A lie.)

"Really! Who did you have?"

"Neither one. Nothing ventured. Anyone asked me how I saw the outcome, I tell them 'dead heat, no question' and leave it at that."

I recall the race very clearly from accounts in the Eagle but of course I was busy selling shirts in downtown Brooklyn instead of sunning myself out at the racetrack. And in those days of my youth I would never place my bets with a bookmaker off-track.

Still I like a story to include me when possible and I have a reputation to maintain as the Ghost of Racing Past. Let it be. It is wonderful to have a common interest. Tanya has a zero interest in handicapping, to the extent she would never even worry (as some do) about losing the milk money. I could walk in rich as Croesus or flat broke as a Bowery bum and neither way get a rise out of my wife. I could mention in passing that I put five thousand big ones on Trigger the Wonder Horse in the 14th race over six miles in the mud and she would say, Well it's nice you enjoyed yourself, Oscar, and never notice a thing.

Of course I know I shouldn't complain. It's to Tanya as her dancing is to me—she is glad for me and does not meddle. She understands I want to go. That's nice and maybe that's all you ask. A lot of wives don't give you that much without taking a little skin off your nose. To enjoy it *with* you, might be asking too much.

"Why do you waste your time talking to me?"

"What choice do I have? You're the only one who will talk to *me*."

"All right, why do I waste *my* time."

The truth is I am pussyfooting it today, fishing around, and really hoping that she will do the work, take the tough hurdles for me.

"Because you like me."

"And so you humor me, correct?"

"Do I?"

"Now you don't be coy. You do humor me. I was turning thirty when you were cutting baby teeth."

"So were my parents. Do I humor them?"

"I'm sure you do. In any event, I am not your parents, I am a social acquaintance, which is different."

"You just don't see it, do you? If you were born the same

day as I was, in the same place, then we would know the same things, roughly. Being older makes you more interesting to me, not less. You've been where I can never."

"And lived to tell it! You mean I've seen the Man O' War."

"And the Roaring Twenties and the Great Depression. Even the War—what can I know about that?"

"Plenty. You don't have to get shot to know what a bullet is. You think that I'm a history book."

"No, a person."

"Well a person, Caddy, knows what he knows outside history. The Great Depression is nothing to me. A label. I saw the breadlines, yes, the homeless souls, Hoovervilles. Someone took pictures, so you can see them too. But I was working. I sold shirts, I sold beer—I made a decent living. So did my friends, and none of us were geniuses. In 1938, Great Depression, I put a down payment on a house. And what's so special about me? "

"I don't know, tell me."

"Zip. I don't sing, I don't dance, and I don't tell jokes. I don't even like the books I read."

"A person knows what he knows outside books."

"Touché I'm sure. Horse, man, and money."

"That's a new one on me. Who said it, Hemingway?"

"Hemingway Wiley, a little old man in the clubhouse. He'll be in soon if you like to meet him."

"Oscar, do you know that way back in May I saw you. Talking to your friend—"

"Hearn?"

"Maybe. With the boy. And I knew you were nice. I could tell you were funny. And that I would like you."

"Funny?"

"A little funny, yeah. And all the time you were pretending not to notice me but I saw you not noticing. So now when you are pretending not to be interested, I can see that you are. And I don't want to embarrass you but it just makes me uncomfortable to pretend anything. I'd rather have it out."

"You can not be just nineteen years old. It isn't possible."

"I'm twenty years old, and never said otherwise."

"You are older than I am, in any case. Tell me please, Caddy, all about the Roaring Twenties."

"Please, Oscar. I've only got a minute more."

"Then let's leave the subject for another day. What if it took more than a minute. Hypothetically, of course. As yet I don't know what the subject is—"

She knows me, this one, she's been stealing my signs from the catcher. It's more like years of friendship between us than only weeks of it. Imagine her reading me like a book in the spring and never said a mumbling word.

But I *don't* know what the subject is, even if she made a face at me when I said it. She declares that I am "interested" in her. To be sure I am. Why is that a subject, however, unless she is interested in me too? If it's a one-way street, what's to discuss? Politeness would demand she leave me alone with it.

Or does a girl make a man declare himself only to shoot him down? Some might, but not this girl—she doesn't need my scalp, or anyone else's either. So what does she need? Therapeutic sex? Dream on.


I am in demand socially, with a pair of invites for the same day. Timothy Myers stayed home from work to watch the Series game and made me welcome to join him downstairs. A nice gesture, and I would like to watch some of it, except there is the problem of Jimmy still. He is cool to me, not welcoming, and it is his house too.

All I can think is Ebbets Field. Maybe he was waiting out the regular season to see if I would come through on my word and in the end pfft, the hell with Oscar. This kind of reasoning is possible with a child—to hold a little grudge and stand in judgment of adults. They don't know they are dirt, no one told them, so they think they are royalty sometimes instead and if you cross them up then it's off with your head.

Anyway Newcombe took a real shellacking and I'm glad I didn't subject myself to it.

I did take up Wiley, however, and joined Himself and Mrs. Wiley for the evening at his place up on Riverside Drive. Rode the train both ways. Nice suite of rooms, with a view of the Hudson and a doorman in the foyer. Stands there like a pheasant under glass as you approach, then pops to life to let you come inside. Mrs. says she feels safe having a doorman down there, but this old trooper couldn't stop a poodle pissing on the carpet.

Very polite lady, who towers over her husband. Does a dinner the proper way, a new set of dishware with every course, a glass for every beverage, and she keeps the coffeepot inside a little tent on the table in case we should want our refills hot. Like her son Noel she would like to see Wiley hang up his bow-tie (not too long before this prejudice emerged). I tried to keep in step with her on most points but here I diverged for my friend's sake. Give the man a helping hand I figured. So I told her, "Whatever makes him happy. Right, Mrs. Wiley? He knows best, I'm sure. And believe me, we do most of his work for him anyway." (That got the little rooster crowing!)

We adjourned to the parlor for brandy and cigars, a real first class operation they run. She left us there, a pair of social lions. Talked politics, for what it's worth. Ike is going to win and everyone knows it. What's more, no one really cares. As Sid pointed out, you look at a Berlin or a Hungary, with all those Russian tanks sitting shivah, and you have to concede we would be having it good even if Francis the Talking Mule was in the White House next year.

A wonderful evening, though once or twice my mind

wandered. Up on Riverside Drive I wondered if down on Battersea Street my telephone was ringing off the hook. And when I got back, late, I tried to see if by looking at it I could tell whether or not it had rung in my absence.

Encouraged one day, discouraged the next, always by some microscopic detail I uncover in our talk. (Which I record and study in the aftermath.)

One thing I know: I do suffer from the condition of too much respect for women. Maybe growing up among sisters, Lilly and Sarah who took care of me and Florence whom I sometimes took care of myself. But to other men, there is no need to wrestle around with the question of women. It can be a game to them, the occasion for fun, as it is with the Duke of Kent or as it was with my old chum Albert Kronstein, who would travel Friday nights to the cathouse in Neptune City. I let him drag me along one time and ended up sitting in his father's DeSoto for two hours.

Albert loved this joint in Neptune City and went there all the time, and if you mentioned respect for women I'm sure he would answer they set the price and he met the price, and leave it at that. Like the Duke telling me up north, "A girl who makes her living being wanted—it's an act of disrespect to respect her."

Maybe I'm not respecting her, maybe I am just respecting myself. After all, she is a prostitute. But whether with her or with a real woman, I'm sure the problem remains the same—easy for some and not so easy for others. You fall on the leaning side, that's all. And so you must give yourself a push forward, play the part, or you sit out in the car all night respecting yourself.

Another question is why a shiksa girl. I should ask The New York Post, but I am asking myself instead. Is it the appeal of a forbidden fruit or just a girl who hits me right? And when they tell you Don't mix with shiks, are they voicing a prejudice or only making common sense? Furthermore, if prejudice cuts both ways on this issue, does it cancel itself out or become twice as bad?

Caddy to me is just Caddy. And no one can say I am a social climber. Used to be you looked at a girl like this and they would automatically assume your motivation was getting into her old man's business. At least I am too far gone to play the young buck with hat in hand. Imagine myself in the posture: "Yes sir, Mr. Moore, I have a very good head for business, honest as the day is long, and just exactly what sort of an arrangement did you have in mind, sir?"

I would have to dress Republican for the occasion, some green and yellow checkered slacks and golfing shoes of the finest Italian leather. Tell him I like Ike, that's right, a kike for Ike. Sky would be the limit for a promising young fellow like that!


We all watched the coal-mining strike on the news and it went off just like a horse race—everyone had an opinion.

Sid: They are out on strike because they hate their work. It's an excuse. They are all secretly hoping none of them ever has to go under the mountain again.

Wiley: It's nothing to them to go under the mountain, they did it all their lives and daddy before them. All they want is a reasonable safety and reasonable dough, like anyone else.

The Duke: What's the difference?

Mr. Nevas: (a late-staying regular of Wiley's, whose vocabulary is enriched by scotch) If it's that hard to get the goddamn coal out of there and so goddamn dirty and dangerous, then probably God never meant for them to get it in the first place. That's why he *put* the goddamn stuff under the goddamn mountain in the first place.

And they say that's what makes horse-racing. I occupied no position in the debate, although not in the same way as Mickey Klutz. I'm sure it does make a difference what we think and what is real, but what can you know from a two-minute news broadcast? Just taps into your bias.

What I saw was how specialized these men and women are. You sit where you live, New York, and assume we are all of a piece from coast to coast, from north pole to south pole the world over. A bagel and cream cheese may be unknown in Texas, yet we all eat lunch.

Then you see these people. Tribes. The coal-miners in the mountains or even the fishermen who come into South Street pier at two in the morning to unload a catch. The ones who spend those dark hours carving up fish and crating them, loading them onto trucks. These men go home after a long day's work when the sun is coming up, one hour before my bell starts ringing. That's not a job, or even a tribe, that's a culture unto itself.

They might as well be living in China, for the hours they keep, and who would understand one but another one?

Still small talk—not the Big Talk—with Caddy. Re-run the Six O'clock News. There's a lot going on in the world and you don't always see it in the paper, I tell her. (The man of parts, the big sophisticate.) Coalminers, I cite for her benefit, and the fishmarket at four in the morning.

"Eskimos," she cites me back, because eskimos are U.S. too, though I am not sure they vote. Maybe Stevenson can turn it around by getting out the eskimo vote while there is still time.

"It's a melting pot, but no one melts. You stay who you are."

"It's more like a stew pot, maybe," she says. Small talking, that's all. "It would work out better if everyone changed lives now and then, changed jobs—like musical chairs."

"Not so easily done. People build up a pension and so forth."

"Did you know a famous writer once argued that everyone in the world should take on a new line of work every seven years? I mean, just for the sake of sanity, and health."

"All except Ike. He should change after four years. But listen Caddy, I changed. I have already launched my new career."

"Not me. I've been a student for a lot more years than seven and I'm ready to try something else. Something where I feel the time is well spent even if I'm just earning money. Because I can always give the money away, to a poor eskimo, or a coalminer."

"He wouldn't take it, I saw those guys. But in school your time is well spent. Look what you learn—change jobs every seven years. I never knew it."

"You not only knew it, you did it. And I never read that in school, I read it on my own, for fun. In school I read stuff like Carlyle and John Stuart Mill. Try *him* some time."

"I'll try him, but I know I can't hang in there on a guy like Hawthorne. I'd rather read the Brooklyn phone directory than the House with Seven Gables."

"The Manhattan book is easier."

"For you, maybe. Lefkowitz versus Smith."

Did not mention my year-and-a-half at college. Some places you impress them with a year-and-a-half, other places you have to know a miss is as good as a mile. And I didn't care to explain it. I spent ten years explaining it to my father, who wanted me so badly to do it. Now I wouldn't try explaining—just hand him the Gables and let him have a go.

Caddy pretends, for my benefit of course, that she is sorry to be leaving New York. But I disagree. Of course she is going and why shouldn't she? She will miss out on the Jockey Club Gold Cup and maybe she will miss our chitchats too. I believe her when she says so. But it's no big deal. She is bound for higher ground and there is no future in lagging back just to chat with the Genius of Racing Past.

A long day to relate. Entitled "A Cup of Coffee with Caddy"—the long awaited. I was up very early for a change and walked the waterfront to do my thinking. And first I thought, Okay I am on the edge of this continent, then took out my thermos. Water a dark green, sun rising a bright orange over Rockaway, seagulls in a chorus line on the early barge.

And I had it worked out, at last. I knew exactly what I wanted, or needed, whatever you call it. To go with this girl one time: no more, no less. If it never happens, what's to keep me from feeling bereft in her absence, as I did in August? But you beat the system, take back the normal, by going once and once only—take the edge off and melt away the magical mystery, so that a girl can become a person to you again and not a raving angel goddess.

Is this idea too crazy? Is it immoral? Do I care if convicted on these particular counts? In the gut I thought to myself, Eureka. Because I can live with this nicely, better than with the alternative positions (nothing doing versus a serious romance). And if she blew up in my face about it, I could tell her I was joking—an idea like that, she would have to believe it. Putting in an escape hatch is what made it possible for me to actually make the proposal later on in the day.

(Which I did do, and will record when I get back here around eight. I just remembered a promise to bring up a pail of chicken chow mein and eat it with Mrs. Vickers. I go from one plate of food to the next, always in the best of female company.)

210

"Last day tomorrow!" (Was my opening line.)

"I hope not. You make it sound like the end of the world. It's the first day of the school year, that's all, on Monday. I'll be back home to visit in less than a month, you know."

"I didn't."

"I'm not traveling to the Aleutian Islands or anything. I'll get back to New York for a weekend in October, and for Thanksgiving. And Christmas."

"Oh yes?"

"What? Did you think we would never see each other again, or something like that?"

"Something like that, yes."

"What a strange attitude. We're friends."

"May it be so."

"So?"

"So, dear Caddy, you are going and you will be gone. Summer camp is over and next comes the rest of your life."

I lost my momentum here, however. It was true I counted down, ten nine eight seven six, and expected the world to end at zero. I forgot it wasn't a game we were playing, but life. Which goes on and on. So I wavered. But prevailed over my weak character with the argument that a decision was taken and it was a brilliant one (in my opinion at the time) and so I went ahead with my plan.

"What does it mean to you, Caddy, to be friends with a man."

"Depends on the man. You mean yourself?"

"Of course."

"Fun, good company, sharing time and experiences. With you it's more fun for me, because you have had more time and experiences to share."

"In that case the best man to marry would be a Methuselah. A relic, who saw the Flood."

"I never said anything about marrying. Except that I

once told you I wouldn't. We were talking about friendship. What does it mean to *you*, Oscar? That's what I'd like
to know. You're so obsessed with our age difference.
That's why I know you must think in terms of a sexual
relationship."
    Such a bluntness—and entirely correct of course. If you
don't think sexual, you don't think mismatch. Just play
with a free hand and enjoy it.
    "Good, I confess. I would like to have a relationship of
that kind, with you—but only once."
    "One time? You mean like one hour, total?"
    "One hour, half-an-hour, I don't know. Whatever it
takes. We get rid of it, get it out of our systems, and then
resume a friendship. Can you see the reasons behind it?"
    "But why once? I guess I can't see them, no. If you want
a sexual relationship, purely for sex, why would you expect the first time to be any good? What if it was just scary,
nervous, or ridiculous in some way. What if the earth
didn't move?"
    "You speak from experience."
    "Not very much. I speak mostly from intuition and
common sense, plus a *little* experience. You have to be
comfortable."
    "So then. You are not interested in my proposal?"
    "In the one-shot plan? Not for my sake, no. It sounds
like the old conquest ritual. A score, you know."
    "Oh but not at all. My respect for you is enormous—"
    "I know that, Oscar."
    "I am clumsy, I realize, and this is foolish the way I
present it. I am only trying to be honest with you, in your
own style of directness. I have considered the matter a
great deal and I reached the conclusion. To be with you
once, in reality, will free me from the *dream* of being with
you. You see, I cannot explain it. Not right now, maybe in
a minute."
    "No, I get it. It isn't such a crazy idea, either. And even

if I'm not interested in it for my own sake, I would do it if you think it is absolutely important to you. Why not?"

"What? You would do this?"

"I don't mind. I am fond of you."

"But it isn't horrible? Grotesque?"

"Not that at all. It's just sex. Something a person will do, with other people, a certain amount. Which is not to say I would do it with anyone. Far from it."

"You would do it for me, however. Not for your sake or for our sake."

"For you. That's right."

"As a favor."

"I am fond, very much so, but not exactly in that way. So yes—for you, as a favor. As in the old expression, granting sexual favors, I suppose."

"Caddy, this is not the way I expected our Big Talk to go."

"What did you expect?"

"That you would laugh at me and say no. And then I would lie and pretend I wasn't being serious. And you would know I was lying."

"Is that what you wanted me to say?"

"No. I wanted to be with you, one time. That's what I wanted. But you make it sound silly."

"It *is* silly."

"Yet you would do it—for me."

"I said so."


Started a temperature on Friday night and by next morning I felt like a rotting cheese. At first I thought it was emotional, and would subside if I slept. So I did and woke up 102. Left alone with my thoughts, by Caddy, and I was too sick to think them.

You can ignore a broken bone, or a cold in your nose, but fever is tough. Fever ignores all protest. And I am a man who has had few illnesses yet has always known how to take his illness seriously. Lying in a room with fever, I am easily convinced I'm in my death throes. Even as a boy this was true of me. It was never I will regain my strength tomorrow and run out to play with the Sondsheim Twins. Always—It's over, I am sinking fast, better bring me in the ginger-ale quick.

Heaven can wait, however. Ginger-ale did the trick again, along with thirty hours sleep. So tonight I'm good and will work tomorrow, and as for my thoughts I feel no urge to hurry. Such an issue could not be decided on the spot, at least not decided in the positive, and yet I can feel that something's gained. It's a giant step forward to have spoken my piece and not only that, to have Caddy reply, Fine by me. It's like a winning ticket in your vest pocket— you know you can cash it anytime.

Kiss goodbye to Caddy on Friday, kiss goodbye to my friend the fever today and enter this resolve tonight—I will let it sit one week. Let it percolate. And then I will call a meeting to discuss the particulars, me myself and I.

Back to the club after my weekend of unmitigated misery and the boys thought I was out living the high life. When I called in sick both days they were sure they had me dead to rights on the Mann Act, fleeing across state lines. One thing—my reputation as a ladies' man is safe with these two.

"Surprised you came back," says Wiley.

"Yes," says the Duke of Kent, "We thought you found a new niche in life."

Naturally I issued a denial across the board, but a denial in the face of these guys is like a losing parimutuel slip on a windy day. The unvarnished fact is I took sick. I never ran off and would not do so if invited—I have a job here. I also had 102.5 Fahrenheit on Saturday and no papers to prove it.

"So what if she *could* be your grand-daughter," consoles Wiley, "as long as she *isn't*."

No alternative but to take it on the chin, keep a dignified face on, jump into my livery and get to work. They'll get over it on their own.


The place Caddy has gone, called Swarthmore, I never even heard of. Why not Harvard Yale, I asked her, and she replies this place is even better! I will check it out when I get up to the library—wherever she goes it ought to be the best.

In the meantime it is as she predicted, life goes ahead and as a matter of fact goes very nicely. There is a little trick in the air that makes me feel younger (or maybe it was losing five pounds in bed with fever)—something special. It's a Munich Oktoberfest air, the top of the line. Not that I'm crazy to be young again. I would just as soon stick.

According to The Post it's about time to be putting shoe polish on my hair, to battle the "autumnal gray." No thanks. My grandfather's hair was snow-white and soft, like goose-down, at the age of twenty-eight and he never put shoe polish. His went white all at once, overnight, when he lost a baby. (Born dead.) A sensitive man, I'm sure, and such things can occur. Glimpse a ghost and your hair stands up straight as a picket fence.

Regardless, I didn't wake up with white hair when Caddy Moore vanished from my sight. I just got sick, from something I ate at the Horn and Hardart. I can't say I'm happy that she is in the state of Pennsylvania—just happy to be alive, to be myself exactly and no one else. Say it's the "autumnal air" but I also know my mental health is unshakable. I have proof.

Because it was trash day here and I came back from breakfast to put out my bags. Just as I am squashing my contribution down into the barrel, my instinct alerts me—

air raid! Sure enough, there is my friend the halfwit up in his windowframe with a nice ripe bag on the launching pad.

"Hold your fire! Listen, can't you walk? You have no legs up there?"

I hope he has legs. The minute I spouted it out, occurred to me for the first time that maybe he has not. Would they put a disabled war veteran on the fourth floor? The day we had a small fire at the house, this piece of work never appeared on the street.

Legs or no legs, he thinks I am a real comic. Up there laughing at me, so I take another crack at it. "You aren't as accurate as you think, with your potshots. And what about the rest of us." Laughs again and sends the slop. His bag tears apart and out rolls the ripe salami, egg-shells, tin cans of tuna—all the usual fare. The man is a nut, a loobie. He is a character not subject to Robert's Rules of Order.

And what do I do? Do I rant and rave and call the cops? Not me, I pick up after him. Figuring it's like the people on relief. Some cannot feed themselves, so we do it. Others feed themselves all right, but can't manage to clean up afterwards. So we do it.

Such is the state of my mental health, that nothing can shake me. I am on the upswing, a philosopher of the city streets. Throw your garbage at me, what the hell, I'll tidy it up. Leave me ten cents tip on a $25 tab, it's no big deal, life goes ahead.

Could be an error, no doubt, the tip. One of those slobs who leaves a puddle of cash on the table. Wiley calls these your trick-or-treat tippers because you never know, it could be good. Sorted out by Sid at the bar, however, the overage on this one was one thin dime. I thought Sidney would weep.

I had no choice but to console him. It's really no problem, I said, my pockets are overflowing with money, I hit the Double pretty big today.

A white lie, and he probably knows I never bet the Double. I could say to him "I don't need it," but Sid understands "I got it" much better. I don't need it, means nothing to him.

Yet another perfect morning. Shirts to Wing Wang, fish breakfast too good to be true, and no one I know in the obituaries. Air so sweet you could breakfast on that, if you were some kind of poet.

Feeling sensational and at the same time still sticking to my deal—don't even examine emotions until Caddy is absent one full week. Not that I need an analysis to know what I feel. I'm as happy as a colt in an April meadow in old Kentucky. The question is why.

A piece of mail from Linda this morning and a nice surprise too. When I saw it I concluded at once a wedding invitation and I was right with Eversharp. She invites her old friend Oscar, her favorite schnorer, to come snore at her wedding to the butcher's boy. Mentions her lovely summer, two weeks at the Delaware shore with her girlfriend, and now the new school year etcetera. And that's all she wrote—just a friendly note of hello, keeping in touch.

I like this note a lot. Makes me feel much better about our whole business. We cleared a way for friendship. Doing it more than once, yes, but only the first time counted, in my book.

A week expired and I went to examine my emotions. The first thing, of the first importance to me, is to know was she being truthful, was she truly willing. A girl is no guinea-pig, and least of all this girl—but was she truthful? She knows me, after all, and could know that a Yes would make the matter more clear to me than a No. No only makes you wish for Yes, whereas Yes can make you think again.

I believe in her sincerity. No one told her she was required to care about me, or what my private preferences might be. So what if I hoped for a Yes? A girl like that, there will be a line around the block, stretching twenty thirty years at least, of those who would love to hear Yes. Doesn't mean she has an obligation to worry about it and smooth all the feathers. She must care, personally.

And I know she doesn't fib. What do I know about her any better than that? It's not her way. She likes to be direct and what could be more so than to acknowledge she does not want to do it, yet will for my sake? It is silly, she says, but still it is all up to you. How could that be a lie?

The decision is clear. It's not a lie or a trick, yet by making it possible to be in bed with her, she made it impossible. She showed how wrong it was. Not wrong because of anyone's birthday or his social background, wrong because it's contrived. It didn't happen. If it should have happened, it would have. It still could, in theory, only it won't since there is nobody now who wants it to happen.

So what becomes of my crush? Caddy is more lovely in my eyes than ever. Such a caring heart, and I have nothing but praise and adoration for her and now she is again among the missing just as she was in August when my heart swung like a boulder inside my chest, and bruised and ached, and so I ask why does it not ache now? Why do I feel lighthearted and happy, if I agree to leave her be? And I do not know the answer, it's that simple. I haven't got a clue.

Changed my mind tonight. It's a good thing I didn't fire off a telegram to Pennsylvania cancelling my order. As far as she knows I took it under advisement and I'm still advising. True enough—tonight's advice is forget last night's advice, it was bad.

What's the argument for suffering a loss like that, when you could instead just go have it. And what *nice* it would be. Sure she voted 51% and not 99.9, but 51% is all it takes in a democracy. Say Ehrlich calls in an order for fifty cases of Lowenbrau—do you send him away if he lets slip that he almost didn't call this week? Certainly not. You ship him the beer fast, before he changes his mind.

What leads me astray on the subject of sex is logic. You try to be logical and to understand. What's the big deal, you say, everyone is naked inside their clothes—as though that makes it null and void. Or when I dreamed my bare girl on the windowsill and awoke thinking okay that's good enough, because you know what it looks like even without seeing.

It's not the same. You cannot be logical on the subject of sex—that's the whole point. It is not a logical subject and if it was no one would bother with it. If you saw yourself in the mirror, doing it, would you expect it to make any sense or to look good? It isn't even emotional, it's physical, like hunger. You might not enjoy watching yourself eat in the mirror either, but do you weigh the pros and cons of your daily bread?

With sex you try to figure the angles, make decisions, and they don't work. You try to get on top of it and can't—it gets on top of you. Does what it does and that's that. So you can forget logic. Flesh has a different reality when it is in the flesh, even if it shouldn't.

Witnessed the return of Billy the Roof today, his first visit to the racetrack in a year. He was out of town, starting a new life, as in the gospel according to Caddy Moore. They trained him to run a machine that prints a circuit, something new he says and I didn't catch the details. Free training in exchange for a minimum of two years on the job. Unfortunately Billy does not like the work now, finds himself sitting in a basement room in Yonkers all day.

"At least it's not the Roof."

"Hell no," he says, "it's the fucking basement."

"Only at first, maybe. You work your way upstairs."

"I can't see taking two years of it, Oscar. No way."

I looked at him and I saw a criminal. Cannot explain this, but I saw a man who was once a criminal, forgot about it, and must very soon begin to consider that option in life again. And really it is to his credit he didn't think of it first, instead of this job in the basement.

"View it as security. People are losing their jobs every day, there's a recession they say. And you can't."

"Too bad! But tell me about yourself, Oscar. You were getting out of the beer business as I recall."

I told him my life as a waiter, so that he could join in the chorus and tell me I am too good for such undignified labor. He just nodded his head, however, and smiled his old blond-haired smile—the one that kept me from ever suspecting he hated the Roof. Maybe anything sounded good to him at this point.

"Well anyway it's great to be back here on a day like this. Like old times. I feel the best I've felt in years, right this very minute, I mean."

"Me too, Billy. It's the air."

"I told them I had The Flu. To get out of working today. You get it?"

I got it after he told me. Asian Flu is going to the post today in the third and Billy will take a ticket on him for the sake of honor, so he can truthfully say "I had The Flu" this after. So you can tell a white truth as well as a white lie in this life.

Billy of course may just be a sourball, who doesn't like it whatever he does. Could be he was spoiled by the life of crime, big money for short hours. In fact yes—that's what

220

he looks for at the racetrack too. In any case I wished him well and gave him Big Sir in the fifth on condition he keep it under his hat. It's easy to start a run out here, as always everyone has an eye and an ear on everyone else.

I am getting to be a regular on the Staten Island Ferry, I just don't keep regular hours. I commute without working, so for this one passenger it's a cruise—neverending luxury cruise. I step off the boat briefly, in accordance with the rules, then hop right back on return trip. Costs me nothing really, to ride the waves all I like, whereas to put a boat on the water myself would cost a small fortune and provide headaches galore.

My boat is on the water already, fully insured. When I want to go out in it, I go, and someone else gasses it up. My private captain keeps an eye out for small craft and there is a bar if I wish to have a drink on deck. You can't beat this arrangement. Some men like to fish from a boat and you cannot cast a line from the Staten Island Ferry, but I am not one of those men—a Fulton Street fisherman strictly.

Today on the boat I put the question of Caddy Moore to myself on this basis: if she arrived tonight on the bus, what would you wish to do? And I don't mind not having the answer. I know that I can't know, and how's that for genius? A genius doesn't waste his time where there is no answer to be found, he sits down with The Morning Telegraph and goes after one that can.

An ocean seen up close is an overwhelming thing and yet it is peaceful. You can very easily imagine dying in that water—just lean over the rail in the dark and it will chill your soul. But close your eyes and hear it slap the side of the boat, and rock it, and nothing could bring you more peace. You relax and pass some time without—in my opinion—wasting any.

By which I mean that not everyone has a mission in life every day. A lawyer defending the innocent, yes, or a doctor healing the young. A schoolteacher. These are some who have an important place and what they do counts for something. Many others, however, do what they do solely in order to keep eating and sleeping in comfort, and stay dry when it rains. They don't change the world, they only keep it going, by selling you a frankfurter or fixing the heel of your shoe.

Even just by standing upon the surface of the earth, or floating across the water, they are participating, and sometimes that is enough. There are a lot of men at the racetrack, for example, who conceive of themselves as having two jobs—making the money is one job and enjoying it (spending) is the other. They don't feel like they failed in life because they didn't cure polio, so long as they are taking care of their own.

"See—I still exist!"

That's the whole postcard. Six words in all, counting the valediction "Love, Caddy." But the girl makes a point precisely.

Caddy writes again, twice inside a week, to say she won't be coming around in the month of October after all. She has mid-term examinations to study for and so proposes we get together over the Thanksgiving holiday. May she phone me up, she inquires, and I say what the hell, let her phone. Maybe we can sit in the Horn and Hardart and hold another serious powwow. Though I am not in a very serious mood these days. (And have not gone near that place since my 102.5.)

But I think of her much as the meeting draws toward a conclusion. Last year I went down to watch them closing up—sweeping out the stalls, hosing down the cinder paths, boarding up on shed row. A lot of horse's asses in trailers, truckloads of tack on the move, and one swipe tossed a load of oats into an empty stall. "Why not let the rats have a jolly winter," he says, and adds a forkful of hay for good measure. No place like home, even for a rat.

Too bad Caddy will miss the last racing dates. (Too bad for me.) Something tells me she won't be back. I don't mean Thanksgiving weekend, she will be back then and she will call me too. But in the spring, in April, she won't be at Jamaica, and she won't be seen again thereafter. That's my opinion anyway, and as usual I would be willing to bet on it.


The boat again tonight, my private yacht for a spin on the sea. They were almost empty on the return trip. I got a strange feeling that the whole harbor was an island of water, surrounded by land, rather than the reverse. Then a moment later the opposite feeling—an open road of water all the way to Europe and the moon marked it out with a strong white line.

An urge to cross. Never glimpsed it, never even took the trouble to imagine what it might be like over there— Poland, Russia, Land of the Four Bears, my father would tease me. It's all changed, God knows that, the old country is a lot older now after the Germans did their work. But still I would like to look at it, and let the record show that before tonight I never had the urge. (And the urge may be gone by tomorrow.)

It would take real money, though. Not for two nickels does one travel abroad to the old country. And in any case the right way to go there would be with Tanya, who *has* been there and has imagined it many times since. Better with her than alone, or for that matter with anyone else. Who else? I mean for an occasion of that sort, who else.

Reminds me, when her brother Daniel arrived in New York, we took him in. And instructions were, leave him be—which I did. By and by, however, I had the idea he should work. Not that I minded in the least funding him, but that he should for his *own* sake, work to forget his troubles.

And I said, I could give you work, get you work, whatever. And he looked at me. He never said a lot, Daniel, before that day or lately either, but after I mentioned work he never said boo to me for two years solid. I racked my brain and thought Jesus, how does a man get a size twelve shoe out of his mouth, and I never. I was sure he was giving me the Silent Treatment.

It wasn't so, as I found out later—all that time I bore a cross and it turns out he didn't even recall the conversation, probably never heard what I said. He was giving the whole world the Silent Treatment, that's all. The world gave him grief and he gave it back the Silent Treatment.

But I remember later that first year Tanya said she wanted someday to go back, and to see Poland after all the horror and Daniel looked at *her.* Same look. And I thought Uh oh, she's in for the Silent Treatment too now, but Tanya said to him, "Don't give me that look, Daniel, I had enough of that face the summer you were five. You don't give me that look."

And instead of the Silent Treatment he laughed and hugged his sister and cried. First time he laughed in America, I'm quite certain.


Visited the library on my day off, and watched a movie near mid-town. At the library I researched the fate of Widmer, the wandering doctor, which I meant to do long ago. Found him on a microfilm with the help of Mrs.

Kearney's friend and there he was, including a picture. An old guy. Defrocked, a suspended sentence, and he has to make good on the money. So it shows you can mistreat your loved ones without fear of reprisal but you can't mistreat the insurance company. I hope he finds work as a waiter.

It seems a long time ago I went. Seems a long time ago that Caddy went too. Times mixes and mingles things up when you spend your time alone and walking. I like that, however, as it is highly conducive to my thoughts. Mickey Klutz says he can get me a good television set for forty dollars and I told him no thanks for now, because I know it keeps you indoors. In January February I can see it—a friend in the dark, a little harmless entertainment. It can also seduce you from the world, however. The boat, the park, even the busy streets—I love it all so long as I am not freezing my ears off.

Anyway, I am in training now for the Olympics—heel-toe walking event. They showed a newsreel today of this year's winner, moving along like a turkey with a stick up his ass. I could beat this guy right now, walking to Penn Station and back, watch my dust. I prefer to take my time, of course, and think my thoughts, but for the Olympic competition I could make an exception.

A break in the Jimmy Myers case at last. Sergeant Fish working the day shift out of homicide! Actually the squirt came up and confessed to me—I never had a clue.

Back in summer, right after our day together at Belmont Park, this poor kid picked up a five-dollar bill on my table. My fault for leaving it lying about—any kid would find it hard to resist. It would not constitute stealing, only weakness, from wanting it too much.

My sister at age five had a favorite doll, Emmy. (Amazing that after all these years the doll's name should come back to me.) Anyway one thing that Florrie would do was drop her lucky penny—always soaked in vinegar and polished till it looked like freshly minted copper—in the big front apron pocket. And this penny she would steal.

Could not resist it. She would go to sleep with the penny safe in Emmy's pocket and wake up with the penny inside her fist. And always confess by the dawn's early light. In my ignorance of the fact that dolls were real and had feelings that were easily bruised, I thought she was a little crazy about this penny that was after all hers. She would cry and beg forgiveness and she would swear to Emmy it won't happen again. But it would.

Knowing all this and blaming myself as well, I would never hold it against my little pal Jimmy. I would have been smart and fair and liberal with him, except that his guilt was so great I never got the opportunity. He hid out from me and that five-dollar bill was the only reason why. I could have killed him when I found out, though not for theft. For silliness, and waste of our time together.

Why he came to own up was a mystery at first. Why not surrender early in the game, and skip the suffering, or else never surrender at all. And the part that *he* could not understand was why I didn't want to scream at him. His mother screams so much at so little provocation that the kid feels cheated when taken into custody by liberals.

"Aren't you going to teach me a lesson?" he says.

"What lesson? You learned it."

"About taking money."

"Tell me this, do you take it from home?"

No response, not even the Fifth Amendment. It's a separate jurisdiction maybe, and he needs to first consult his attorney.

"Well then *if* you take it from home, do you give it back?"

"No."

"Yet my five dollars you return. Why?"

"I never meant to keep it, to steal it I mean. But I lost it. Spent it anyways. And I never got five dollars all at once again till now."

"I believe you. So you don't need a lesson you already know. If you are here to make amends, that proves you gave yourself the lesson without help. And someone who learns by himself, a smart boy, might deserve a little reward, no?"

No. I tried to give him a dollar bill, but I was in the wrong to do this and he would not accept the money. I didn't insist. Maybe he thought I was testing him for greed still. Or just his sense of honor—presents himself for punishment due, not for reward and praise. And I should oblige and punish him, except I can not, I am so glad he came clean with me.

"But tell me this, my friend. If you know to bring my money back, why don't you bring your father's money back too? What's the difference?"

"I don't know. What?"

"I'm asking."

"I don't know."

"As far as *I* know, there isn't any difference, so if you can manage to figure one out, let me know. Meanwhile I thank you very much for your honesty, sir, and can I offer you a cold drink?"

I bring out the lemonade on a small cork tray (one of two I took home when Sid was getting rid of them last week), up over the shoulder in the classic form. Even with the finest service, however, he drinks guilty. He is not yet purged, merely confessed. Doesn't ask for a single refill, so I'm stuck with the rest of this batch.


A busy night of dreaming. Most are gone—you throw them back in and shovel sleep over them—but the last one sticks. It was Caddy showing up at my place, in the very early morning, with a wild look of danger in her eye. An expression I never saw there, to be truthful, nor in anyone else's eye either. Out drinking all night and feeling restless, she comes to demand *her* hour in bed with me. Gets in the bed, too, geared for action—hip naked under her coat like Miss Rheingold in Saratoga.

I will not try logic on this one. It's sex and it's a dream, two strikes against. But I kicked her out and sent her home. She looked like a kid to me—the Caddy that was in the dream looked a kid to the me that was in the dream. Left with tears on a dirty face, just as Jimmy did yesterday, and in fact the faces got switched out in the hallway so that she *was* Jimmy going down the stairs. Like I say, forget logic with a dream.

I won't say it constitutes a decision. A dream does not try to clarify, it tries to confuse. But I will record another dream I experienced twice before, in which the sex did take place. I am one of the principals involved but the other one isn't Caddy, it's Tanya Lehman—my wife as I knew her in school. (The black coat and lace-up boots exactly.)

And it is very odd that a dream can steal your virginity (which she kept as long as she kept Lehman, I happen to know) and yet not tamper with your black overcoat or the front stoop of your father's house in Brooklyn.

Funny looks I'm getting at the ferry-slip. You would think a regular commands a little respect. Instead I am a suspect. Of insanity perhaps, like the ones who ride IRT all day with no destination in mind. Or of criminal activity. I could be dropping off a load of opium every day at Stapleton, then coming straight back to make my daily deposit at the Chase Manhattan. That's how they eyeball me down there, as though I'm Albert Anastasia. No one understands a man of leisure, who happens to exist in harmony with the stars, so I must be up to something fishy.

Nothing could be farther from the truth. I'm a real straight-shooter, honest John, hardly even betting my money at the racetrack these days. I have a nice time but am too lazy to handicap. I lack ambition. I am content. I'll stick. (Wiley speaks: "Last is not least unless it's less.")

I might be looking for winter work and I might not. It has to fit my schedule of free mornings and free evenings, and it requires a majority vote. I can wait till spring if necessary, though I would prefer to work a shift and keep my hand in. Last winter I stayed in the cave, this year I am feeling more sociable.

Not in the mornings sociable, however, or the evenings. In the *afternoons* sociable, so invite me to high tea. I'll bring along the watercress sandwiches.


A very remarkable telephone call, just concluded, from Caddy long distance. Of course I was delighted by the call and protested the expense. She says she has a trick for cutting out the phone company, getting the call for free. No one minds putting one over on the Bell Boys but I doubt you really can—they know all the tricks and then some.

But what a conversation to have and on a public wire. We must have burned a pigeon's ear with this one, at the very least. I never said such things in my life, much less over the telephone to another state.

"You haven't written me once," she says, "so I had no choice but to call you."

"To learn your fate?"

"To say hello and hear about the stable. And learn my fate—I almost forgot our half-hour of sin."

"Caddy I don't think you can even joke about these topics over the telephone wire."

"Sure you can. It's a free country. You can definitely talk about it on the telephone, Oscar, though I'm not sure you can *do* it on the telephone."

"Definitely not legal to do it, telephone or otherwise."

"Says who?"

"Just read your morning paper. Oh they agree that if you suppress it, ignore it, don't get it, then you're a mess. But they also agree that you should not do it when you're young, can not do it when you're old, and you better not do it without your wife, so who isn't a mess? One man in twenty? What do you think, really?"

"I don't know. I'm not old enough to vote. And my mother says I'm too young to even know my own mind."

"Yes well I'm 98.6 and I don't know either. Why not a prostitute?"

(Cannot explain how we got going like this, but we did, and kept going, word for word.)

"No reason, I guess. I mean, if you want one."

"Correct. If."

"So?"

"So do I? I don't sometimes and sometimes I do. Or I think that I should—that it's healthy."

"It's normal, anyway. It's what men do, I think. But why not a woman, Oscar? I mean, one who isn't a prostitute?"

(This trick—she leaves herself out of the equation and so do I, and it's not a problem. She is not bootlegging a message past me, just talking.)

"Can't meet one. And if I do then I'm stuck. I mean that she isn't a prostitute only, she's also a woman."

"You mean that she wants to eat dinner and go out to the movies."

"But exactly. That's *exactly* what she wants to do. Not approximately, you understand—exactly." (Linda Stanley.)

"And you value your solitude."

"I seem to, yes. I'm sure I don't know why."

"It really doesn't matter why, does it? Well I vote for the prostitute as long as you tell me all the details afterwards."

"I'm frightened of them."

"Sure you are. They know what's going to happen and

you don't. But if you find out, then I'll know too."

In this same vein to the end—it's serious and it's all a joke. And excepting the very start, when she cites our half-hour of sin, there is no mention of ourselves. Nothing. We slipped right past it somehow, but unanimously. Maybe the old man hit the hobnail on the head again: take your time and everything will take care of itself naturally. Save the work and skip the agony, that's the old man's daily double.

Nashua easy as pie in the Gold Cup. I like this horse, and not because he made me money. I did that myself, with help from the dumb bunnies. How anyone could find another horse to bet at the two miles is far beyond my feeble powers of comprehension, though I will say this: if there was no one stupid there would be no one smart either, because you don't need Einstein to know it's all relative. That's parimutuels in a nutshell, so be glad for the dumb bunny and be kind enough to accept his dumb money. They cover a genius like myself with glory.

You hear some talk of Swaps as Horse of the Year, but it's bunk until he beats this guy and I don't see his people too eager for a shot at it. Once burnt, twice shy, especially at a distance. Swaps is a speed horse, a Hollywood character. Nashua is a worker, a winner. He carried a lot more weight in this race than he carried here last year, yet lowered his time nicely. Show him Swaps again and he'll run through a brick wall with a piano strapped to his back.

Responded to Caddy's complaint by dropping her a line about the Gold Cup—the inside story.

A fire off Coentes Slip round ten o'clock last night. I heard the fire-boats coming and saw everyone run for the docks, so I took myself up the metal staircase to the roof, to gain the Pisgah view. It's twenty degrees colder on top and a freezing wind blasts off the open water, but it was worth it standing ringside for this battle of the monsters.

In this corner a huge tanker showing a sheet of fire off one flank, and dark gray rolling smoke. The surface of the waves aflame and voices among the mixed lamps on the water yelling Get back, back up, she's gonna blow any second. She didn't, though, just kept on burning.

While in the other corner, hailing from the boat basin on the Hudson side, a pair of big fire-boats that parked a couple hundred feet off the Slip and launched twin geysers at the fireball. Gigantic streams of heavy water—you saw them arching across the harbor like foam rainbows and you heard them thump against the burning boat.

They got it snuffed, then it flared again, then snuffed for good. Winner and still champion, Bertha III. Quite an achievement to make a fire extinguisher like that, but I guess you better if you already made a boat that holds half a million gallons of oil—and leaks. They do incredible things every day in this city, always some new structure is scraping the sky, yet something's lost when something's gained—these monsters are a little out of control.

Anyway the smoke kept rolling through the neighborhood streets all night, so that you tasted it on your tongue. And it stank, like a cheap kerosene. Came right in through your closed windows, of course, and I wondered if it could spontaneously combust. It was still there in the a.m., doing nothing spontaneous but drenching and fouling the air, and though I fled down to South Street early, to the diner, I found it there too, naturally enough.

At the scene of the crime, Coentes Slip, I saw the ship burnt on one side, blackened, and the waves oily. Otherwise no sign—nothing to show that monsters had clashed in the dark.

It's tonight and the taste of kerosene is still on my tongue. In my dinner, everywhere. Maybe the chill can knock it out—they say temperatures maybe below freezing this week. So starts the cocoa season, and I had Jimmy and sister Bea for treats and a game of checkers.

Many times I offered to play him and he refused—doesn't go for "games like that." (Me neither, but there is no one to play chess with.) But now sister wants a game and he changes his mind. I should make him stand in line for such stinky behavior, except I am going very easy for a while. His conscience is still too soft and until he forgets the five dollars I believe it's best to spoil him.

How will I know he forgot? Easy: when he is a hog again. As long as remains polite and turns down a second donut, I will know he's feeling guilty, like nothing belongs to him anymore. Except me, when sister is in sight.

The one single most charming aspect of Caddy is her honesty. Saying what she means and meaning what she says. (Also the best proof she was willing to go with me one time, for one hour, solely for the sake of my peace of mind.) And such calm, to assume the act will not ruin her life, such an unselfish attitude. The truth is I am proud of her. In examining my emotions that's what I find more than anything else. Not left lonely, or sadly disappointed in love, but proud. I will write again to tell her so.

It is rare to be so honest, to always speak the truth aloud. Not everyone will out-and-out lie, yet very few will consistently speak the truth out loud. Doesn't usually pay. Even look at myself and my wife during all those years. I am an honest man, I think so, but you do not say what's on your mind because it's pointless. Nothing changes.

If it stands a particular way between people, it stands that way for reasons, the natural shaking down of personalities. So if you complain and get a change put into law, it's only a superficial change and never a change of heart. If you have No Complaints, then at least no one is blaming *you*.

Tanya's brother had a bitter time, an unspeakable tragedy visited him. He must have been a different man beforehand, because he led a different life. Wife and the two children in Poland, active in the Resistance, a speaker on public occasions, prominent citizen who kept a dozen chickens in his backyard and grew a garden. When he came to the U.S. bereft of his family, Daniel had nothing to say. And he still has nothing to say ten years later.

For a few years, 1948 to 1952 I would say roughly, he went around with a nice woman named Irma, a tall sophisticated lady who worked at a magazine uptown. Daniel was a sophisticated man himself, of course, university-trained, a professional engineer. They were "friends" and never married and in 1952 she died at the age of forty-six. Another tragedy for him, disease. Since then there has been no one that I know of.

He works like a dog, makes a load of money, and never sees a friend. He never comes round to visit except on holidays when we plead, and then he sits quiet, nothing to say. Makes an effort with the children, my nieces and nephews, but hides behind language to keep it simple. I happen to know he talks perfect English—I have heard him on the telephone on a business call more than once now. It's a different Daniel—precise and quick and *pushy*.

He won't heal. He doesn't want to heal. To do so would be unfaithful to his past and his principles. The world does not merit Daniel's forgiveness, but what about him? He deserves something from himself. And also what about me? I never get close to this brother. I don't even try because it would be too *difficult*. Mind your own business, says Tanya, and I appreciate her point of view. Yet the man is suffering.

Not that I hold it in my power to cure Daniel Lehman, whose sole ailment is reality, but I could go thirty forty years and never utter the truth—that I love him, that I worry and care, and yes that I am very curious to know more about the War and Hitler and the camps. That I want to hear from him, and to help him.

Sure I might fail to help, but it is also a failure not to try. It is like not caring. So we could go through life like two lanes on the highway, close together, same direction, and yet we never touch. It's very sad to me.

And Caddy Moore would not let it happen. She is only a child, full of high spirits and high hopes. Illusions I'm sure. She might cure my brother-in-law all the same—she might unlock his heart by being simple, and saying whatever comes to mind. Where I think, Be careful not to jog an unhappy memory, she would not think at all.

She would say, Tell me. How did it happen, such a terrible thing, and how does it feel? She might make him want to tell, although Daniel I admit is a tough nut to crack. A stone.


I'm sure that two lovers can miss like ships in the night. As with baseball, it's a game of inches. Tanya and I had been in the same room (and as it turned out very much alive in each other) and yet we nearly missed altogether. We both know how close I came to never even saying hello, much less "Will you have me?"

Caddy will never miss out that way. She will know it when she sees it and she will speak up, straightaway, the whole truth and nothing but the truth. A rare child.


I interviewed this morning, on DePeyster Street. The title is Superintendent, for two apartment buildings, fourteen units, make your own hours. That's why I answered it—good location, good pay, and your own hours.

The work I don't mind. Locks, garbage, stray cats, plus a little janitorial. But he says I am to be "on call"—someone has a problem, they phone me up and I come running. This I don't feature. The trouble-shooter, have mop will travel. That ain't my idea of make your own hours.

I reasoned with him. How's about no emergencies. A real emergency you call in the police or the fire department, anything else can wait a day. What about no hot water, he says. Heat up a pot on the stove in that case, that's how it used to be done. That's how we did it in my family, even after I was born I remember. By the time Florence was born we had running hot water, though. It was so hot my mama would let it run half a minute and then put it in a cup with her tea-ball.

This job is mine on his terms, not mine otherwise. Fair enough, I told him, and call me if you change your mind. I changed my own since this morning, however—I don't want it anyway. Who needs it? You might meet a few nice people and you might not. But if you do it will never be high tea with muffins, it will be fix the lights, fix the sink, and fix the cat while you're at it, she just dropped another litter down in the coal-cellar.


While I seek one new career for myself, Jimmy is seeking two. He is torn. On the one hand he's becoming a comedian, who writes his own jokes.

"If a train is a choo-choo, what's half a train?"

"A choo."

"Gesundheit!"

Wunnerful wunnerful. He has a dozen of these and he works on them, to perfect his timing. (But expects you to find it just as funny on the tenth time through.) All his pals are learning jokes, asking one another why the moron threw the alarm clock out the window and so forth, but only Jimmy cooks up his own recipes. So he's invested and Bee-bee better laugh or she gets a kick in the shins from him. She laughs, to avoid the kick, and he is convinced it was very funny. A genuine despot.

His alternative career, a strongman. I am not sure how he will parlay this into a living, though I know he plans to be Mr. America, the one and only, and endorse Wheaties or Strongman Toothpaste. A true believer, Jimmy. He got his hands on a pamphlet that preaches flexing the muscles. Look in the mirror and flex, sit at your desk and flex—every moment spent relaxing is a moment lost and never to be regained. Jimmy sits in my room with his jaws flexed and his palms pushing against each other (never failing to overturn the sugar bowl) and his legs tense. He's an eel. A skinny strip of bone and muscle who barely feels free to borrow a hand from himself when it's time to move the checkermen.

Worse, he is a proselytizer. It's not enough he should be a strongman, he wants me to be one too. Checks my biceps: not too bad, he pronounces, but could be better.

"Jimmy, you know what? I'm not worried about anyone kicking sand in my face at the beach. I don't go to the beach."

"Someone could assault you in a dark alley."

"I don't go in dark alleys either."

"Come on, Oscar, danger is lurking everywhere. A man has to be ready for it."

"You're right, I'm sorry. A man must be ready. But let me flex in private, later on."

I played a little game with myself, a guessing game— what will Jimmy Myers be when he grows up. His old man is a security cop, Federal Reserve on Liberty Street. A standing-around job, Jimmy won't go for that. He is his own hero anyway, and will strike out in some new direction. Definitely has the chutzpah to be a comic, and the will to become Mr. America the muscleman. Anything. But I had a terrible thought from this game I played.

Possibly because I had Daniel on my mind a lot lately. But whatever he might be, or could be, there is also a damned good chance a kid like this will be killed in war. A good shock I gave myself because it's true—he is the kind that does. However smart he will not be a college boy and he isn't a shirker, he'll want to stick his nose into something.

Adventure! See the World! Join the Army! He could join it Monday, be a hero Tuesday, and get blown up on Wednesday morning. I am upset to entertain the thought, yet won't blink it, that life for many kids is just the dance of death.

Jimmy very much alive, thank goodness. I had a bad daydream, that's all, and it evaporated in the new morning sunlight. And now that I am unemployed, he seems to be back on a regular schedule. I knew things were running smooth again when he came with me to the final race-date—willing to be seen with me in public!

Of course he was disappointed to miss "the girl with the red horse" so I let him know the girl was in Pennsylvania and the horse was in Maryland, both freshening. Then Wiley put him to work at the waiter-station and placed him on salary. Money is funny. This was nothing alongside the profits from his empty bottle empire. Hear him talk about the easy money in the park, the bottles already collected and waiting in trashcans, and the goldmine at the base of every tree. But now a *salary*.

He is still on the strongman kick. It is his great goal to pick up "thirty pounds of pure muscle" and so he travels each day up to Cortland's Drug Store with a penny to weigh in. As he weighs all of sixty pounds to begin with, it may take him a while to put on the thirty additional, though not for lack of effort. Jimmy interprets the daily reading as constant proof he is not doing enough, and so redoubles his output of flexing and tensing.

I help out by accompanying him to Cortland's and treating him to a malted milk with an egg tossed in (unbeknownst to him, as he has an inflexible rule against the ingestion of eggs) telling him a rich milk drink is how the prizefighters build up weight and muscle. Eat well, train hard.

He will pick up a few pounds I'm sure, and get some muscle tone. As for thirty pounds, that's next year or the year after—when he is taller. No problem. Just a matter of time until he's selling us Strongman Toothpaste on television. And now here's Jimmy Myers for Strongman Toothpaste!

I am offered the chance to travel south, with Mickey Klutz. It's warm, he argues, and the ponies will be running. I told him I would give it some thought, and I did. In fact I already had before he spoke out and I won't preclude the possibility of two weeks in his spare room in February. (Air fare is surprisingly cheap.) For now I'll stick it out. I'm not afraid of winter after all and will be most comfortable down here on the reservation.

Like Herbie. Fullblooded Passamaquoddy Indian from the state of Maine who drove truck for me, and who always took off whenever he got a little cash stockpiled. He would go back home—called "down on the reservation." Conditions were terrible there, with open sewage, unheated shacks, and they would hunt in the woods for their food, or steal it. And booze, of course. But it was home to him and that's where he always went.

I used him when I could, each time he came back around. I knew he would come and go, but I wanted to help him out and whatever went on up there in the forest he never drank on my time. He never missed a single delivery, chipped a fender, or shortchanged anyone a penny, honest injun.

The ambulance was here in the afternoon and they carried Mrs. Vickers down on a stretcher. She was looking pretty bad, maybe the worst. I don't know anything more, although I asked and will keep asking. A very sad business. If she is stuck in the hospital awhile, I have got the time to pay a visit, where others who work might not.

Much colder weather. I brewed up my chicken soup—was hard at it when we heard the siren. Like everything else (including a human being) it's mostly water. Add in whatever you have around, some cold rice, a few potatoes, vegetables, a pound of boiled chicken meat, and of course the salt. I keep tasting it, and nothing I drop in seems to ruin the taste. Simmer till hungry, that's my recipe.

Jimmy had a big portion. I explained him how Jack Dempsey used to train on homemade chicken soup for all his big bouts, and then switched over to red meat for the two Tunney fights. Lost them both before he figured out the problem—he was missing his chicken soup muscles.

I don't mind inventing a little story if it gets him to eat good food. Otherwise he fills up on root beer and licorice, and Strongman Cocoa.

Marconi, the landlord, poking around Mrs. Vickers' flat. Not a good sign, I would have to say.

Mrs. Vickers is dead. A stroke did her in, very sad. Her offspring came here to clear out—two ladies not much younger than myself, arrived together in a Chevrolet.

Dying has to be a trick. When my own mother was in

the hospital and dying day by day, she said, "What if I never see another snow fall?" And she did not.

Yet if she was going in winter she might say instead "I'll never see the dogwoods bloom or the forsythia in Prospect Park." Because it wasn't the snow she planned on missing, it was life. She always hated the sight of snow as a matter of fact, but what you say is determined by the small circumstances, things of the moment, like Tuesday versus Thursday. What you *feel* is determined by larger circumstances, that don't change.

Marconi left a kid in the empty flat with a can of paint, then returned himself with floor oil and a mop. They will wash the windows and double the rent, count on it. Curious who my new neighbor will be.

Caddy on schedule, due back on turkey day. She will call here on Friday morning "to make a plan."

More plans in the offing. Very pleased to hear from Wally Wiley. He has a fistful of tickets for Sugar Ray in the Garden after New Year's and includes me in on the party. Boys night out, he says, a few close friends for dinner and the fights. Jack Dempsey's restaurant, of course, he will buy the dinner and I am to provide cigars for five.

My girl arrives from Pennsylvania to eat turkey at the family estate, and ventures to Manhattan next day to eat tunafish with me in the Horn and Hardart. I love that.

Looking terrific. I never saw her in a coat before, otherwise unchanged. But like a Jew, she came down here just to worry about me. Am I working? Am I happy? What will I do next? I do not worry about her, however—I care, but see no cause for worry. This kid has got what it takes.

Hasn't lost her knack for conversation, either. Whatever it is, she makes you feel it's worth saying, and whatever you say she can convince you said it perfectly. So I spilled out a few of my latest daydreams to her, and went back over the fall racing season, plus Jimmy's big muscle campaign, and she listens, and laughs, and is entertained. Someone like Caddy can be having the time of her life elsewhere and yet still mean it when she says she misses me, and misses the racetrack. She is full of life, that's all, spilling over life. And I can joke with her:

"Tell me, what is the Statute of Limitations on our half-hour in bed together? What if I change my mind?"

"I might change mine too, then."

"I won't ask—you know I'm kidding you. But tell me, do you have a boyfriend at school?"

"Guess. I'll make a pokerface and you guess the truth."

"Some pokerface! I say you have *two* boyfriends with that face, and ate the canary too."

"Some guess. You're off by two boyfriends and a canary, Oscar. You must be a really bad poker player."

"Or else you are a good one."

Like old cohorts we gab, and my heart is perfectly safe. In fact, my heart is uplifted. The die is cast and I don't mind—I cast my share of it. And I *want* her to have a boyfriend, providing he is worthy. I want her to have whatever there is in life, times three. I do not feel jealous or left in the dust, I feel the decision we made was absolutely correct.

Talking of my days as a "steeplechase jockey" at Coney Island, I was amazed to find it was Dutch to her. She never went to Steeplechase Park in her life.

"Then what gave you the idea?"

"Of riding in the steeplechase? Someone told me they let women ride there, that was all. It's the only place that does, really."

"If it does. Better check your facts before you ship out. It might be they run a few races for Ladies Only. Because that's a rough circuit from what I hear. And so was Coney Island, a wild ride. You wouldn't believe this ride—nothing like it in the world. My father was more impressed by this, as an engineering feat, than by the Brooklyn Bridge. The Bridge doesn't *move*, he would say, but look at these horses. And they would go, Caddy, into the buildings, back outside, around the shooting galleries—everywhere, and fast."

"Is it still there?"

"You want to go out and practice your steeplechase technique? I don't know. They would be closed now, in any case, for the season."

"Take me in the summer?"

"Maybe. We'll see. If you're around next summer—and if it is still standing. I don't know."

As with Jimmy Myers and Ebbets Field, I lacked the sense to say a simple No. It's why they didn't elect me mayor, because it's okay to be stupid but you must at least learn something from experience. Why not be direct? The truth is easy and leaves no marks. (Or if it does, it leaves them on the other guy.)

Yet it would seem silly to say at my age, No I can't do it, I am a fugitive from my loved ones, and my friends on Ocean Parkway might see me, not to mention my enemies. Did Tanya settle up across the board? For all I know, I could owe money. But I kept this sour note to myself, and kept our exchanges on the high note.

"I'm ready for your report," she says, "about life in the red-light district."

"Nothing ventured. I finished with red lights when I gave up my Plymouth and took to my feet."

It was so nice of her to come visit me. In New York just four days and everyone wants a piece of her on the Island—school chums, relations, horses and dogs—and yet she journeys down here and even insists on greeting Jimmy.

So she popped a bicep at him, he popped one back, and

they asked me to be the Judge and Jury. A lot of fun, and I had no choice but to call it a draw.

Still feeling elated with Caddy's visit, and with her report on life at college. She has got what she wants there, a "work study" where she helps out at a sanitorium of some kind—old wackos like myself, I bet—and gets a course credit for it. On top of that she has been learning the Russian language, as she prefers the bumpy road.

I doubt they will allow her to ride any horses in England, but she does not doubt it, so maybe she can convince them. For some reason everyone believes there is enlightenment in merry old England, and an English accent means you know it all. How can you have injustice or folly in such a civilized land?

It's bunk. An English accent means you're English, that's all, and they are just the same as us—a box of mixed biscuits. The Russkies too, I'm sure. Why not?

"Is she your new blondie?"

"Is who?"

"The girl with the horse."

"The girl with the horse is closer to your age than mine. She is a friend of mine, that's all. A friend of yours too."

"What happened to your other blondie?"

"Nothing bad. She's a friend of mine too. I just received a Christmas card from her yesterday, as a matter of fact."

"I thought Jews didn't celebrate Christmas."

Straight from the shoulder, with this one too. Maybe he has been taking directness lessons from the girl with the horse.

"That's what she said, on the card. 'I know Jews don't celebrate Christmas, so I'll just say happy holiday season from Linda.'"

"I didn't know her name was Linda. I knew she wasn't a Jew, cause my ma says a blondie can't be a Jew."

"Not usually. Sometimes, though—I do have cousins, blond."

"I like the new one a lot better. She's pretty. And I bet *she* won't send you a stupid card."


Freezing cold in the harbor, a fierce wind and zero sun. It looked like a wild ice-storm was about to break from the sky at any second, so we all felt a little apprehension out on the water. I huddled up behind the glass most of the way, holding onto my hat with one hand and a cup of ice coffee with the other.

Much too cold and windy to read the paper, as a proper commuter should do. Of course I ain't a proper commuter. It's just a short snort of a workday for me—the time it takes to turn the boat around, load a few, and shove off for the mainland.

We passed close up to the garbage scow on our way in, and I got a good look at the captain's face, up front in his look-out house on the tug-boat. A real sea dog, puffing on his pipe and staring out over the water in one of those black-billed hats with the gold insignia.

You could say he is nothing but a garbage-man, although for all I know he is First High Admiral complete with power to wage war on the high seas and marry the willing. What I saw was a contented fellow who wouldn't change places with anyone. Past retirement age already I would guess, but they will have to shanghai this guy to drag him down from his outpost.


Record the new tenant. A man about thirty, possibly less, who works at the Aquarium. Quiet, pleasant fellow, and a bachelor. Jimmy didn't like it at first because he and his gang had gotten their mitts on a key and were using the empty place as a clubhouse after school. Also during, at least once. They would sit in there telling jokes and flexing their muscles, I'm sure, and God knows what else. Then the new man, Hansen, invited the whole bunch to come in free and see the fishes, so now they forgave him for living and are all budding aficionados. Jimmy wants a little tank of his own, with a few goldfish to feed. Time for a career change maybe—after months of flexing he registers a gain of one pound on his good days and sometimes not even that, as he fluctuates. He is stronger I'm sure, but may have a tapeworm inside.

I experienced a wonderful dream—full of wonder, like a masterpiece of painting. Only a picture (a still life), of Caddy on the track with Mandan, in soft sunlight at Jamaica Park.

It was snowing past my window when I awoke and the snow did not seem real. Real was the summer stillness at Jamaica, blue sky on a green crop of trees, and of course the girl. I heated up last night's coffee and took my cup back to bed, and watched the snow dropping down to the street—thin paper flakes like a white ash. I am someone who loves to gaze. Someone who loves the pictures in life.

My next career I'll be a camera. But I do love the pictures I walk past, faces I see, even in the a.m. when nobody smiles and you would guess that all joy was banished from the world. Caddy on a horse, the captain of the garbage barge, the fire-boat geysers—they stay with me in such a nice way. It's why I have come to enjoy walking around. For years I went everyplace in the car, and saw nothing under the sun except concrete and my fellow cars. Now I don't mind an ugly picture either, as long as there are no cars in it.

Life goes along and it doesn't matter, not for the likes of

me. The likes of me can stay in bed drinking coffee. Because in this country a few get more and a few get less but most people get the same deal. An education if they want it, a job, and then you must locate a woman. And enjoy the time to the best of your ability. Life can be exciting, exceptional, for the select few. Caddy for example might make it to England, or the French Riviera, and she might marry the King of Siam and write her memoirs. But most of us are not special that way. I was never going to marry with Grace Kelly or win an Olympic medal, not even in the turkey walk. I am the kind of citizen who must take life as it comes, one day after another, just as I feared. Except it's not so bad.

What you miss out on isn't much. Big bucks, fame, glamor—that's all sad stuff, sets you up for a fall. The little things are what give you grace. The pictures, that anyone walking past can appreciate, like the beautiful child, harbor seas, the hobo in summertime. You are alive and so is everything around you and all you need now is the right cigar to go with it.

I don't mean to say that luxury isn't nice to have. I mean this: your house might cost you thirty thousand dollars and your new sofa three hundred, the suit you wear can run a hundred dollars and the maid fifteen per diem. But the cigar is less than one dollar and the cigar is the luxury.

The rest you toss out, like the eight nags who are fated to lose a horse race. The last horse is the cigar and that's the one you want to have.

Life is a fountain, or so I said last time I scribbled. The Great High Lama knew his stuff after all. But reading it back it sounds like sour grapes, like something an envious man might say to conceal his envy. Whatever it sounds like, it is the truth—I begrudge no one nothing, and least of all Caddy, who is my personal entry in life's sweepstakes. Yes she is the kind who could have it all and may she own it.

The mass of men lead lives of public transportation, says the great sage Wiley, and he means the same as Thoreau meant with his pond in the woods back in tenth grade. Me too. I took no satisfaction until I walked away and I'm sure the ones who stay might suffer. A few will turn to drastic measures to rise above the mass.

How does an everyman grab Page One? Simple. Jump from the top of the latest skyscraper, some hunk of showy architecture, and you might at least die famous. You could also try to get a little something accomplished—walk through a door and shoot an evil man to death. Shoot Hitler, shoot Mussolini, shoot Senator Joe McCarthy. That makes a noise.

And such things will happen but it is a shame for all concerned. This desperation is not necessary, things are not so bad as they seem, and you have to figure it out for yourself. It's a mood, that's all. Yes, life goes along one day after another all the way down to the grave, but listen: it's not the days going along that constitute a problem, it's the grave. The days are fine.

Wonderful to see my friend Wally Wiley. He brought along the others, nice men, knowledgeable, and we ate chops in Dempsey's as planned. I drank a glass of beer, we lit cigars, and strolled to the Garden in fine high spirits. Yelled ourselves hoarse in a meaningless prelim, then settled in for the title fight. A sad event, however.

Ray Robinson was the best ever. I never saw Jack Johnson or some of them, but I saw Dempsey, and Benny Leonard, and Joe Louis, I saw Henry Armstrong fight many times. None was the equal of this guy. A dancer with fast feet, fast hands, a picture boxer who could yet unload the concrete on you with either hand. An artist by reputation well deserved, but a very big hitter too, who kayoed a hundred good fighters, a list of big names, champions. And he was also much tougher than people give him credit. Excepting the night he collapsed from the heat while fighting light-heavy, no one ever stopped this man. Ever.

And he loses his title to this bull by the name of Fullmer. It's nothing against Fullmer. He's got to use what God gave him and God didn't give him much. He can't box, he can't punch, but he is very young and strong. He rushes, he pushes, lunges. He fights like a bread truck, coming at you in the street. After a while you get tired of dodging and hitting and you just get run over.

Robinson never liked to fight this style, yet he always knew how to beat it. Speed. Throw a lot of very precise leather and skip away, like the LaMotta fights. It takes energy, however, and conditioning. You can't get by on half a can.

Sad to see the great man end like that, mauling with this clumsy force, pushing him away all night and trying to lift tired arms. It's five years since he retired—five years ago he had enough. He was old then, or so he decided for himself, and a layoff never helps a fighter. It killed Louis the same way. Being a little old and then the layoff, you come back a *lot* old. Much older than if you never stopped.

What the hell, we all said it. It's only a prizefight and Robinson had his day no doubt. I wasn't hit once the whole night, myself personally, it only feels that way.


It was my intent to sound Wiley out last week, and I did, except he derailed me with his humor, as per usual.

"Did you ever see a prostitute?" I asked him.

"Yes I saw one," he says. "As a matter of fact I saw two, standing together, in Times Square."

I let it go at that, as we had very little time apart from

the others, and I figured let the whole idea go while you're at it. But it wasn't the idea which accosted me on my walk today, although the idea might have predisposed me. She was a plain girl I would say, an ordinary face under a hatbrim, who sold it to me like aluminum siding, and I bought it the same way. A tall girl with a very nice figure (you could never guess in her street clothes) and she recommends herself out of the blue, "I'll show you a nice time."

"Oh yes?" I said these syllables and meant not a thing. When she spoke up in my direction, I didn't suspect her in the least—I expected to answer left on 42nd Street and straight up Fifth Avenue.

"Try me," she says, with a sincere eye, like a girl from home, not a monster. It's why I didn't know what she was at first, even when she spoke her piece. I must have looked as though I was mulling it over, as she kept up, "Not everyone's clean but I am. And I'll give you my best price."

$9.95 plus tax, I'm sure. Because that's what it was, a sale going on, and furthermore she had a room on this very block in case I was rushing to an important appointment. That's what did it. Oh sure, yes, an appointment mid-town—if I don't make the board meeting by three it'll be six million right down the drain. My only appointment was with the streets, same as her, so we teamed up then and there.

It was not so bad and I'm not sorry I went, so long as there are no medical repercussions. I am not guilty. It was sex, as Caddy puts it—something people will do a certain amount, and we did it. If I want to do it some more, I have a special number I can dial any time. "I trust you with this number," she says. Me and the men of the 69th Regiment Marching Band, I'm sure.

Yes she knew her business and I'm glad she did. Helps you forget that it's the strangest moment in your life, and you do forget it. But they should make you pay up front, before you even see the room. I liked least the paying. Not the money itself. But all was said and done and you suit up like intimate friends and then comes the invoice. So you may have thought you were people and now you know otherwise.

I did what I did and lived to tell it. Will I tell it to Caddy, who says she wants the lowdown yet may turn seasick when she gets it? I almost believed this—that I did it for her, so as to bring back the inside story—but I was just making excuses in the aftermath.

Counted up the months since Linda Stanley's last stand and acknowledged the obvious: I built up a need. After all, I am used to a light schedule, but not the celibate life.

Lazy. I don't walk enough and I don't scribble much these days. You go to put down your latest thought and find you do not necessarily have one. So I sit too much and eat too much and have only crazy ideas, like this one. Give Tanya a call on the phone and invite her over for a bowl of soup. As though she was twenty and we were just about to commence our courtship, and do it, all over again.

Yellow roses from Baumgartner's, a thermos of tea in Prospect Park, or a sitdown in Effie's Tea Room. Talkies at the old Strand, roller-skate in Greenwood, chop suey and fireworks at Coney Island on a Tuesday. A million things we had fun doing, before we settled down.

Let it be, a little nostalgia never killed anyone. And it's no great secret why. Washington Lincoln had a birthday and so did I. Washington is about two hundred, Lincoln one hundred, and I just hit fifty. I'm half-a-century around the oval and look at me: lazy.

March 11. Wiley called with work uptown, his neighborhood on Riverside Drive. He has contacts everywhere, but I told him no thanks, I'll stick. Another month and they will be running at Jamaica, and I can eat beans till then.

"Don't disturb me, Wiley, I'm on sabbatical."

"Suit yourself, professor," he says.

Sabbatical. A long long sabbath. Everyone should take one now and then, not only the professors of truth but the waiters and the jockeys, the cops and the robbers. And how come no sabbatical for the poor slobs who sit up in an office getting rich?* It takes a lot out of you, getting rich, more than will show.

Not that I've ever been rich, but some things you can know anyway—things I learned out on sabbatical.


March 19. Insert this funny note from Caddy—

I really almost had a boyfriend this time. He looked all right and could count from one to ten backwards, but when I told him I wasn't interested in going steady he couldn't handle it.

I explained it as well as I could. What if my friend Oscar changes his mind and demands his fifteen minutes in bed with me? What then? You see I must keep my options open.

But Paul doesn't understand about options, he wants to have me stuffed and put on his pillow like a teddy bear, so I said there were plenty of teddy bears around and sent him on his way with a letter of recommendation for his excellent backwards counting.

Love,
Caddy

So I wrote her back at once complaining that my hour was reduced to a stingy quarter-hour, and generally at-

*Hear, Hear.

—Walter Ford

tempting to match her high spirits. Although I think of her frequently and always fondly, I can honestly record that I never think in terms of a "sexual relationship" as she once called it.

In fact I will also record the following oddity. That I do have the urge sometimes, quite naturally, and the one I picture in my mind is Tanya. Never Caddy or Linda Stanley, who was real, nor the tall one, who was both real and recent. Nor Marilyn Monroe on the merry month of May, or Miss Rhinegold who misplaced her underwear during luncheon. I can barely recall my bare girl, even if I am looking right at the blue and orange curtain across her old window. It's Tanya, and that's who it is.

Not at the dinner table or waving bye bye in the early morning. Tanya naked, rising from her bath. My new sex symbol is my wife—true more than once.


Once or twice I sharpened my pencil and sat here with the book open. It's the second week of April and I only wrote once since the Ides of March. I'm not shirking on my homework, it's just that nothing much is new. I am doing more cookery than last year at this time, that's a change. I like cooking for myself, as you save money, eat better food, and the place smells nice. But why list recipes? I don't even have any, I'm a junk pitcher, mix it up and keep them guessing.

I could enter Jimmy's latest. He has become a freeholder in the Yukon Territory, putting together a parcel of land inch by inch, but literally. They are putting deeds in the cereal now—a piece of gold paper worth one square inch of land comes in each box, so that he has got five square inches of his land already. Maybe it's a phony, or in a rotten swamp, or maybe there is three hundred miles of ice between each inch and you can't get a right-of-way. But he feels good about owning this turf and assures me I am in for a share if gold is discovered under his plot.

What else? I shared a chess board twice with the new man, Hansen. I enjoyed myself—a good man. But not a good chess player. I need Morris for that.

That's it, all the news that's fit to scribble. If I come up with more, I'll be back, but just now I have no interesting thoughts. (Maybe I never had any, and now I don't even try.) I'm finished thinking. It's all worked out, my philosophy of life: life is a fountain, no more no less.

Rejoined the working classes today. My favorite time of the year, the early spring races at Jamaica. The first day in January is not a New Year—it's the start of nothing, the deep freeze. It's April when the world re-opens, that's the new beginning, as designated by God and the Devil alike.

We had a roster change, as Mickey Klutz will not be reporting for duty. He went on from Hialeah to Kentucky and will stay put there for the present. Wiley had a note inviting us down for Derby Day, with mint juleps on the house. Something to do with a lady, I'm sure.

It's a different atmosphere in the clubhouse without Mickey Klutz. We are all unique, of course, but some are more unique than others. And the new man is not a man at all—the beardless youth, Wiley tags him, and daringly so, as the kid's old man is a big stockholder. (That's how he comes by the job, sent down to dip his toe in the waters of experience.) He parts his hair in the middle like McSorley's bartender, and knows it all.

Wiley thinks he don't know a thing, including how to comb his hair, and so presents the kid with a gift-wrapped ten cent comb for a joke. Lucky for the kid he came up with a smile. If not, he would never survive a week in the room, stockholder or no stockholder.

May 2. Watched the fight on television, the rematch from Chicago with Robinson and Fullmer. Hansen and I sat downstairs with Timothy Myers and Jimmy—men's night.

Started out a carbon copy of the first bout. Sugar Ray in better shape and doing more (make Fullmer look as clumsy as he is) and yet you could not envision Robinson holding on to the fort over fifteen gruelling rounds.

No need. To all the world this Fullmer looks carved from stone, a butte from Utah, a plateau of solid granite. No one has ever had him down—pushed him, knocked him, or tripped him to the canvas. He doesn't *go* down, no more than a cornerstone. But in Round Five of this one, Sugar Ray put a left hook on his chin that must be the single greatest punch in prizefight history. Had to be.

An ordinary fighter fielding this blow (perfectly timed and placed, full leverage from way down) would sift away like sand, and wake up two three minutes later. A punch like that makes you miss out on a little American History. This Fullmer nearly made it back to his feet. He was wobbling sideways like a Russian dancer when they tolled the number ten. So a clean knockout, Robinson is once more the champion, and the world is set right until further notice.

Hansen can't see the fights, can't see caring too much who wins. First time he watched a fight. And I'm sure I surprised him with my ringside personality, as contrasted with my chess face. Timothy Myers likes the fights, likes his beer. He pulls for Gene Fullmer because Fullmer is white and that's that. Not a bad fellow but simple. He keeps it simple, black and white.

I have to admit I'm no better. Black versus white, I will always root black, automatic. In the old days, when the white guy was Jewish, I might make an exception.

May 4. Visited Elaine.

May 10. I found a way to get rich on Hartack again. When General Duke scratched out just before the serious betting began, the race opened up, with a number of good possibilities. Yet no one was looking to Iron Liege, Calumet's number two or three, who was not at all up to it the Derby Trials. Even Kramer never suspected.

Shoemaker made his mistake—stood up in the irons at the sixteenth pole and that cost him—but I was already past sweating it. Neck and neck with two hundred yards to go, I am comfy with the formula. Hartack. This kid asks 110% from his mount but he knows just *how* to ask, and so he gets it.

And Kramer crying where can he get a thousand bucks, but I know where. "In your pocket, you crumb. You took the action, now take the heat." Because I already planned on sharing the wealth. New mitt for Jimmy, so he will throw something besides a rock at the kittycat, and a lovely saddle blanket I had my eye on for Caddy. Why not five hundred in an envelope for Tanya, she could need it by now, and I know Walter can always use a single.

But see what life will turn on. I'm sure it's no different with a world war or the general election. A pebble on the ground, General Duke steps on it, and the shape of history is altered. Take it at the flood.

A number of years since I did any business with Coney Island. Goes back to before the War, excepting a few times with Walter, and I can't say I missed it. Coney Island is for the young. You must be young, or crazy, to brave the masses, although I can well recall the argument we would make—"There's plenty of room in the water." And we would go, and never be sorry. There *was* water, and food, softshell crabs at Feltman's while the mob thinned out, then head home on the train around dark. Nice.

This week I felt the urge. The whole world is ready for Coney Island suddenly, because we are on a hot streak—two straight days of humidity. I'm sure the Culver Line will be loaded for bear tomorrow morning, with all the palefaces, and they have boats leaving from here, Battery Park, that loop the loop too. It's a procession, and I can't make it, my hands are tied.

I would gladly put my face in the sun and float on my back with a cigar high and dry, like early times. Eat a plate of softshells and who knows, maybe ride the steeplechase. I would love to take Caddy there, and stroll down Surf Avenue with the hoi polloi. Of course it is not an option, as she likes to say. Though she will be here soon, and I will be seeing her.

Instead of Merry Old England she has latched on with a professor of hers, who will be spending his summer in Italy, digging up old bones.

> It is very significant work, Oscar, to find an old bone in the ground. Some people think that even a dog can do it, but a dog can't say which bone it is, or how old. And if it's old enough and hasn't much flavor, the dog will leave it in the bushes. And imagine, it could be Julius Caesar's kneecap!
>
> I'm really going, as you know, to build up my biceps for the return match with Jimmy (tell him: September, to the death) and to get tan and gorgeous in case you claim your two minutes in bed with me, and to master Italian and see the world and to bring you Julius Caesar's kneecap as a souvenir.

She will do it, of course she will. She'll show up in the fall and meet me for chicken soup and tuna, with her Roman sun-tan and a few dozen suitors in her wake. She will come down here and sit with me and chat about the summer's racing. And she will guaranteed arrive with some old hunk of Genoa butcher-shop bone and tell me with her pokerface, here, for you Oscar, Julius Caesar's right knee.

Caddy off to Europe. She was looking very mature in her "digging togs"—a blue skirt and a red silk scarf around her neck. And she should look mature because by the time she comes back to America she will be a voter.

They age very quickly between 19 and 21. At 19 they can still live home where at 21 they inherit the earth.

July 2. Seeing Jimmy today made me aware I have been seeing him less. No problem, however, we are still pals and I am still in line for a full share of the gold up north. He's growing up, that's all, and like a young animal a growing boy will get what he needs. So if he needs me he'll come round, and otherwise not.

I will nonetheless record that he has added six pounds or so of new "pure muscle" and that his mama is not as quick to scream in his face these days. Commands a little more respect with so much pure muscle, and with something else he's got going for him, a presence. If he does go off to war they will have to make him an officer, and maybe he will survive it after all.

July 26. Commiserated this a.m. with Bulkitis over a cup of coffee. All month long we have been hearing the rumors about the teams moving west. Unbelievable that they could do this, least of all Brooklyn. The Dodgers in sunny California is a fish out of water. Not only that they have been such a great team but also a team that stands for something, and as far as I am concerned they can only stand for it at home in Brooklyn.

258

So now we read the Giants will probably be going too. As much as I love to hate the Giants I can't see them shifting either, from the Polo Grounds. They belong here too. It's all relative—you cannot have the Dodgers without the Giants the same way you cannot have Marshall Dillon without a few black hats down at the saloon.

But nothing is sacred and what's more nobody cares, except the nobodies. Bulkitis and I must hang together, conjoined by fate as friendly rivals and now as teammates in defeat. And the worst of it is Tanya, because no one would believe a grown woman can mind a development inside the world of sports but they don't know my wife. This is the Brooklyn Dodgers and she can mind. Her heart's blood—and the whole damn team walks away.

Money is absolutely no excuse. They talk about the gold in California, the packed houses and so forth. Would Ben Franklin polish off the Declaration of Independence and then sign on with the Russkies for a higher percent of the take? High and mighty pronouncements, for sale to the highest bidder? Forget it.

And then some people are saying, Wait till next year and they will be back. I say not a chance, my poor dear friends. The past becomes past fast in this world, and that's one worthy of Wiley himself. A real spouter.


August 1. Packed for the Spa. My last ferry trip until the fall, and to break a habit I spent my morning walk on Staten Island—poked around a few hours. The ferry men, who consider me every kind of lunatic already, were astonished to see me disembark and walk away. Like the sun not setting—it made them sit up and take notice. What can be the meaning! I saw them pondering all the little mysteries of the universe.

Across the Narrows from Brooklyn, facing Fort Hamilton, is another fort on Staten Island that looks like a cross between a Roman temple and a shooting gallery. As a matter of fact it is a shooting gallery and you can see the guns poking out at the water, in case the Russian fleet should happen to float up in the Bay. Battery Weed they call it, and no visitors welcome inside, as it is the genuine article and all the guns are loaded.

But they tell a story that the last boats out of here in 1783 (bound home for Great Britain after they lost the war) got a nice Bronx cheer from the peanut gallery onshore. The British guys had signed a treaty of course, and the war was officially over with, but they decided to let one go just the same for the pure hell of it, and because they didn't care for the raspberry.

And the cannonball fell in the drink with a tiny splash and that was it, just another hole in the water. The last shot fired in the war for our independence and it's not such a long time ago. After all, we are still a young country, compared to almost anyone else.

# AFTERWORD

This odd, flat enigmatic note on the subject of Battery Weed, or the Revolutionary War, comprised the final entry in Oscar's journal. I suppose if he had known they were also to be the closing words of a book, he would have labored over them a bit or perhaps tacked something on that was more like an ending *per se,* something to round off or polish up the sentiment.

However, it is a story that to a certain extent I can finish for him, as the rest is largely known. The mystery was not exactly solved, yet simply ended on one level the day my uncle returned. I don't have the exact date, although I could look it up easily enough, for it was in October of 1957, approximately two months after the "Battery Weed" entry, and it was the day the Russians launched their first Sputnik.

My father's best joke, in fact, was that the Sputnik went up into orbit on the same day Oscar Carnovsky touched down. And this one-liner created an escape-hatch for Oscar, for he could smile and answer quite simply the question that so many would ask, namely where had he been?

"In orbit. I just touched down."

"How was the view from up there?" was inevitably the next line, establishing the joke, as opposed to the serious heartfelt inquiry.

"Fine, you see a lot."

And so on. That he should have touched down on that particular day in history merely highlights for me the extraordinary distance between those years and these. We are always nostalgic for the days of our youth and those were mine (I was seventeen when my uncle re-entered the atmosphere at Linden Boulevard in Brooklyn) yet the changes really have been immense.

Just as the automobile—a luxury in Oscar's boyhood and an innovation then in American life—had become ubiquitous by 1955, as much is true for the computer today. When was it invented? Surely no one except I.B.M. and Uncle Sam could have had them thirty years ago, where now to lack one in the home is considered a malediction upon one's offspring. It is moving quickly to the point where men will not go hunting or fishing in the woods without a micro-computer to plot their movements; to chart the previously arcane patterns of fish and game, factor in the sun and shadow, tell them when to stop and rest. They won't trust their feet anymore.

Certainly this office would be an empty, impotent husk if they carted our twelve terminals out to the elevator tomorrow, for we are all plugged in now. The eyes of America are on one sort of screen or another constantly, and the ears of America are clogged with transmitted sound. We are doing business while decanting untold decibels directly into the brain, and no one even seems to mind.

But what of the brain itself in the midst of such electronic buffeting? These plugged-in persons we see—are they really *in* there? They man the cash-registers and the little tin cars and very likely they are manning the nuclear controls from sea to shining sea, but are they safe? Are we safe?

It seems unlikely. We are not safe. And that is the biggest single change since Oscar's time, or the time of his great escape. The Bomb existed then (albeit not in such gay profusion as now) but I am not referring to The Bomb, or to extinction in a literal sense. I mean that for Oscar it was possible to be anonymous, private, to move through the world without quite being a part of it. Walking away was more feasible then, although I recognize that is an odd compliment to an age.

Today the world impinges more. Our vacated souls are simply awash in media swill. We seem intent on lopping off all the rich corners of existence; a new electronic product is announced and twenty minutes later we are told that "half the homes in America" now own at least one. Of whatever it is. And our incomes, fingerprints, and parking histories can be summoned up on screens that flash from coast to coast in an instant. Today a computer would find my uncle an hour after he left home, a dot on a grid somehow, and stipulate his return.

I have digressed. It was my intention to discuss the journal, and to add to it a few details and commentaries for the curious reader. As I have said, the journal comes to an end yet has no "ending." I have also argued that there was an artistic thrust to it, or a catharsis in it, and I contend now that it was in this way completed after all. Clearly Oscar's investment in it waned as his resolve to return, though always unmentioned, must have germinated and grown. Toward the close his entries are spaced in time, occasional, and they treat mostly of the sporting news, which to a lesser extent does appear throughout.

But there is a loss of interest, or a loss of the need to crystallize his interest, or to celebrate his pleasures, or to belabor his thinking any further. Having finished with his journal, he was soon to finish his sabbatical as well, sixty-odd days later, as the two were firmly linked. Perhaps they were simply the same thing, one expressing the other in words, as Oscar intended. That is not very profound of me, I know, nor is the observation that the true conclusion to this record exists in history, in action: Oscar's return to Tanya.

Oscar never saw it this way, never made explicit the import of the journal to the journey, although he did carefully preserve it. He certainly never saw himself as an artist, holing up in a garret where he could be freed from bourgeois restraints and purge himself through the performance of a work. But he was purged. Never sour or even reserved after his return—quite the reverse, he was remarkably ebullient—never bitter by anyone's account, and he never again wandered away. He often remarked that my aunt was the best thing in his life and on his deathbed rambled incoherently about her beauty, his heart full even as it was failing.

Perhaps the most remarkable aspect of the journal to me personally is this: here is an accounting of one man's daily life, his darkest thoughts and doings mingled with his best, and though I may squirm in embarrassment whenever I am mentioned and become "Walter" or "my nephew Walter," nevertheless there is nothing in all these pages to make me love my uncle less, or admire him less I should say. To me, and despite all his protestations, he was a very special man.

In any event, with my acquisition of the document, the Three Big Mysteries of Oscar Carnovsky were laid to rest, the case was closed, and yet I had many questions still, an ongoing curiosity, and so one month after I had gone through these pages a fourth time and had allowed them to settle into the empty recesses of my mind, I made a couple of pilgrimages. The first of these was to Brooklyn, to Albemarle Road where my aunt was now living alone, as no doubt she will for the duration.

I thought to take along my sons, as I would on later visits, but this time decided to see Tanya by myself, so we could speak freely. Tanya was not related to me by blood and I had never felt a strong tie to her. She prepared food, and cleaned the mess, and had never made it possible to know her, so I didn't. For that reason, I suppose, she was surprised to hear I wanted to come out and talk.

This reaction convinced me she had not taken the trouble to know the contents of the box she handed me at Oscar's funeral. If she had perused the journal, she might have chosen to suppress or destroy it—might simply have failed to execute the bequest. And she would not have been surprised that I came with questions. So it was possible Tanya knew very little of what Oscar had done while "in orbit." Having seen the two of them function as a couple, this seemed not unlikely to me.

It was May and we sat on white wicker chairs in the small yard behind the house. Tanya was a gardener and had her early flowers up, primroses and daffodils, and her early vegetables were staked or marked, her hedges trimmed; even the gravel was neat on the walk. About her person, she took less care. I could discern in her face the bone-structure that had made her a beauty and her eyes were still quite striking. She had kept up her weekly dancing, and walking ahead of me with the tray of drinks she had the muscular calves of a thirty-five-year-old woman. But she had made only a cursory pass at her flyaway hair and bound it in a rubber band, affected no makeup or jewelry, and though she had been expecting me wore a simple cotton house-dress with frayed hem and a pocket that having come unstitched at one corner, hung down in a red triangular flap.

From this carelessness, moreso than from the cleverness of her plantings, I had an impression that she would respond honestly to my questions, openly. She had no reason to do so, for these were sensitive, private matters and I was certainly no confidante of hers, yet I hoped she would have equally no reason not to, which proved to be the case. Tanya was not the least bit evasive—she was perfectly happy to reminisce, and held nothing back in the name of dignity. Her attitude toward the appearance of family history was indeed the same as was her attitude toward her personal appearance, namely that she had not imagined it could matter to a living soul, either how she looked or how her marriage looked, to others.

The problem was it hadn't looked that odd to *her*. To my astonishment, she had not examined the eight-hundred-day hiatus very deeply at the time it occurred, nor had she done so since. It was an aberration, she conceded in her own terms, but no big deal, as Oscar would have put it.

"Like taking a trip, he said. You know, you take a trip and then you want very much to come home."

"But things just aren't done that way. It's irresponsible," I sputtered a bit.

"He was not such a responsible guy always, your uncle Oscar. He was always out for fun. And he wasn't having much, I couldn't tell you why not."

"So he left you."

"Not at all. He went for a ride, that's all. Now, Walter—*now* he has left me."

"It must have hurt a great deal, it must have been terrible at the time. Do you remember it?"

"Of course. Do you think a woman forgets her own life? I remember everything, from the age of five or six. And I wasn't such an old hen, you know, I was forty-four years old the year Brooklyn won the World Series. You know what else? I remember every game of that World Series too."

"So do I."

"Good. Come here, and I'll show you what I looked like at the ripe old age of forty-four."

We went inside and she pretended (I thought) to rummage around after a particular photograph in a hatboxful of shots ranging from old brown-tints to four-at-a-crack carnival snaps to crummy modern polaroids. At last, "casually," she dug it out and passed it to me, a color enlargement that could have been Rita Hayworth, or someone like that, in the early Fifties. A rich cloud of black-and-rust hair framed her handsome face; she wore one of those bell-shaped skirts that elaborate the hips, and a white cotton blouse.

"Maybe *that's* why he came back!" I exclaimed. I believe I was expected to marvel and so I did. This was at the same time contrived and absolutely candid. I may have contrived the utterance, yet the sentiment was perfectly genuine. In my recollection of those years, Aunt Tanya had looked no such way; she had been an avuncular appendage, the somewhat elderly lady who had married my mother's brother and was therefore sometimes around on holidays.

"Bubi, I know why he came back. It's why he could leave I never figured out."

"You must have asked. He must have said."

"Oscar?"

"He must at least have apologized."

"I'm sure," she said, echoing the intonation of a phrase I associated particularly with Oscar himself. "He must have."

Tanya was being neither evasive nor coy. There was simply little to reveal. Oscar (as I apparently knew better than she) had left "for no reason"—quite explicitly—and in just that same spirit he had returned. For no reason, or none that could be given.

Yet my uncle was more than a fundamentally decent man, he was an absolutely moral man, and so he could not have returned in a frivolous state of mind. I am sure he knew that coming back at all meant staying, and never walking away again, and I will wager he was giving that very matter a great deal of thought in the long silence between August and October of 1957. He would be returning for no reason other than that he wished to do so, to be there however in a spirit that was new—as though he had been there before under duress, or through circumstance, and would thenceforth be there by choice.

"He was gone a long time. He must have had jobs, made

268

friends—did you ever meet the people he knew at the
time?"

"I never saw Oscar's friends. You know the kind of
people he liked to run around with—horseplayers. He
never brought them around. When Oscar came back, it
was like he never left, except for the business. I tried to
keep it going, hired help, but it had slacked off. The
business depended on Oscar. When he came back he was
surprised we still had it. He hadn't taken the trouble to
check up! And he didn't want to build it back up again. He
had a job—is this what you're curious?—as a waiter. In a
restaurant."

She spoke the word "restaurant" as some might say
"cesspool," or "whorehouse." What a jolt it must have
been to Oscar, his own wife looked down on waiters!

"But he did it."

"Yes, eventually. And the business went back up, bigger
than ever, so it was worth a little something when he
finally sold it. As you know, he retired at sixty-five anyway."

"Promptly."

Indeed Oscar and I had celebrated the occasion together.
I was in my thirties and married by then, and I had long
considered Oscar more than a relative—a friend. Retirement, so depressing a prospect to many, absolutely exhila-
rated him. In a sense he could walk away again after all.
Not from Tanya (he had never walked away from her, I
don't think) but from a schedule, the things that hem one
in. He went back to riding the ferryboats then, and playing the horses. As a matter of fact we celebrated his retirement in the clubhouse at Belmont Park. Oscar despised the
new Aqueduct and never ceased to lament the closing of
Jamaica. But if he knew a soul in that clubhouse, or if they
knew him, it was not at all evident.

"Prompt to the minute," said Tanya. "He learned from
his horses how to get quickly out of harness."

"Forgive me all my questions, Aunt Tanya, but I'd ask a hundred more if I knew what to ask. Is there any more to know, anything else to tell about that time?"

"It was a long time ago. Not that I don't remember it, but it is almost thirty years. You could have asked *him*."

"Oh I did. He never answered."

"Exactly. So you know I did. I will tell you one thing, though. Your uncle, despite being in the liquor business, never went in for drink, but he loved a good cigar. The biggest tragedy in Oscar's life was the overthrow of Cuba. He didn't have such a terrible hard life, you know. But in the year he went without his Havanas—maybe it was longer, year and a half—that was his biggest complaint. He tried the other ones. Brazilians, Canary Islands, and every damn thing. But he never stopped moaning about it until he made a connection."

"A connection?"

"You know, black market. Until he got the cigars. And he was not disappointed in them, either, they were just what he wanted, and he never complained again, about anything, until his heart attacked him."

Tanya shuffled around in the top compartment of the hutch and produced two cedar cigar boxes bearing the seal of the Cuban government, now under Castro of course, and each containing fifty Rafael Gonzales Coronas. Proof that you can't take it with you.

"They will be fine," she said, "each one fresh inside. Age won't make a difference."

"For me? No, Tanya, thanks. I don't smoke them."

"Smoke them the hell, Walter—you can sell them on the street anywhere in New York for five dollars apiece, maybe more. Right down here at the corner candy, it's true. Havana Specials."

"You sell them, Tanya, or I could sell them for you. It's your money."

"The money. No, if you don't want them I'll keep them

around. They give off a nice smell, as long as you don't light up."

Oscar had returned acting for all the world as though he had never gone, or as though he'd gone to work like any other day and returned on schedule. Honey, I'm home. As though a man was sent out for coffee, vanished for over two years, then walked in with the containers, sat down, and without one word of explanation began to sip his coffee. The missing years were simply missing: they didn't exist anymore.

Which led me on to further inquiries and eventually to a second pilgrimage, back to Oscar's old haunts, to the place he lived during those years, 10 Battersea Street. But first came my quest for the missing persons, or the persons from the missing years. The most intriguing, and the most likely, was the woman I had actually seen at Oscar's funeral—a very attractive woman in a dark suit whom no one had seemed to know. She had remained on the periphery of events and was never accounted for by any of the relatives. No one, myself included, much cared. At the time (ignorant of the daybooks, though I held them in my hand at graveside) I noticed her more for her striking good looks than anything else. I have never seen a woman my age, which I guessed her to be, who looked so stunning.

Later I arrived at the theory that this mystery guest might well be Caddy Moore, or Caddy Ormsby-Gore by now; that either they had remained friends somehow, or perhaps, alternatively, that living in the city she had seen the notice in the newspaper and recognized the name. The name on the notice was not the one by which she had known him up to the time the journal left off, but for all I knew she had participated in his deliberations that autumn and knew the whole story.

I preferred the theory that they had stayed in touch—that although Oscar never took his ten minutes in bed with her, he did take pride and keep tabs, and that no doubt she did fulfill his grand sense of her worth, her fate. I liked the idea very much, that there was a deep abiding affection between them, but neither was it a totally wild assumption. Their rapport may have been unique, but it did not strike me as trivial. And the woman I saw at the funeral service *was someone,* she *was there,* and although all my inquiries yielded no clue as to her identity (or because of that) it seemed all the more plausible she was Caddy. If not, then who else?

I am no detective and my spare time is limited. Nonetheless I made, over the course of several weeks, every effort to locate the people who had known my uncle in his Fish incarnation. Wally Wiley, Mickey Klutz, Linda Stanley, Jimmy Myers: I was sure some of these people, perhaps all save Wiley, were still alive and would talk to me about those years and share their memories of Oscar. I did not even doubt he might have maintained those friendships too, after Sputnik, as there was nothing in his relation with Tanya to hinder him.

I used the phone-books, chiefly, making hundreds of calls (that varied in oddness, I assure you) to homes listed under a correct surname and now and then the Christian name or first initial as well. I combed obituaries on microfilm at the New York Public Library, and thank Christ for alphabetization at least. With Jimmy Myers I went so far as to examine the lists of Vietnam War casualties (in case Oscar's premonition had unhappily proved out) and found three of him. And in the end I wandered the city streets a bit; asked around at Belmont Park, at Aqueduct, and in the Battery Park environs.

The result: the past was past fast, as Oscar articulated. The old guard was gone and little was retained in the changing over. I did find a Bulkitis who recalled the old news-stand (long since removed) and who told me that most of the family was now living in Connecticut. And Wes Farr, son of the trainers Will and Wesley Farr, recalled for me that his father did employ a girl, or maybe two of them, walking hots and swiping back in those days when it was still a great novelty. He could show me detailed records, Farr said, of every horse the stable had handled in New York State going back to 1946, but as for stable employees—the non-payroll people, hangers-on and part-timers—it was hopeless.

The neighborhood from Fulton Street to Battery Park has changed, like everything else, and far from being able to walk through Oscar's rooms (as I had naively imagined myself doing) I discovered the very street he stayed on was gone. It was this detail, the wholesale absence of Battersea Street, and Number 10, that lent to my proceedings an almost spectral aspect. In effect I was knocking on doors in a ghost-town, asking after Oscar's shade—or the ghost of his ghost really, since the Oscar who had resided here was already half spirit, a displaced soul in earthly limbo.

Time can take funny bounces on an errand of this kind. My sense of where in time and space I stood varied from moment to moment, as did my sense of who exactly I had set out to find. I had seen Oscar just six weeks prior to his death, for lunch, and I had talked with him over the phone even more recently, as we laid our Saratoga plans. These were fresh memories, as were the images of my uncle upstate last August, where my two boys and I shared a lakeside cottage with him a few miles from the Saratoga race course. That Oscar, heavily wrinkled, his eyes and hair gone iron-grey, a strong man now yielding to a gathering roundness in the middle and a new thinness in the arms and legs, was the Oscar I thought I knew. The only one.

But in my searches I became aware that I perceived him as someone long gone—a long time dead—and I realized then that the real Oscar, the most current one that is, had been displaced by the old Oscar, the one who came back to life in the pages he had accumulated for eight hundred days back in the 1950's.

I was not looking for Myers or Klutz or any of those people really, nor was I looking for Oscar Carnovsky, my uncle whom I knew so well. I was pursuing the other Oscar, Fish I suppose, a man I now knew even better and yet who lived so long ago, at a time when for a time I did not in fact know him at all.